DEVIL'S DANCE

The David Spandau Thrillers by Daniel Depp

LOSER'S TOWN
BABYLON NIGHTS
DEVIL'S DANCE *

* available from Severn House

DEVIL'S DANCE

A David Spandau Thriller

Daniel Depp

This first world edition published 2014
in Great Britain and 2015 in the USA by
SEVERN HOUSE PUBLISHERS LTD of
19 Cedar Road, Sutton, Surrey, England, SM2 5DA.
Trade paperback edition first published
in Great Britain and the USA 2015 by
SEVERN HOUSE PUBLISHERS LTD.

Depp, Daniel author.
  1. Spandau, David (Fictitious character)–Fiction.
  2. Private investigators–California–Los Angeles–
  Fiction. 3. Motion picture producers and directors–
  California–Los Angeles–Fiction. 4. Hollywood (Los
  Angeles, Calif.)–Fiction. 5. Suspense fiction.
  I. Title
  813.6-dc23

ISBN-13: 978-07278-8433-6 (cased)
ISBN-13: 978-1-84751-542-1 (trade paper)
ISBN-13: 978-1-78010-587-1 (e-book)

All Severn House titles are printed on acid-free paper.

Severn House Publishers support the Forest Stewardship Council™ [FSC™],
the leading international forest certification organisation. All our titles that
are printed on FSC certified paper carry the FSC logo.

Typeset by Palimpsest Book Production Ltd.,
Falkirk, Stirlingshire, Scotland.
Printed and bound in Great Britain by
TJ International, Padstow, Cornwall.

PROLOGUE

Chekhov's rule about the use of plot devices is this:
that if a gun is introduced in Act One . . .

C aptain Midnight said to the man,
'Get that dog away from me or I'll kill it.'
MacArthur Park in Los Angeles, on a gray overcast
afternoon in early spring.

Deets sat on a bench by the pond eating a pastrami sandwich
and looking out across the lake. His view of the downtown LA
skyline was slightly impeded by that stupid geyser they'd put on
the middle of the water. Deets hated that geyser, squirting like an
old man with a lousy prostate, a reminder of things to look forward
to. It was a shitty day but the park was still busy, Asians and
blacks and Latinos milling around. Deets reckoned that at least
half of them were there doing something illegal. The place was a
goddamn supermarket for weapons and drugs, and the pond itself
was like a night deposit for guns and body parts. Every now and
then the police dredged it looking for someone gone missing.
Deets wished he could be here one time to see it. It was the only
reason worth coming.

Deets was a big guy in a dirty rumpled brown suit and wore
thick heavy-rimmed spectacles. When you first saw him he looked
stupid, then you got closer and realized there was something strange
about the eyes. You looked in there and you could see the gears
whirring, but the machine itself was designed by Hieronymus
Bosch.

Deets had pulled his sandwich out of the greasy bag and was
chewing on it, staring into space and dripping juice down the front
of his jacket, when the faggot came over with his little dog and
sat down on the bench next to him. The faggot was having one
of those little mincing conversations on his cell phone, talking
about what Ronnie did or did not do with Albert at the party
Saturday night. Deets could feel his stomach turning. The dog sat

in the faggot's lap. It was one of those little dustmop dogs, one of those little yappy ones, the ones that make you as nervous as they are. The dog looked up at Deets and Deets looked down at the dog. The dog sniffed and smelled the sandwich and began to bark. The faggot made no attempt to shut the dog up, he just let it bark and talked louder into his phone.

That's when Deets threatened to kill it.

The fag stopped talking and stared at him.

'What?'

'You heard me,' said Deets. 'Get that yappy little shit-eater away from me or I'm going to pop its head off like a Christmas cracker.'

The faggot just stared at him, his mouth opening and closing but no sounds coming out. Then he finally said,

'You can't say that.'

'Why not,' said Deets through a mouthful of pastrami and rye. 'You going to call a cop? Go ahead. When was the last time you heard of anybody going to jail for threatening the life of a canine, hah? The constitution don't extend to animals. I could kill your fucking dog and eat it in front of you and maybe, just maybe, I'd do six months of soft time in jail. And that's only if the fucking judge is a PETA member or something. You think the county of Los Angeles is going to spend the forty thousand bucks it would take to prosecute, house, and feed me just because I killed and ate your fucking little lice-ridden ankle-huncher?' Deets took another bite of the sandwich. 'No, I do not think so.'

The faggot kept trying to talk, opening and closing his mouth, trying to form words. But nothing came. Tears welled in his eyes.

'Timothy?' said the cell phone. 'Timothy, what's wrong, what's happening?'

Timothy picked up the little yapping dog. It snapped and snarled at Deets. Timothy tried to clamp his fingers round the dog's snout but it broke free and bit him, went on snarling at Deets, who just sat there and stared into space and chewed his sandwich. Timothy was crying in earnest now, shaking, trying to keep the dog from leaping out of his arms.

'Timothy? Darling? What is it, what's going on?' said the phone.

Timothy wrapped his arms around the struggling dog, crushed it to his body, walked away sobbing.

Captain Midnight took another bite of his sandwich, drank some of his cream soda.

Malo had been sitting on a bench farther down the path. He was a large black man in a well-cut suit and expensive shoes. He carried a folded copy of *Time* magazine. He got up, walked over, and sat down where the fag had been.

'You still just as much of a people-person as ever, huh, Deets.'

'I got tired of you sitting over there like a fucking idiot waiting for him to leave.'

'Suppose he comes back with a cop?'

Deets gave a kind of pastrami-muffled chortle.

'There's two guys over there been dispensing dope all afternoon like they was the fucking Walgreens. Over by the water fountain there's a bloodstain where some cholo got offed last week with an AR-15 in a drive-by. If we sit here long enough, somebody is liable to try and steal one of our vital organs. You think the police are going to put all that stuff on hold while they investigate a threat of grievous bodily harm on some faggot's terrier? Anyway I fucking hate dogs. Fucking filthy beasts.'

'You a cat person, then?'

'Nah, I fucking hate them too.'

Deets ate the last of the sandwich, drained the can of cream soda. He wadded it all up, dropped it on the ground next to him, took out a filthy handkerchief, and wiped his hands.

'What have you got?'

'You can do the Marmont, right?' Malo asked him.

'Stevie Wonder could do the Marmont,' said Deets.

'It's a simple B and E. Guy will be out all evening, you got plenty of time. You can do the key card?'

Deets snorted. This sort of question was beneath contempt. He was fucking Captain Midnight, for fuck's sake.

Malo ignored the snort and went on.

'Inside there's a laptop computer somewhere, I don't know what kind. On the computer there's a manuscript, or parts of one. Somebody's memoirs. You'll be able to tell. I want you to copy the thing and then I want you to leak it to the press. You've done this often enough, I don't need to explain it. Use them friends of yours.'

'It's not blackmail?'

'That don't concern you. You leak the info a little at a time. I want you to stop I'll tell you. When I do, I better fucking hear skid marks, you understand? I hear you going all entrepreneurial on me and they going to find your head bobbing in that water over there and your ass somewheres up in Bakersfield feeling lonely. Whatever you make on the deal you get to keep.'

Deets eyed Malo suspiciously. Smiled, said,

'This don't sound right. You want me to steal this shit, sell it, and then keep the money. Excuse me if I'm worried about getting fucked.'

'Man I work for ain't interested in the money. He just wants it out there.'

'And anybody traces the source it comes back to me?'

'That would be your problem,' said Malo. 'You old enough to hold your own dick and you ought to know who you can trust and who you can't. Anyway we both know you clearing enough to make it sweet so don't ask me for no motherfucking tea and sympathy.'

Deets made that snorting noise again.

'In and out, no fucking around like last time. No cute little tricks. No silver bullet. You go in, you get what you got to get, then come out. Yes?'

'You de boss,' said Deets in his sambo accent.

'Don't you get funny on me, Deets. After that little trick last time, only reason we called you is we can't find nobody else this late.'

Deets laughed.

'Only reason you called me, baby, is because I'm the only fucking one who can do the job and we both know it. I'm Captain Midnight, remember. You go take your pickaninny shuck and jive and play it for some other guilty honky. I know what I'm worth.'

'One of these days, Deets,' Malo said as evenly as he could manage, 'I'm going to kill you, you sick, fat-assed racist motherfuck.'

'You ain't going to do shit as long as you need me. And since I'm the best, that's going to be a while yet. That just frosts those big black balls of yours, don't it, Malo? God, I love that. Now that you done give me ol' massa's message, you can go back off to the cotton fields and fuck your sister or something. By the way, you goddamned nappy headed Arkansas porch monkey, don't you ever threaten me again.'

Malo shook his head, gave a bitter laugh, stood up.

'You forgetting something, sambo?'

Malo looked at the folded magazine in his hand. Deets smiled. Deets held out his hand and Malo started to give it to him, then changed his mind, went over and dumped it into a trash can, walked away.

'You stupid black cocksucker!' Deets called after him.

Malo gave him the finger over his shoulder and kept walking.

Deets cursed and mumbled to himself and went over and stared down into the trash can. It was filthy, there were bees and flies all over. God knows what he could catch. He stuck his hand in and fished around. An old Korean woman walked by, stared at him.

'What the fuck are you looking at, you ignorant slope,' Deets said to her.

Deets pulled out the envelope, now soaked in god knows what. He opened it, took out the money, wiped off the individual bills, then tucked them into his jacket pocket. He was cursing Malo and thinking about that so hard he stepped in dogshit. He yelled, jumped into the grass to do a little foxtrot trying to wipe it off. Back on the sidewalk he tried to kick a fat pigeon who was just asking for it, but he missed and nearly fell down.

It was that sort of day.

ONE

The Chateau Marmont is maybe the last hotel in the Western hemisphere to still use keys. Real keys, the metal kind, the kind where you want to break into somewhere you make a copy in a bar of soap or something, or, what the hell, you just pick the bastard. There was likely a master key somewhere in his bag, but it wasn't worth looking. Deets stuck in the picks and thought about a late-nite breakfast at Canter's when he got finished.

A fucking blind coon piano player could have done it, so he couldn't feel particularly proud. Malo could kiss his pale and dimpled ass, Deets was going to treat himself when he went in. It took him less than five seconds with his mind primarily on a bagel with cream cheese, lox, and onions.

This of course is why he got the Big Bucks.

He was a fucking super hero, no question about it.

Captain Midnight went into the dark hotel cottage. He closed the door, took a small flashlight from the messenger bag he carried, shined it around while he hummed 'New York, New York'. What he was looking for, the laptop briefcase, was over near the desk. He zipped it open, took out the computer, sat it on the desk. Checked his watch. He was okay on time.

He turned on the computer, waited for it to boot. It asked for the password. Fuck that, I laugh in the face of passwords. He got out the notebook file containing a couple of dozen of his very own special start-up disks. He selected the right one, slid it into the computer, rebooted. It shut down, hummed, woke up. Now, rather than some asshole start-up program, it circumvented all that crap and shot him directly into the system files, and from that a list of every file on the computer.

'Hurrah,' said Captain Midnight. 'I am clearly a god among common mortals.'

Captain Midnight searched the computer screen desktop, leisurely glanced through a few files. It didn't take long to find it.

He plugged in a flash drive, downloaded the file onto it. It took just a few seconds and he was done. He ran a quick file check to see if there was anything he'd missed.

'This is just too easy. Where is the challenge, I ask you? Where is the poetry?'

Checked his watch again. Still good.

'Let's have a little fun then, shall we?'

He took out a large Snickers bar, unwrapped it, chewed on it while he leisurely browsed through files.

'Boring . . . boring . . . boring . . . Aha!'

Photos. Captain Midnight opened the file. Some old family shit, lots of photos of some bozo with curly blond hair and a beard. Captain Midnight thought he remembered the guy from somewhere. Then Captain Midnight found some photos of nude women. He brightened up.

'Oh, you naughty boy.'

Every guy had them on his computer somewhere. This was really the best part of the job. Captain Midnight looked through them, pleased.

He copied these too.

When he was sure he'd gotten everything of interest, he shut down the computer, closed the case again, and put it back in the briefcase. He double-checked around the room to see if he'd forgotten anything.

Nope.

He sighed. Now was the best part of the job. It was the only reason he did it. Everything else was just fucking dull. One of the perils of being a genius.

He went around the room and touched things. Opened drawers, closets, suitcases. Touched pants shirts jackets hanging. Touched folded underwear, opened a cotton hotel laundry bag and moved his hand around in the contents of that. Went into the bathroom, touched the toothbrush, the electric razor, the still damp towels, the toilet seat. Opened the little Dopp kit and handled the bottle of pills, the condoms, sniffed the bottle of cologne.

Oh yeah, oh yeah.

Went back into the bedroom, took a brand-new folded white shirt from a drawer. Pulled out the pins, the cardboard, unfolded the shirt, and laid it on the bed. He unzipped his fly, pulled out his dick, and whacked off onto it. Just a few hard quick strokes and bam, he was done.

Ahh god, ahh god . . .

Stood there for a few moments in bliss, weak, the room spinning a little.

Finally tucked away his pizzle. Carefully refolded, repinned the shirt exactly the way he'd found it. Put it back in the drawer.

Then said to the room,

'Congratulations, you have just been fucked by Captain Midnight. Heigh-ho, Silver, and away.'

And was gone.

TWO

J erry Margashack stood in the dining room of the Bonaventure Hotel with a hundred or so people he hated. He hardly knew any of them, but the ones he did know he despised, and he figured the odds were in his favor concerning the rest. He was more than a little drunk, but this wasn't unusual. The room was full of film distributors, sucking-up critics, and the other industry types who always come to these things. There'd been a private screening downtown and they'd all adjourned here to swill the producer's booze, score dope, and try to get laid.

The film, Jerry's film, the one he'd (in theory anyway) written and directed, had done great in the advance screenings with very little tweaking. The people who did the numbers were happy. They'd nailed domestic and European distribution already – that's where the bread came from to make the film in the first place, they'd pre-sold the shit out of it – and now it was a matter of trying to conquer the rest of the world. This explained why geeky looking people from around the world were allowed this evening to come up and tell him how brilliant he was. Which was the last thing he wanted to hear.

There was a blonde halfway across the room trying to make eye contact with him.

'That bimbo almost wearing the red dress is going to get a hernia if you don't respond,' Annie Michaels said to him.

Annie was his agent. He hated her too but, like most everybody else in this hellhole, she had him by the balls in one way or another.

'I hate her,' Jerry said.

'You know her?'

'Nope.'

'You hate everybody.'

'My experience is that it's better to start out that way,' he said, slugging back some of the champagne in his glass. 'That way there's nowhere to go but up.'

'So what do you think,' she said to him. 'You should be happy.'

'Fucking overjoyed.'

'Everybody loved it. You're a hit.'

'I don't want to be a hit,' he said, taking another drink. 'I want to be the guy who made a good film, which this fucking well isn't, by the way.'

She grabbed him by the arm, led him off to the edge of the crowd out of earshot.

'Do not do this,' she said. 'Not now, not here. You want to whine and act like a fucking child, fine, go back to the hotel and get shitfaced again and tell your woes to the toilet.'

'It's a piece of shit, Annie. It's not my film. Not after Frank had the fucking second-unit director – an imbecile, by the way, whose idea of dramatic resolution is to cut somebody's head in half with a chainsaw – reshoot those desert scenes without telling me about it. Then the bastard recuts it with a fucking Cuisinart. I'd take my fucking name off the thing if I thought I'd still get my money. Where is the rest of my fucking money, by the way?'

A guy who looked oily enough to be a second-string studio exec came up, took Jerry's hand.

'Congratulations, man!' said the exec. 'Great flick. It must feel good. Long time getting recognized by the Establishment, right?'

'Sure,' said Jerry. 'You bet.'

'This has got Oscar written all over it,' the exec said. 'Best Director, Golden Globes for sure.'

'Who won last year?' Jerry asked him.

'Huh?'

'Who got the Globes for Best Director last year?'

He thought. 'Jesus, I can't remember.'

'My point exactly,' said Jerry. To Annie he said, 'Where is he?'

'Who?'

'You know goddamn well who. Frank. Where is the fucking weasel hiding?'

'I don't know,' she said.

'Is he here? Where is the motherfucker? He's got to be here somewhere, the shitass.'

Jerry drained the champagne, grabbed another one, took a healthy hit, went off in search of his prey.

Frank Jurado, the producer, was talking with a group of money people. Saw Jerry approach.

'Here he is, the Golden Boy,' said Jurado. 'Big congrats.'

'Fuck you, Frank. Where's my money?'

'We'll talk,' said Jurado, throwing a warning look past him at Annie. 'Go enjoy yourself.'

'Fucking right we will. We could also talk about why you hacked my film to pieces, and why you've got me stuck like a hamster in the Chateau.'

'Nice cage for a hamster,' said the money guy with a Latin accent.

'Fuck you too,' Jerry said to him politely.

Annie came up, took Jerry's arm, and tried to steer him away.

'Not the time or the place,' she said to him.

'No? When is the time and the place? It's never the fucking time or the place.'

'You just told the largest distributor of US films in Latin America to go fuck himself.'

'I want my money. Unless that fucking greaseball pachuco motherfucker has my money, I don't want to talk to him. I want to talk to Frank, who's the slimy motherfucker who actually does have it.'

'You'll get your money. You know the deal. You'll get the rest of it when the foreign distribution deals are all clear.'

'When will that be?'

'You go around telling the people who can get your money to go fuck themselves, it's liable to be never.'

'I don't trust that bastard.'

'Fucking hell, I don't trust him either. Nobody trusts Frank. You're not supposed to, honey, he's a producer. But he's put you finally on the map. This time last year you were fucking happy to see him. Where were you? Oh yes, now I remember. You were

in Wisconsin trying to get somebody to loan you enough money
to rent a camera so you could make a film about cheese.'

'It was a film about a dying craft. It was a film about the nature
of art and dedication.'

'It was a fucking film about cheese, Jerry.'

'It was a fucking film about cheese,' he repeated softly.

'That's right. So now just get slightly shitfaced on free champagne and try to score with one of these bimbettes who are circu-
lating around like mayflies. I'm going to go back to Frank and
see if I can curb the stroke he's having about now.'

She left. The blonde came up. Extended her hand. Jerry took it.

'Hi, I'm Terri.'

'I'm Jerry.'

'I know.'

'Terri and Jerry. It sounds like a cartoon.'

'Do I get to be the cat or the mouse?'

'You can be either one, as long as you're interested in cheese.
I know a great deal about cheese, and I look forward to sharing
it with you.'

THREE

Jerry arrived in a taxi at the Chateau Marmont, got out with
Terri the blonde.

In a dark Mercedes sedan, the Chipmunks watched him. They
were three young Armenian men in their mid-twenties to early
thirties. Araz, Tavit, and Savan.

'What does she look like?' asked Tavit, struggling to see her
from the back seat.

'Not bad,' said Araz.

'Fuck not bad,' said Savan. 'She's fucking hot is what she is.'

'Fucking actress, you think?' asked Savan.

'Or a model,' suggested Tavit.

'We wait a couple of minutes we catch her naked, what do you
think?' said Savan.

'Oh yeah,' said Tavit.

FOUR

Inside the cottage the girl was indeed very much naked and Jerry was just about to climb on top of her. When there was an ungodly erection-killing pounding on the door. Jerry cursed, climbed off of her, pulled on one of the Chateau robes, and went to the door. He was ready to kill whatever asshole was on the other side of it.

'Whoever this is,' Jerry shouted to the door, 'I'm fixing to break your nose, just so it comes as no surprise.'

He flung open the door. The Chipmunks.

'You're not breaking nobody's nose tonight,' Savan said to him as the Chipmunks pushed themselves into the room.

'And just who the fuck might you be?' Jerry asked him.

'We are,' volunteered Tavit, 'the accounts payable department of the Baldessarian Investment Corporation.'

'The Bald—' started Jerry. Then it hit him. 'Oh, you mean Uncle Atom. You guys would be the Chipmunks.'

'We'd prefer,' said Araz, 'that you gave us our due respect and not use that name.'

'The Chipmunks?' said naked Terri from the bed.

'Cover your titties, honey, we have company,' Jerry said to her. 'Atom Baldessarian, a loan shark out in Eagle Rock. Armenian mafia. These are his nephews. They're famous.'

'Armenian mafia?' said Terri, covering her tits.

'There is no Armenian mafia,' said Savan.

'There's no Eagle Rock, either,' said Jerry.

'I still don't get the Chipmunks,' said Terri.

'Alvin, Theodore and Simon. You know.'

'The cartoon,' said Terri. 'How cute.'

'Hell of a Christmas song too,' said Jerry.

'You need to be taking this seriously,' Araz told him.

'I am taking this seriously,' said Jerry. 'Or about as serious as a man can be having this sort of conversation with his dick poking out of his robe. Can I help you gentlemen?'

'I still don't get why they're called the Chipmunks.' She smiled at Tavit who smiled back. Savan hit him on the arm.

'Ross Bagdassarian, an Armenian, wrote that song,' said Jerry. 'He created the Chipmunks. He was a cousin of William Saroyan, another famous Armenian.'

'How do you know so much about Armenians?' she asked. 'Are there famous Armenians?'

'There are many famous Armenians,' Tavit declared to her proudly, whereupon Savan said to him,

'Shut the fuck up, will you?'

'Uncle Atom says they always forget our contributions unless we remind them,' said Tavit.

'Yeah and I'm reminding you you're a fucking idiot,' said Araz. 'Where are the things?'

Tavit held up a small children's knapsack with little bunnies on it. Tavit's idea. Tavit had a sense of humor.

'Here.'

Handed it to Araz. Araz nodded toward Jerry. Savan and Tavit grabbed Jerry and dragged him to a chair, sat him down, pinned his arms.

'You owe Uncle Atom thirty-seven thousand dollars. With ten percent interest a week, and you're three weeks behind, that's—'

Savan stopped to figure it. It took a while.

'Forty-nine thousand, two hundred and forty-seven,' said Terri. 'I used to work in a bank.'

'I told Uncle Atom he would get his money.'

'You told him that two weeks ago,' said Araz.

'Look, why don't we go rough up the guy who owes me money? I'll take you right to his house. I'll help you slap him around and then we can give Uncle Atom his forty grand.'

Araz reached into the kiddie bag, pulled out a small blowtorch. Jerry's eyes widened. Araz lit it. Jerry's eyes widened considerably more.

Araz pulled Jerry's robe aside, exposing his nether parts.

'Jesus,' said Tavit.

'That explains a lot,' said Savan, looking at Terri, who was also staring at Jerry's prick.

'If you gentlemen have finished staring at my private parts – in what can only be described as a rather homoerotic fashion, I might add,' said Jerry, 'I would like to talk about the matter at hand. So to speak.'

'The matter at hand,' said Araz, 'is that you owe Uncle Atom forty thousand big ones and you don't have it.'

'This is not being very fucking proactive,' said Jerry. 'We all want you to get your money.'

Araz turned up the blowtorch, moved it slowly toward Jerry's crotch. Jerry struggled.

'Ohlordjesus,' said Jerry, trying to back his way up the chair. 'One more week. Just one more week.'

The smell of faintly singed pubic hair.

'Oh goddamn,' said Jerry.

Terri let out a yelp. Savan said to her:

'It'll be fried tuna for you, you let out one more screech.'

Terri shut up.

Araz moved the blowtorch in and out until Jerry couldn't stand the pain and yelped.

Araz took the blowtorch away. Set it down, still burning. Looked around. Spied a bowl of fruit. Took a banana, dumped out the rest of the fruit. Smiled to himself.

Reached into the knapsack again, came out with something wrapped in butcher's paper. Opened it up. Two oval-shaped fleshy objects.

'What the fuck,' asked Terri, 'are those?'

Jerry stared at them. 'They would be, if memory serves me, a pair of ram's balls.'

'Sheep nuts?' asked Terri.

Araz put the fruit bowl on the floor between Jerry's feet. He placed the ram's nuts in it, then artfully wedged the banana between them.

He picked up the blowtorch, looked at Jerry, then started to barbecue his artwork. The smell of lamb and fried banana filled the room as it sizzled. This combined with the slightly less intense smell of the singed hair on the inside of Jerry's thighs.

Terri got up, ran to the bathroom, puked.

When the ram's balls and the banana were nothing but cinders, Araz turned off the torch. Looked down at Jerry, who had a huge sign of relief on his face. He said:

'Give Uncle Atom his money, otherwise we come back in one week and finish the barbecue, right?'

Araz put the torch away. As the Chipmunks left, the very naked Terri came back into the room. Savan and Tavit stopped for an admiring moment until Savan clouted Tavit in the head and they all left.

Terri sat down on the edge of the bed.

'This sort of thing a typical evening for you?' she asked.

'It's starting to look that way.'

She looked down at Jerry's exposed crotch.

'I don't suppose you still could . . .?'

'No, honey, I don't think so.'

'Shame.'

She got up, grabbed her clothes, went back into the bathroom. Jerry gently prodded his burnt regions. It hurt.

Terri came back in, dressed.

'You should give me a call when the swelling goes down,' she said.

'Will do, honey,' said Jerry.

She kissed him quickly and then left.

Jerry sat for a bit. Then stood up painfully, waddled gap-legged over to the phone. Punched a number.

'Hello, room service? You all got anything for burns?' Listened to someone. Checked his balls. 'I reckon it's still just first degree. Thank God for small favors, right?'

Hung up. Eased over to his laptop, opened it up, began to write in his journal.

FIVE

Annie Michaels' assistant, Sylvia, first thing in the morning, was opening up the office. She made coffee, sorted through a pile of mail, turned on the computer. Did what she did every morning – looked through the RSS messages of internet articles about Annie's clients.

In a Hollywood gossip blog, the big reference about Jerry, Jerry's past, Jerry and that guy whose screenplay he supposedly stole.

Oh shit.

She picked up the phone and dialed Annie.

SIX

Annie was at home, doing her tai-chi class with Roberto.

'Ju have to imagine like you holding a gray fru. Then you move it from one side to the other.'

'I am holding the gray fru, Roberto.'

'No you not. Is like you hold a basset ball. You must hold a gray fru, not a basset ball. Ju got to concentray.'

'I am concentray, Roberto. I just don't see why I shouldn't be able to hold a fucking basset ball if it's more comfortable. Look, I want some inner peace, Roberto, I don't want lessons in fucking fruit handling.'

'Ju got to work hard for inner peace.'

'Is there some way to inner peace without me feeling like fucking Marcel Marceau every fucking time we do this? And I'm going to have some inner peace, Roberto, I shit you not, if it kills the both of us. You got that?'

'We going to Push the Monkey now.'

Her cell phone rang. She grabbed it. Roberto threw up his hands and rolled his eyes.

Sylvia.

'What is it?' said Annie. 'I'm about to push the fucking monkey or something.'

Sylvia wondered if this involved sex or drugs, then remembered it was Annie's tai-chi day.

'I did the internet scan as usual this morning and there was this thing.'

'What thing? What fucking thing?'

'About Jerry Margashack. You said to call you if there was ever a thing.'

'Sylvia, darling, if you don't clear the shit out of your throat and tell me what this is, I'm going to come down there and extract it with a machete. Is it bad?'

'Well,' said poor Sylvia, 'it's not good.'

And she told her.

'Shit,' said Annie.

Hung up.

'Ju got to concentray,' Roberto said to her again.

Annie dialed a phone number on her cell phone.

'No, Roberto, I got to deal with my fucking asshole clients who seem intent on trying to kill me. By the way, you're fired, I hate this fucking shit. Pack up your fruit and your monkeys and go.'

To the phone:

'Let me speak to Frank . . . Who do you mean who is this? Are you fucking new? Are you fucking fresh out of the cradle? Tell him it's Annie.'

A moment. Frank answered.

'Frank,' she said, 'we have a thing.'

SEVEN

On the soundstage during the remake of *The Lady Eve*, the male and female leads were doing a scene. The director called, 'Cut!' then looked at the director of photography. 'Was that good?'

'It was famous,' said the DP.

The male lead said, 'Was I close enough?'

'You were close enough,' said the female lead.

'I can get closer,' said the male lead.

'Not unless,' said the female lead, 'you've decided to play both roles wearing my underwear.'

'Food for thought, of course,' said the actor.

Spandau and Anna were just off the set, watching the scene on a monitor and listening through headphones.

'Our Oscar-winning cinematographer says it was famous,' the director announced. 'I guess we're okay. Are we okay?'

'We're okay,' said the DP. 'Can we eat now?'

'I think we can eat now. Our producer is on the set. We have to ask the Suit.' To Anna: 'What does the Suit say? Can we eat now?'

'The Suit says eat,' Anna told him.

'Are there any more Suits here?' the director asked her.

'I'm the only Suit present,' said Anna.

The director announced loudly,

'You hear that? The Suit says eat! We eat!'

'Lunch!' cried the assistant director.

They broke for lunch.

'What do you think?' Anna asked Spandau.

'It looks good.'

'You think the chemistry is working between Regina and Bill?'

'It looks great to me. But you're the Suit. I am merely the Suit's boyfriend.'

'I am the Suit, aren't I?'

'And a damned fine Suit you are too. I'd like to fondle your buttons but not until you feed me something.'

'Is food the only thing you ever think about?'

'Sometimes I think about really disgusting sexual acts, but only on a full stomach.'

'Ooh, let's get you fed then.'

'Then do we have time to go back to your office and do kinky things on the desk?'

'I have a one-thirty meeting.'

'What if I eat fast?'

'I refuse to have afternoon sex with a man who has ketchup on his shirt.'

'It was only just that once. I'll wear a bib.'

He reached for his cell phone.

'Do not touch that phone,' she said. 'We made a deal. One lunch without either of us using our phones.'

'We said talking. We didn't say anything about checking. Walter's out sick again. I'm still playing boss.'

'How many days is this? Is he on another bender? Or did he get married again?'

'He's at home. I'm starting to get worried about him.'

'I'm sure he's making passionate love to a bottle of scotch.'

'That's pretty harsh.'

'Harsh, I think, is him staying shitfaced and expecting you to do your job and his.'

Spandau checked his phone.

'It's him,' she said. 'I knew it.'

'He wants me to come by the house.'

'He needs his drinking buddy.'

'That's not going to happen.'

'He'd like nothing better than to ruin us and get you back on the sauce. Then he has you all to himself.'

'Can we not have this conversation?'

'Don't let him do it, David. We have this great thing going. Don't let him fuck it up.'

'You act like he's some kind of Svengali. He's a friend of mine.'

'He's a fucking selfish and manipulative drunk, and he knows you're the only person who can stand him.'

'So,' said Spandau, changing the topic, 'you want to go to Canter's? What do you think about a nice artery-clogging pastrami?'

'I mean it, David.'

'What are you doing, Anna? Are you threatening me? Are you threatening to leave me?'

'I'm asking you to look out for yourself, for once.'

'You keep asking me to give up the house in the Valley, move in with you. Well, this is why I don't. I keep waiting for the other shoe to fall. I'm not one of your old boytoys, Anna. I've been a grown-up for a while now. If you're not happy, I can manage.'

'That's not what I meant.'

'Anna Mayhew the famous actress is used to having her ass kissed.'

'But not by you.'

'That's right. Not by me.'

'You sure you're not waiting for Dee to come back?'

'You know what? Why don't you have lunch with one of the actors who need a speaking part. I'm sure they'll let you shit on them all you want. I don't have to.'

Started to leave.

'Don't go,' she said. 'I'm sorry.'

'You're the one who seems determined to fuck this up, not me. I've been as faithful and sober as a goddamned Mormon since I met you. What is it you want, Anna?'

'I don't want to lose you.'

'Then let me live my life. Let me do the things I have to do, instead of becoming the sort of goddamned parasite you seem to want.'

'David . . .'

He left.

EIGHT

A short while later Spandau pulled up at Walter's house in his black BMW. Got out. Rang the bell. No answer. Called on his cell phone.

'Hello, sport,' answered Walter.

'You want to let me in?'

'Is that you? Fucking maid's took a powder. Don't know where she is.'

The door opened and there was Walter, still talking on the phone. He looked like shit.

'So nice of you to come calling,' Walter said into the phone.

'Quit farting around, Walter,' said Spandau, and pushed past him into the house.

'Testy,' said Walter, following him inside. 'All not right at the old Augean stables?'

'Walter, I am in no mood for you to be showing off your superior education. Do you have anything to eat? I missed lunch thanks to you.'

'You can see if the maid left anything,' said Walter. 'Normally she steals me blind.'

Walter followed him into the kitchen. Spandau opened the fridge, got hit by the smell. Closed it.

'When did the maid leave?'

'Don't know, sport,' said Walter. 'Maybe two weeks. Left when I suggested she find me a woman for erotic purposes. Can't imagine why she'd find that offensive.'

'When was the last time you ate?'

'Don't know that either. I've been ordering things on the internet. People just keep coming to the door.'

'There are easier ways of killing yourself, Walter.'

'Are there?' said Walter. 'And here I am thinking I was efficient.'

Spandau looked through the cabinets, found some packaged stuff. Later Walter was sitting at the kitchen table eating microwaved ramen noodles. His hands shook. Spandau took another bowl out of the microwave.

'What is this?' asked Walter.

'Ramen noodles.'

'Japanese, is it?'

'Supposed to be.'

'Why do they make them all zigzaggy like that?'

'I don't know, Walter. So they don't slide off your chopsticks. Just eat it. Please.'

'Your hostility is ruining my appetite.'

'I think it would be the chronic alcoholism doing that. What the hell am I going to do with you? You need to go in for another dry out. You want me to arrange it?'

'God no. They want me to quit drinking.'

'I can't keep doing this.'

'Didn't ask you to do anything, sport.'

'You asked me to come here.'

'Entirely work-related. Nice cushy assignment for you. Frank Jurado.'

'You're kidding.'

Walter broke into a wheezy laugh.

'Thought you'd enjoy that. Just wanted to be able to see your face.'

'Last time I saw that bastard he had two goons drag me into an alley and beat the shit out of me.'

'Thought you'd appreciate the poetry of it.'

'I'd appreciate getting my hands around that sonofabitch's neck.'

'You might have the rare opportunity. He's got trouble with a director of his. Guy's also a client of Annie Michaels.'

'Ball-buster Michaels? This just gets better and better. It's like a reunion of all the people I'd expect to see in hell. Why me? They both hate my guts?'

'I keep telling you, there's no such thing as hatred in the movie business, only box-office receipts. Nobody gives a shit who hates who as long as you give them what they want. In this case you're the only guy who can do that. After that Cannes crap you're famous now. We can stick them for a bundle.'

'You're serious? You expect me to take this?'

'Oh come on, sport. You're just dying to get in there and strike a few licks.'

'Who's the client?'

'Jerry Margashack.'

'What sort of trouble is he in?'

'Don't know, sport. Said they'd rather wait and tell you.'

'I like his work.'

'I know.'

'Anna is right. You really are a manipulative bastard.'

'Anna should know,' said Walter. 'She's got you high-stepping with your balls in her gentle but firm grip.'

'Don't you start too.'

'She thinks I'm a bad influence, does she?'

'She knows you're a bad influence.'

'The serpent in the garden.'

'No,' said Spandau, 'just a hopeless drunk and my friend, that's all.'

NINE

S pandau hadn't been back to the two-bedroomed house he owned in Woodland Hills for over a week. In theory he and Anna weren't living together, but compared to the estate she lived in just off Sunset, it felt ludicrous to invite her here, so he didn't, and ended up spending more and more time at her place until the line between guest and resident got itself dissolved.

He parked the BMW in the drive, went into the house and the dry, musty smell of a home now feeling unloved. He and Dee bought the house just after they were married, lived in it until she'd finally given up on the marriage and found her own place. Like all marriages it began happy then got away from them. Spandau had been a stuntman when they'd met, working for her father, Big Beau Macaulay. As risky as that profession was, at least it was one she knew and could respect.

Then Beau died and the injuries Spandau had accumulated in rodeos and mistimed stunt gags started taking their toll. He'd taken the job with Walter, better hours, good pay, safer, no long-distance film shoots. Except Dee had hated it. Hated the way it changed him, hated the acts that were required of him. It was a

profession of dishonesty, she said. Spying on people, getting them
to trust you, then betraying that trust one way or another. Trust
was everything to Dee. She couldn't see how he could hold a job
that violated the very things he was supposed to care about most.
Ironically, he was having that same battle now with Anna. She
wanted him to quit. He was having a hard time explaining why
he couldn't, though in fact he'd been thinking for a long time
that he should.

Spandau went into his office. Dee called it the Gene Autry
Room. It was the second bedroom, they'd meant it for a child,
but the marriage showed strains early enough they avoided that
mistake. Spandau was free to work mainly from home if he
wanted, so the room became an uneasy combination of office
and personal museum. Dee simply called it his 'macho crap' and
probably that's what it was. Things from movies he'd worked on,
rodeos he'd competed in, rare books on the American West, Indian
totems, even a few collectible guns hanging on the wall. A large
poster of Sitting Bull frowned down upon all this from his view-
point above a rolltop desk where the phone and computer were
hidden. Spandau opened the desk, listened to his messages on the
answering machine. Nothing that couldn't wait. Sitting Bull
seemed to be glaring at him with still more disapproval than usual,
as if considering Spandau an impressive fuck up even for a white
man.

Spandau went into the living room. The furniture looked shab-
bier than he remembered. Through the patio door he could see
how badly the yard needed mowing. Somehow everything went
to seed after Dee left, especially Spandau. The divorce damn near
killed him. He'd pulled a Walter and nearly drunk himself to death
until he met Anna the previous year. She'd been good to him, but
there were indications he was about to screw that up as well.
Spandau went outside to check on the pond he built after Dee left
him.

He'd installed a turtle and some large goldfish. A poor excuse
for a family but the best he could manage. Then raccoons began
coming down at night and killing his fish, and every so often he'd
come out in the morning to find a stiff golden corpse or two, half-
eaten or perhaps just mangled for the hell of it. He was drinking
heavily and it didn't take much for him to see the bandit-masked

critters as symbols of pure evil, furry devils, examples of all that was worst in the world. One night, tanked, he'd fired off shots from an antique Navy .44 into the trees. He woke with a mighty hangover the next day but thankful he'd not been arrested or had the rickety weapon blow up in his hand.

The fish swam around happily. A neighbor fed them when he was gone. They saw Spandau and waggled toward him to be fed. He went inside and brought out the fish chow, scattered some lightly on the water. They gobbled. Spandau did a quick count, none seemed to be missing. Maybe the raccoons had given up, moved on. He felt relieved. The turtle had vacated a long time ago, having correctly tagged Spandau as a bad risk.

He went into the garage to check on his truck, the pride of his life, a 1958 baby blue and white Apache shortbed, kept lovingly in cherry condition. It had been Beau's and Beau had left it to him when he died. He opened the door, climbed in, ran his hand across the leather seat. The Red Pecker Bar & Grill baseball cap was still there. He put it on, opened the garage door, cranked the engine. It balked for just a second before it turned over and ran fine. Spandau turned on the AM dashboard radio, eased out into the street, and went off for a short drive. Waylon Jennings sang 'This Time' and Spandau warbled along with the old outlaw, pretending, at least for as long as the ride lasted, to be an earlier and better version of himself.

TEN

S pandau pulled up in front of the Coren Investigations office on Sunset. Found a parking spot in front, looked over across the street at the small French bistro. Julien, the owner and chef, was posting up a new menu. He looked at Spandau and Spandau looked at him. Spandau crossed the street and made a show of examining the menu.

Spandau cleared his throat and said:

'I see you have the Daube Provençal again.'

'That's right,' said Julien.

'With the orange peel?'

'No,' said Julien, 'not with the orange peel.'

'Ah,' said Spandau.

Julien moaned and rolled his eyes.

'Don't start with me, David. How many times do we have to go over this? Americans don't like the orange peel.'

'It's not authentic without the orange peel. You said so yourself. You're from Provence, you said your own mother never made it without orange peel. You said, and I quote, that without orange peel it's just fucking beef stew. Did you not say that?'

'We are not in Provence. We are in America. And Americans do not like orange peel in their daube. I tried it and it doesn't work, everybody complained.'

'That's fine,' said Spandau. 'I have no ethical objections to you putting beef stew on the menu, as long as you call it beef stew and not Daube Provençal.'

'You have to be practical. You don't understand cuisine. It's a living thing, you move it around, it adapts, it changes. That's the beauty of it.'

'So when are you going to adapt beanie-weenies and call it cassoulet?'

'Kiss my ass,' Julien said in French.

'I'm just saying.'

'I've worked with Alain Ducasse and I refuse to accept criticism of my art from a man wearing cowboy boots with a Versace jacket.'

'In their own humble way, these boots are a work of art.'

'This tells me everything I need to know. If Walter didn't tell you how to dress or what to drive, that'– nodding to the Beemer – 'would be a Ford Fiesta and your jacket would be from Sears.'

'You, my friend, are a snob.'

'If preferring that which is beautiful to that which is ugly means I'm a snob, then I'm a snob. I don't understand why Americans think beauty is undemocratic.'

'Didn't Gainsbourg once say that ugliness is superior to beauty because it lasts longer?'

'Serge also drank himself to death and dumped Jane Birkin when she began to wrinkle. And do not ever quote Serge Gainsbourg to me because you're not French and you will never understand him. When are you going to bring Anna back in? She's the only intelligent thing you've done since I've known you.'

'I can get beef stew anywhere.'

'One day she's going to wake up and realize she could be with a Français.'

'Ah, but she's a Texas girl, and she knows that once you've had cowboy there's no going back.'

Julien pulled a disgusted face.

'You make it sound like a social disease. I'll call you when the beanie-weenies are ready.'

'Please do,' said Spandau, and went back across the street.

ELEVEN

When Spandau came in Pookie was at the reception desk and Leo Reinhart was flirting with her. Pookie was young and beautiful and would often remind you she'd gone to a good school back east. A healthy portion of the money her father sent her each month went to antique and exotic clothing. Spandau took a look at what she was wearing and said,

'Grace Kelly.'

'Right,' she said. 'What movie?'

Spandau thought.

'*Rear Window*?'

'No, no!' she roared. '*To Catch a Thief*. Look at the purse, it's a dead giveaway.'

He turned to Leo. If Pookie generally reminded him of Audrey Hepburn, it was Leo's fate to be cast as Jim Hutton. Tall, gangly and shy, he played online computer games and was hopelessly outclassed by Pookie, with whom he was in love.

'Aren't you supposed to be out watching Ullman on that insurance thing?'

'He's in the hospital. He fell off the roof of his house cleaning the gutters.'

'We can assume then that he was fibbing about being paralyzed?'

'Well the thing is now he actually is. Which brings up a kind of weird philosophical point. He was lying to the insurance company but now he isn't anymore. So do they have to pay him anyway?'

'You mean like the movie,' said Pookie, 'where the guy is tried for killing his wife but it turns out she's not dead so he gets a kind of mulligan to go ahead and kill her for real?'

'Yeah,' said Leo.

'I don't think it works that way, children,' said Spandau. 'Most likely once fraud is proven his policy will be considered dead, which means at the time he fell he technically didn't have any insurance.'

'Bummer,' said Leo. 'You want to see the tape? I got it on my iPhone.'

They all watched. It was painful.

'You'd think a guy that fat would bounce or something,' said Leo.

'Look at his face,' said Pookie. 'I wonder what was going through his mind.'

'Second thoughts about being too cheap to hire one of the neighborhood kids to do it, I would imagine,' said Leo.

'Okay, hatchlings, enough fun and games,' said Spandau. 'Tomorrow we watch kittens in a microwave, but today there's work.' To Leo he said, 'Send that to Derek Bell at the insurance company. What are you doing now?'

'Nothing.'

'Did you clock out?'

'God, you sound like Walter. Management offers you a crumb and you immediately become a class traitor.'

'There's a thing called the work ethic.'

'Were you thinking work ethic when you spent that three hours over lunch last week at Ago's?'

'That was purely in the line of duty. It comes under public relations, schmoozing the clients.'

'Anna is thinking about hiring her own boyfriend to do what exactly?' asked Leo.

Pookie, ever conciliatory said, 'Shall we not cloud the issue with facts?'

'Meanwhile,' Spandau said to her, 'I want you to fix an appointment for me with Frank Jurado.'

Her mouth dropped open.

'Oh my god. So it's true. You're actually going to work for him again? Didn't he like try to kill you or something?'

'Yes, but we're all professionals here.'

'You're just using this as an opportunity to get your hands on him, aren't you?' she said, delighted.

'Just do what you're supposed to do and stop meddling in the affairs of management.'

'You're going to beat the holy crap out of him. I can see it in your eyes. Gosh, I wish I could be there.' She turned to Leo. 'You see? This is why I came to Los Angeles. Everything is a movie.'

'Let's just hope this one's more John Wayne than Woody Allen,' said Leo.

Spandau glared at him and went into the office and shut the door.

TWELVE

S pandau stopped at the gate to Jurado's office building. There was a camera watching. He leaned out of the car window and pressed the button.

'This is Ground Control to Major Tom,' he said when the speaker crackled.

'What?' said a young female voice, not amused.

'David Spandau to see Frank Jurado.'

A pause. Then:

'Any of the spaces on the right.'

The gate opened and Spandau drove through into the parking lot. He wedged the BMW between a Range Rover and an impeccably preserved baby blue 1965 Ford Fairlane. The Rover would belong to one of the executives, the Fairlane to somebody's hip assistant. That's the way these things worked. Status had to be preserved one way or another, and you couldn't have the flunkies aping the bosses.

Spandau crossed to the door into the building. There was a lock and another camera here too. They made him wait this time.

Spandau whistled 'Leaving Cheyenne'. Finally they buzzed him through.

The receptionist was about twenty-five and looked like Louise Brooks if Lulu had gone in for piercings and tattoos. There were rings in her nose and ears and a red and blue macaw covered most of her left arm. She wore a severe black dress and a look of unbridled hatred toward Spandau.

'Quite a security system you've got,' Spandau said, giving her his best smile. 'You expecting a jihad?'

'You can't be too careful,' she said coldly.

'I don't have to stand in front of an X-ray scanner, do I? I always forget to bring a rolled-up sock.'

She stared at him and it took her a moment to get the joke, which made her hate him all the more. She was sexy in that Suicide Girl kind of way and was used to staring most men down. Spandau had an unfair advantage in that he didn't like either her or her boss and he wasn't in the mood to hide it.

'I'll let Frank know you're here,' she said, turning her back to him and walking away before the sentence was finished. It was an effective dismissal. Spandau wondered if that was practiced or she just had that kind of timing.

She hadn't bothered to offer him a seat or a drink. Spandau sat on the edge of her desk because he knew it would irritate her the most. There were just some days when it was good to give into your baser instincts.

She came back out and saw his ass on her desk and stopped and glared at it for a moment, during which she realized: a) he'd done it to piss her off, and b) by reacting to it she'd already lost ground and surrendered the advantage.

She sucked her teeth, sat down at the desk, and pretended to arrange some papers.

'Frank will see you now,' she said without looking at him.

'That's real sweet of you, honey,' Spandau said to her and went into Jurado's office.

Jurado was at his desk and Annie Michaels sat on the sofa, thumbing through a copy of *Vanity Fair*.

'Are you going to be a prick about this?' she asked Spandau before he got entirely through the door.

'Probably,' Spandau said. 'Anyway that's one of the options.

The other two were not showing up at all or physical violence. None of them have been ruled out yet.'

'Look,' said Jurado, 'we're all professionals here.'

'Funny,' said Spandau, 'I was saying that very thing earlier and it didn't sound convincing then either.'

'Why don't you sit down?'

Spandau towered over the desk and it made Jurado nervous.

'I'll stand,' said Spandau. 'I don't intend being here that long.'

'David, what is it going to take to get you to put the past aside.'

'Can I have a puppy?'

'This is a fucking monumental waste of our time,' Annie said.

'I thought you'd feel that way. That's why I came.'

'Frank . . .' she said.

'Let's cut to the chase on this—' said Jurado.

'God,' Spandau interrupted, 'I just love it when you do movie talk.'

'We have a job for you,' continued Jurado, 'and aside from how you feel about me, you wouldn't be here if it hadn't piqued your interest. It's Jerry Margashack. You know Jerry Margashack, right?'

'I know of him.'

'You like his work?'

'I have a weakness for stylized violence and sexual perversion.'

'Is that a yes?'

'I think he's probably a twisted bastard but he's also probably a genius.'

'You're right on both counts. He is a sick bastard and he is a genius. Like all geniuses he is a pain in the ass and his own worst enemy. We announced we're releasing *Wet Eye* next month, and the day after that this appeared on the internet.'

He handed Spandau a copy of the article. Spandau scanned it and handed it back.

'Is this true?'

'Did he rip off somebody else's screenplay? Who the hell knows. Who cares. It was a damn good movie, and it was fifteen years ago.'

'Okay, so what? Why would you need me?'

'And this appeared two days ago.'

He passes over another article.

'Sexual misconduct with a production assistant. Settled privately out of court, no big deal about it. Except the timing, that it comes out now, after *Wet Eye* has garnered all this buzz. We think it's Oscar material.'

'And you think it's a smear?'

'Putting a film in the running for an Academy Award is like running for a public office. You invite the entire world to look at you and pass judgment. This shit has nothing to do with the quality of the film, but the fact is that the public won't give an Oscar to someone they don't like. They want their contenders to be squeaky clean. None of them are, of course, but the point is they want to think so. It's still a country that likes to consider itself moral.'

'I was under the impression the Oscars were chosen by one's peers.' Spandau was being contrary.

'Oh come on,' said Jurado. 'You know as well as I do half the selections are made by wives and grandchildren.'

'What do you want me to do about it?'

'I want you to find out who's doing it and I want you to make them stop.'

'How am I supposed to do that?'

'You get proof against whoever is doing this, they'll stop. This shit happens all the time but it can backfire against you if you get caught.'

'You think it's one of the other contenders?'

'Duh,' said Annie from across the room. 'It's Mel Rosenthal. The cocksucker is renowned for this kind of crap. It's got his paw marks all over it.'

'You know this sort of thing is impossible to prove.'

'I just want him made nervous enough to stop,' said Jurado. 'You start seriously nosing around and anything you find we can leak to the press and turn the game around. We might even be able to use this to our advantage. Big Bad Melvin attacking poor little Jerry. We'll spin it somehow, we just need the bastard to stop.'

Spandau nodded sagely.

'This,' he said, 'brings us to the big question as to why I should do this, since I hate your guts.'

'How much would it take to buy your affections back, David?'

'You're joking, right? I can't believe even you are stupid enough to say that.'

'Look,' said Annie. 'Jerry is my client. He's a good guy and he's in trouble. His career has been in the dumper for the last ten years, and this is his shot at getting back into the game. There's been the drink and the drugs and every other kind of excess, he'll admit to that. But he's trying to straighten out his life. He's made this brilliant film and now there's Rosenthal trying to ruin him, not because he hates Jerry or anything, but just out of cold blood, because it'll give him a leg up for the Oscars. You think that's fair?'

'This isn't about me,' said Jurado. 'Okay, so you hate me. But Jerry deserves a fair deal.'

'You two rehearse this, did you? You go to the Polo Lounge for breakfast and sit and figure out how to pluck at my heartstrings?'

'Actually it was dinner last night at Dan Tana's.'

'Why me? If I thought Mel Rosenthal was trying to fuck you over, I'd be selling tickets to the event.'

'Oh, you know why. You're connected, you know everybody in the business. People talk to you when they won't talk to anybody else. They trust you, and you've got a track record. We live in a closed world, David. You know that. You're on the inside. You're one of us, whether you like it or not.'

'We can't farm this out to some sleazy private dick in Burbank,' said Annie. 'If you don't help Jerry nobody can.'

'What happens if I say no?'

'If this shit keeps up, and it will, then we pull the film,' said Jurado. 'There's no point in wasting the money and subjecting the film to the negative publicity. The bad guys win.'

'The bad guys? Jesus, coming from you, that's priceless. You had two guys take me out in an alley and beat the shit out of me.'

'I do what I do to make things happen. There's nothing personal in it. You got between me and my film. I can't let that happen.'

'Yeah, the films are great but your actors end up killing themselves.'

'Look, I know Bobby Dye was a friend of yours, but I didn't kill him. None of us did. He fucked up his own life without any help from us.'

'Meaning you didn't pull the trigger, you just left the ammo lying around.'

'Bobby Dye made everybody a lot of money. Nobody wanted him dead. Look at it that way.'

'And now Jerry Margashack is the latest meal ticket. And what happens to him if you pull the film?'

'We cut our losses.'

'How do you sleep at night?'

'I don't. I work until one or two in the fucking morning, dealing with shit from every film we've got going from all over the world. I take a pill to get to sleep, and I sleep maybe four hours if I'm lucky and then I take a pill to wake up. Contrary to my doctor's suggestions I will do this until my liver fails and my eyeballs fucking turn yellow. At that point I'm either going to retire to an island in the Bahamas or I'm going to off myself like your pal Bobby Dye. I won't know until I get there. Does that answer your fucking sanctimonious fucking question? Do you want to help this guy or not? I have a job to do and I'll fucking do it, even if it means cutting Jerry Margashack loose to sail with the tides. You know this and I know this and he knows this. It's the way the game is played and I don't have the time or the patience to let you stand here and pretend you're fucking Peter Pan or the moral voice of the universe. So what's it going to be, because I have a meeting in five minutes.'

THIRTEEN

Spandau entered the darkened Bar Marmont half blind from sunlight. The hostess asked if she could help and Spandau blinked at her like an emerging mole. She laughed. It was a good laugh, he wished he could see where it came from. He told her he was there to meet someone. She asked who. From the back of the bar a male voice shouted, 'Where the fuck is my drink?' and Spandau said he believed he'd located the party in question.

Jerry Margashack was in a table at the far corner of the room, happily inserted between two young and very beautiful women.

He had his right arm draped around the neck of one of them, the tips of his fingers absentmindedly brushing the nipple beneath a thin blouse. His left hand was around a glass of bourbon, holding it on the table as if it might decide to run off on him. The other girl had her hand on his thigh and was whispering something into his ear. Jerry cackled and raised the glass to his lips, where the ice banged against his nose and it dawned on him it was empty.

Spandau walked up to the table and Jerry eyed him warily. There was that look of a man who's used to bar-room brawls, but Jerry's face lightened a bit.

'You Spandau?'

'Yeah.'

Spandau offered his hand. This created an ethical dilemma for Jerry, who could either release his glass or the girl's breast. He released the breast and shook Spandau's hand.

'You look like they said you'd look,' Jerry said to him.

'So do you.'

'They said you looked big and stupid but not to worry about that.'

'They told me you'd be drunk and rude but not to worry about that either.'

Jerry gave one of his belly laughs.

'Ladies,' Jerry said to the girls, 'I hate to end this, but we have gentlemen's business to transact.'

The girls looked Spandau up and down. One of them said to Jerry, 'Let's do get together later. You can bring your friend.'

'Well, I don't know if he wants to.'

'You want to, don't you,' the other girl said to Spandau. It wasn't a question.

'I do, I really do,' said Spandau. 'It's just that I'm self-conscious about the skin disease. It's not as contagious as it looks.'

Jerry hooted again.

The girl with the recently freed knocker wrote a phone number on a napkin and tucked it into the pocket of Jerry's shirt. 'So you don't forget.'

'Absolutely,' said Jerry, which meant either he was certain to forget or certain not to. He didn't specify.

The girls got up and passed close to Spandau but made an effort to avoid body contact. Spandau sat down and both men did what every other guy in the room was doing, which was to watch them leave. They were tall and gorgeous and knew how to make an exit. It was worth watching.

'Skin disease,' repeated Jerry. 'You are a character. You're not a fucking writer, are you?'

'Nope.'

'Good. I hate fucking writers. Where you from. You look like you might just be a Good Ol' Boy.'

'I grew up just outside of Flagstaff.'

'Ranch?'

'In its more optimistic moments.'

'I'm from Texas myself.'

'I figured,' said Spandau. 'You were humming "Yellow Rose" while you played her tit like a bagpipe.'

Jerry gave a laugh so big that it morphed itself into a fit of wheezing. 'Shit,' said Jerry when he'd recovered. 'You done any cowboying?'

'I used to do some rodeo. Too old for it now. I keep breaking things.'

'Rodeo, goddamn, that's something. I always thought you bastards were crazy. I grew up riding but, damn, I do not like falling off a horse. What events?'

'Bulldogging mainly. I tried broncs early on but, as one of my friends used to say, that's a short career and a hard dollar.'

'That how you busted that nose?'

'One of them. It's been busted about five or six times. Last time was when I came crashing through a breakaway wall too high and about knocked my brains out on a stud.'

'You do stunt work?'

'Used to do that too.'

'No shit. Who'd you work with?'

'You remember Beau Macaulay?'

'Oh hell yeah, everybody knew Beau. He was the best, man. The real thing. Goddamn shame when he died. His like won't be around again, let me tell you. This is a town full of pissants and faggots now. Ah shit, I guess it always was, come to think of it. Have a drink.'

He flagged down a waitress, ordered a George Dickel. Spandau ordered the same.

'George Jones used to drink this stuff,' Jerry told him. 'You like George Jones?'

'About the way George Jones liked George Dickel.'

Jerry broke out into 'It Was a Good Year for the Roses' in a passable imitation of George Jones. Most of the bar watched and a few even applauded. Jerry ignored them. Then he said,

'Well, I thought they were going to send some goddamn greasy little man or another fucking powder-puff.'

'It's not too late. I'm not sure I'm going to take the job.'

'You're right goddamn uppity, ain't you. How come?'

'I happen to think Frank Jurado is an asshole.'

Another hoot.

'You and me both, brother! Hot damn, I have found a soulmate! What I wouldn't do to ram a hot poker about a foot and a half up his ass. I would too, if I didn't think he'd enjoy it. What'd he do to you?'

'I crossed him a couple of years ago and he had three guys work me over and dump me in the middle of the street.'

'Well,' said Jerry, 'I can see how that might put a crimp in your working relationship. Here are them goddamn drinks. They are about as slow as Christmas in here.'

The waitress never got as far as setting Jerry's whiskey on the table. He intercepted it and took a desperate hit. Sat back and rubbed his forearms, one after another.

'I think we ought to get shitfaced. Flush that motherfucker out and stomp his sorry ass.'

'It's a thought I've considered more than once.'

'To huevos, and trying to hang on to them in Hollywood,' Jerry offered as a toast.

They drank.

'The whole goddamn thing is like that now. Goddamn crooks and bean-counters. But you're right, it didn't used to be like this. I mean, the suits were always bastards, but at least they knew something about movies. Nowadays it's all two-column book-keeping and bankable stars. Screw making a movie, let's get a bunch of bankables and throw their glossy asses together and just stare at 'em. A goddamn fashion show. Maybe that is what people want now. I don't know. I swear to god I don't.'

'You're bankable enough. There's a lot of good talk about *Wet Eye*.'

'Bankable my ass. The only goddamn reason that film got made is because Cory Pernell wanted to do it. Up to that point nobody'd touch me with an eight-foot Russian. I've been persona non grata here for the last decade. Cory heard about the project. Goddamn Jurado and that bunch, they just wanted to option the story, get somebody else to write and direct. Old Cory, man, he stood his ground for me. He's a tough little fucker. Crazy, though. A goddamn lunatic if there ever was one. He's got a tattoo on his pecker, you know that?'

'There was a rumor.'

'It's true! He showed it to me. You know what it is? The opening words of *Ulysses* by James Joyce. "Stately plump Buck Mulligan . . ." That's what he calls it, his dick. Old Buck Mulligan. "Me and old Buck Mulligan banged the shit out of those two broads." You know what he said? Said he wanted the rest of the novel on it but he couldn't stay hard long enough.'

Another fit of laughter.

'He's a goddamn lunatic, but I love him, I truly do.'

Jerry laughed again, shook his head, took another long pull at his bourbon. 'You going to take the job?' he asked Spandau.

'I'm thinking about it.'

'That would be fine,' said Jerry. 'You and me could have some fine times together, I figure, just as soon as I could get a few drinks down you and get you to pull that plug part of the way out of your ass. But I won't help you.'

'Why not?'

'Oh, a bunch of reasons. I have no information to give you, and I don't like the idea of you and your pal Jurado poking around in my private life, which is exactly what this is. You work for him, you don't work for me. You find out I like to stick nickels up my ass while pulling my pud, that info goes to him, not to me, and wouldn't I just be the biggest chump on the face of the earth to help him do that. Anything he finds through you, you think he wouldn't use that at some point? The bastard already has me tied up like a hog. No thank you. But mainly, you know, I just don't give a shit. Jurado wants to hire you, it has nothing to do with me. He doesn't give a fuck about me, he's worried about his goddamn film. Me, he'd throw to the dogs in a heartbeat and you and me both know it.'

'You don't care about the film?'

Long pull on the bourbon, drains it. Holds the glass up and wriggles it to get the attention of the waitress. 'You want the truth or the Hollywood version?'

'Something that resembles the truth would be refreshing.'

'I don't give a shit,' Jerry repeated. 'I don't give a shit about Jurado, I don't give a shit about these rumors, and especially I don't give a shit about the film.'

The new bourbon came. He didn't bother to ask Spandau if he wanted anything. The waitress put it on the table, took his old glass, started to leave but Jerry motioned for her to wait and downed the bourbon in one shot while she watched and he gave her back the glass, tapping the rim as a signal for still another.

She laughed, looked at Spandau, and said, 'Is your friend going to get wild?'

Spandau said to Jerry, 'Are you going to get wild?'

'Most likely,' Jerry said, putting his head back to stare at the butterflies on the ceiling.

'Well,' said the waitress, 'it's a dull night anyway,' and left.

'You said yourself this film is going to revive your career. It's interesting that you don't mind somebody trying to sabotage it. It's not a quality you often find in directors.'

'It's not my film.'

'You wrote and directed it. It says so on the film canister.'

'I wrote a movie and I directed a movie. Now the movie that I wrote and directed is not necessarily the movie that everybody will see. You know how this works.'

'You didn't get final cut.'

'I did not get final cut. I did not get script approval, I did not get a decent percentage of the back end, I did not get shit. I was a desperate washed-up old fuck making a movie in Wisconsin about cheese. Cheese, I shit you not, and telling myself it was somehow a work of art when, in point of fact, it was the only thing anybody would give me money to do. I worked for the Wisconsin Society of Dairy Manufacturers and now I work for Frank Jurado. I by far prefer the manufacturers of cheese – blessed are the cheesemakers, as Jesus says – but I'm in hock up to my ass and Hollywood beckoned. I lifted my balls and placed them

gently in Satan's hand. I used a Racine-based lawyer who specialized in agricultural suits to negotiate a fucking movie deal with
the biggest shark in international cinema. We work with what we
have.'

The drink came.

'How many is that?' Jerry asked her.

'Six,' said the waitress. 'We're running a pool to see how long
you're going to remain upright.'

'What's yours?'

'I'm thinking eight. You haven't eaten anything and you seem
determined.'

'Ten would be about right,' said Jerry.

'Shit,' said the waitress. 'That would mean Aidan the bartender
gets it.'

'Tell Aidan he's a fine judge of serious drunks,' said Jerry, 'but
if you'll give me your phone number I might be tempted to take
a dive for you.'

'You think you'd remember it?'

'Good point,' said Jerry. 'Does a double count as one drink or
two?'

'I'll have to ask,' she said.

'I'm a goddamn prisoner,' Jerry said to Spandau when the
waitress had gone again. Jerry tilted his head and went back to
staring at the ceiling. 'Why the fucking butterflies, I wonder? Not
that I don't like them or anything.'

'You said a lawyer in Racine negotiated your contract. I thought
Annie Michaels was your agent.'

'Well, she wasn't exactly on then and I hadn't heard a word
out of her for two years. I met Cory at the Banff Film Festival
when they were doing a retrospective of my old stuff. Cory
asked if I had any new projects and I sent him *Wet Eye* and he
loved it and wanted the option. I needed the money quick so I
let this guy in Racine do the deal, then all of a sudden the
goddamn film is in play and I get this call from Annie screaming
at the top of her lungs telling me what an idiot I am. Annie
takes the project to Jurado and Jurado and Cory do a deal and
there is a hell of a mess because the lawyer back in Racine
didn't have a goddamn clue and wanted ten percent. Anyway
Jurado buys him off and Cory drops out of the project and all

of a sudden I'm stuck with Jurado, who basically owns the whole thing lock, stock and barrel at this point. I don't have approval on anything, I don't have shit, I'm basically thrown into indentured servitude until the fucking film is released. No, excuse me, until even after the film is released because I'm obliged to go tarting my ass around for publicity. The whole setup was a mess and now I'm holed up here at the Marmont on Jurado's dime waiting for him to do something. The bastard owes me money but it's tied up and I'm too goddamn broke to tell him to kiss my ass and leave.'

'What do you think of the film?'

'You mean the version I saw? Or the version he's got some other fucker re-editing and reshooting right now? We fought like hellcats and I did a version I wasn't entirely ashamed of, then I found out he reshot some things and did at least one more edit that I never saw. It looks like Helen Keller directed it. I don't know. It's the biggest piece of shit excreted by Hollywood since *Myra Breckinridge*, which won't do my already mostly submerged career any good any way. So why don't you ask me again if I care.'

The waitress came back with another drink. By this time Jerry was staring at the butterflies again.

The waitress said, 'Everybody insists that doubles count as two, not one. Which I suppose makes sense.'

'Uh huh,' said Jerry, closing one eye, as if trying to single out an individual species of Lepidoptera.

After she put down the napkin and the drink, Spandau noticed a phone number lightly penciled along one edge. Jerry was very still now and Spandau noticed that he was snoring ever so slightly. The waitress noticed it too.

She shook her head and laughed. 'I guess I lose all around. Should I call him a cab?'

'When he wakes up, just have somebody point him up the hill to the hotel,' he said. 'The sorry part is, he's already home.'

FOURTEEN

Spandau pulled up again to the gate outside Jurado's compound. Leaned out, stared into the camera without pushing any buttons. Finally the same irritated female voice as last time said, 'Yes?'

'David Spandau for Jurado.'

'You don't have an appointment.'

'Honey,' said Spandau, 'if I need an appointment then I'm turning this car around and good old Frank can kiss my patootie.'

There was a pause. The gate clicked open.

Little Lulu was standing guard next to her desk when Spandau came in.

'He's in a meeting,' she said. 'You'll have to wait.'

'Don't think so.'

He walked past her. She made no move to stop him but just glared. Spandau pushed open Jurado's door and Jurado was sitting barefoot on the sofa, trimming a toenail with a pair of office scissors. He looked up at Spandau, shook his head, then went back to his operation. Spandau sat down in one of the chairs. Jurado whittled away at the toe for a while, and when he couldn't stand it anymore he said,

'I'm going to fire the girl who does my pedicures.'

'I would,' said Spandau. 'Don't take this the wrong way, but I've seen more attractive nails on a tree sloth.'

This seemed to have struck a nerve. 'She leaves them too long. I keep telling her. They get snagged in my socks and my wife complains it's like sleeping with a bobcat. What do you want? Are you going to do it or not?'

'I'll do it,' said Spandau.

'Good,' said Jurado. 'I'll have my attorney make the arrangements and cut you an advance check.'

Jurado daintily dropped a handful of fragmented toenail into an expensive-looking leather wastebin and pulled on his socks. He stood up and looked at Spandau as if surprised he was still there.

'One more thing in the contract,' said Spandau.

'Whatever, take it up with the attorney.'

'He can't negotiate this one,' said Spandau. 'I'm going to hit you. I didn't want to sucker-punch you so I decided to give you some advance warning.'

'What the hell are you—'

Spandau hit him. He'd wanted to break his nose, but that would have been difficult to explain. So he hit him in the stomach, in the solar plexus, not nearly as hard as he would have liked. Still it was rather satisfying. Jurado curled up like a boiled langoustine. He wasn't making any noise because air could neither get in or out. Jurado stood there and Spandau eased him over to the sofa.

'Don't fight it. It'll get better in a minute or two.' Jurado had a petrified look on his face. 'It always seems worse than it is.'

Spandau knelt by the sofa and put his face close to Jurado's.

'If you ever, ever again get it into that shit-filled head of yours to have somebody, anybody, threaten me or try to rough me up or even so much as brush dandruff off the shoulder of my jacket, I am going to forget they even exist but I will make like a homing pigeon to you, you miserable asshole, wherever you are, and I will start breaking things, beginning with a BMW tire iron for a creative rearrangement of your disgusting smirking face, and work my way down your body until your repulsive fucking toenails will be the only things that aren't cracked. If you are listening to me, I want you to nod.'

Jurado nodded.

'Good,' said Spandau. 'Two things. I'm going to take the case, but any information I find about Margashack that I don't think is relevant to the case, I keep to myself. The other thing is that whatever amount you agreed with Walter, it's going to cost you twice that.' Spandau stood up, with his booted foot pushed the wastebin over next to Jurado. 'This is just in case you feel like puking.'

Spandau eased out, closed the door softly behind him. Lulu was sitting at the desk. As Spandau passed she couldn't resist one last glare, but this was interrupted by the sound of her employer retching violently into a one thousand dollar Louis Vuitton trash basket.

FIFTEEN

The Chipmunks' van pulled off the street and into the alley behind Atom's Meats. There was the usual grab-ass between Savan and Tavit. All the way up from Laguna Beach Savan had been ragging Tavit about sex.

Tavit was twenty-three but Savan said he was convinced Tavit had never even touched a naked woman, much less ever bonked one. Tavit protested that he had. Savan was trying to get names, dates, details, and when Tavit didn't give them Savan used this as proof of his virginity. Actually everybody in the van knew damned well Tavit had scored at least once, with a fat Native American waitress at one of the reservation casinos. He'd nailed her in the back of this very van, and then spent a hypochondriac week irritating the hell out of everybody, certain he'd contracted every STD known to mankind. Savan just liked tormenting him, it helped pass the time, and Tavit was one of those poor schnooks who encouraged it by confusing mental cruelty with male bonding. Tavit thought he was being playfully ragged but in truth Savan had simply never liked him.

Anyway they both irritated Araz, who kept turning up the van radio in an attempt to drown them out, but they only talked louder. There was just no way to stop them, they were like fucking kids, never took a goddamn thing seriously. Now they were going to see Uncle Atom and it was guaranteed either Savan or Tavit would do something to piss the old bastard off. Araz was the oldest and it would be him that Uncle Atom laid into. He was supposed to be in charge.

Just before they got out of the van, Savan licked his index finger and stuck it in Tavit's ear.

'Goddamn it, Savan!' yelled Tavit, frantically wiping at his ear with the cuff of his jacket.

'A wet dick in your ear,' Savan said to him. 'This is as close as you're ever going to get to sex.'

'Will you make him stop,' Tavit said to Araz.

'Stop it,' Araz said to Savan, halfheartedly because he didn't much like Tavit either.

'Maybe you like it up the poop chute,' said Savan, goosing Tavit in the ass with his thumb.

'I mean it!' said Tavit.

'Will you leave him the fuck alone,' Araz said to Savan.

'What?' said Savan. 'What did I do?'

Araz pushed the buzzer and in a moment Omar opened the door. Omar was a large man whose acne-ravaged face had over time been augmented with a collection of knife wounds, one of which had severed a nerve so that the left side of his jaw drooped. He was inclined to drool and kept dabbing at the corner of his mouth with a handkerchief. He always wore the same dark-blue suit with a pattern of dandruff sprinkled across the shoulders that never changed either. Araz couldn't help being fascinated by it, like Omar had glued minuscule bits of dead skin to the cloth in some complex array that made sense only to him. Not that Araz was ever going to broach the subject, since somewhere in his right jacket pocket Omar had a six-inch switchblade that could be drawn, opened, and used to extend a man's smile by a bloody three inches before anybody knew what had happened. Araz knew this because he had driven a poor bastard to the hospital and left him outside the emergency room with a rather too late warning about saying anything critical of Uncle Atom within Omar's hearing. Omar was Uncle Atom's right hand, and carried a knife because a gun was too fucking expensive to toss if the cops were onto you.

When the door opened they were hit by a blast of chilled air and the pasty smell of fresh dead flesh. They passed through the curtain of plastic strips and into a large room full of hanging flayed and dismembered animals and men standing at tables hacking at dead things with cleavers and large knives. The Chipmunks followed Omar through the dangling carcasses back toward the office. On the way Savan picked up small raw chicken and tossed it blindly over his shoulder to Tavit, who caught it without thinking.

'Goddamn it, Savan,' said Tavit but shut up and placed the chicken back on the rack when Omar glared at him.

Uncle Atom sat at an old gray metal desk, counting half a dozen piles of money with the aid of an ancient hand-crank adding machine. Atom Baldessarian hated technology nearly as much as

he hated spending money, and he hated spending money nearly
as much as he hated people, which was considerable. The office
itself consisted of the desk, two metal filing cabinets, two metal
chairs, and a metal bookcase that held some audio cassettes and
a circa 1978 cassette-playing ghetto blaster. On the walls were
posters diagraming the various cuts of meat and a giant photo of
Charles Aznavour on the wall above Uncle Atom's head. Armenian
folk music came tinnily from the boom box. Araz knocked and
pushed open the door.

'Come the hell in,' said Uncle Atom without looking up.

Araz went warily halfway in. Tavit and Savan stood behind him.
They were all scared shitless of the old man but as the eldest it
was Araz's job to do the talking.

Finally Atom looked up. 'Are you going to stand there like a
fucking *apush*, giving me pneumonia? Where's my money? And
where the hell have you been?'

'It was late?' Araz meant it as a statement but nerves let it
escape as a question.

'How am I supposed to know you didn't get hit over the head
and robbed?'

'All of us?' said Araz.

Atom counted some money, mumbled to himself, gave the
adding machine handle a good crank.

'A little Jew kid with a cap gun could take down the three of
you. I don't trust you to pick lint off your dicks, much less run
around overnight with forty-five thousand of my dollars. Where
is it?'

'He didn't have it?' Araz wished to hell his knees would stop
shaking and these statements would stop coming out like he was
playing fucking *Jeopardy*.

'How much did he have?'

'None?' This came out almost as a squeak. Pathetic.

Atom stopped cranking and stared at him.

'What the hell is wrong with you?' Atom asked him. 'Are you
afraid of me?'

'No,' said Araz.

'You're not afraid of me?' Atom asked again.

'No,' said Araz.

Atom got up slowly from the desk and moved around it toward

Araz without taking his eyes off him. He moved up close to Araz and Araz blurted,

'Okay, yes, I'm afraid of you.'

'Good,' said Atom. 'You should be afraid of your elders, they know more than you. Always be afraid of people who know more than you, you understand?'

'Yes.'

'In your case, this would be practically the entire world. It's going to be a hard life. Come with me.'

Atom moved past him and out the door. Savan and Tavit jumped aside to let him pass. They all followed him out onto the butchery floor.

'What do you see?' Atom asked them.

It was obviously some kind of trick question and nobody wanted to fall into it. The Chipmunks all looked at each other.

'MEAT!' shouted Uncle Atom. 'You see MEAT! You're in a butchery, for god's sake, what else are you going to see? What do you see again?'

'Meat?' Tavit repeated.

'Good. Yes, meat. Maybe you're not a complete retard after all. What is the significance of meat?'

'People eat it?' said Tavit, feeling encouraged.

'"People eat it,"' repeated Atom. 'Come here.'

Tavit came forward and Atom grabbed him by the scruff of his neck and pulled him over to where the head of a sheep lay on a table. Atom pushed Tavit's face right up next to it.

'Would you eat that?' Atom asked him.

'No?' said Tavit.

'Why not?' said Atom.

'I dunno,' said Tavit. 'It's not cooked or something.'

'That's right. If it was cooked, it would be FOOD, right? But it's not cooked, so it's MEAT. Understand?'

Everybody nodded but they clearly had no fucking idea what he was talking about. He let go of Tavit.

'MEAT. Everything that is alive in the world is MEAT. You understand this? It is not butterflies, it is not cute little kitties with big round eyes, it is not people, it is not you, it is not me. It is MEAT, nothing more. All living things are nothing but meat. I want you to be clear on this. You think this sheep has a soul?'

'Not anymore,' said Savan. 'It's dead.'

'Thank you, you fucking *apush*. No, this sheep does not have a soul. This sheep never had a soul. You don't have a soul. I don't have a soul. You went to school, you went to church, they told you all these things have a soul. They lied. None of these things have a soul. They're just meat. It's all just meat.'

Atom looked at Araz.

'You're the smart one. You're thinking about God, aren't you?'

'No,' said Araz.

'Don't lie to me, you little turd. I can read your mind. You're thinking about God. You're thinking that God gave everything souls. You're thinking that Uncle Atom is wrong, that there are fucking souls floating around all over the place. But I am here to tell you that you are wrong. Ask me if I believe in God. ASK ME!'

'Do you believe in God,' Araz said to him.

'Of course I believe in God. God exists. I know, because I've seen him. I've looked right into his eyes. And you know what? God doesn't care. God doesn't give a shit about you or me or the butterflies or the little kitties. And if God ever gave us souls, then I was there on the fucking day he took them back.'

Atom began to unbutton his sweater.

'I was a boy,' said Atom, 'the Soviets wanted my country. That shitass Stalin. We Armenians, we're a brave people. Even the Turks couldn't wipe us out. We fought like bastards. We're tough.'

Atom took off the sweater. He began to unbutton his shirt.

The Chipmunks looked at each other. And then it hit them. They all looked at each other and then glommed onto it at once: they were going to see it. He was going to show it to them. His back. The family legend.

Uncle Atom's back.

'The Soviets, they had tanks, machine guns, fucking airplanes. We had old rifles and ammunition that had turned green. Sometimes we fought with swords. Can you believe that, swords?'

Atom took off his shirt.

'We resisted. We weren't just going to let them walk in, take over our country. We're a proud people, we're brave. We fought back. We knew we would lose, but we fought back. My brothers fought back. I fought back.'

He hands the shirt, the sweater to Omar. Reaches down to grab the hem of his undershirt.

'The Chechens were the worst. Like animals, monsters. We'd been given money to buy rifles, my brothers and me. We crossed the mountains carrying the rifles on donkeys. We were stupid, we were young. It was a great adventure. We fought for the freedom of our people. We got five kilometers into the mountains before they caught us. Actually they'd been watching us all along. They just weren't in a hurry. The same man who'd sold us the rifles sold us to the Chechens. He was a good businessman.'

Up and off comes the undershirt.

Atom turned.

From the width of his shoulders, from the base of his neck to his waist, his back was a mass of scar tissue. Araz thought it looked like the top layer of bubbled, melted cheese on a tray of lasagna.

'They cut their heads off, my brothers' heads. Whack, whack, just like that. They held me as I watched. I waited for them to kill me too. Then one of the Chechens said he needed to shit, but there was no toilet paper. The Russians never gave them enough toilet paper, he said, they were constantly wiping their asses with leaves and grass. So they held me down and tore off my shirt, and one of them took a knife and cut my back and peeled off strips of skin. It took a while. I'd scream and when I'd pass out they'd slap me until I woke up. Then they'd continue. They showed me the four long strips of skin. I was young. The skin was soft and there was no hair. They said now they had something to wipe their asses on.'

He'd pulled off his undershirt, let them see, now pulled it on again. He'd made his point.

'They left me. I just lay there. I couldn't move. I wasn't dead, I wasn't alive. What I remember was the flies. You see any flies in here? Hell no. Flies are disgusting. They have shit on their feet, they lay eggs in meat. Maggots.'

On with the shirt.

'It was hot. The flies came. I watched them crawl all over my brothers' heads, climb in and out of their mouths, climb down into the necks of their bodies. Then I realized they were on me too.

All over my back. I couldn't move. I could hear them, the buzzing. Flies will do this. Flies will do this to any sort of meat, you leave it sitting around long enough.'

Tavit had been pretty good. You could only hear him barely moaning through most of Uncle Atom's little show. He even made it, though moaning like a sort of hum, through the display of Uncle Atom's flayed back. But the fly thing was too much for him. The idea of that back, that back, flies laying maggots in it . . .

Tavit retched and projected a hefty arc of semi-digested Dr Pepper and a hot pastrami on rye onto the floor about four feet away.

Uncle Atom said,

'Go get something to clean that up. Spray it down, then scrub it with some disinfectant. All I need are the health inspectors on my ass,' and pulled on his sweater.

Tavit wiped his mouth with his sleeve, then quickly shuffled into the back to get something to clean up his puke.

Uncle Atom said,

'That's when I realized the truth about meat. My brothers, they were just meat. I didn't see any souls flying out of their bodies when their heads were cut off. The Chechens, they didn't have any souls. I was laying there, looking at the flies crawling all over the dead bodies of my brothers, and I felt nothing, so it was clear I didn't have a soul either. Meat. It became very clear that we were all nothing but meat.'

He buttoned the sweater, straightened it out, straightened the sleeves.

'It took me months. Laying on my stomach. My mother changing the dressings, the doctor coming to paw me. When I was better, as soon as I could put a shirt on my back, I went back out. I'd get in close to the Russian camps. I had nothing to lose. I had no soul. I was fearless. I was a boy, but I had grown men following me. They'd all lost sons, had wives and daughters murdered or raped. None of us had souls anymore.'

Tavit had come out with a pail and water, paper towels and a mop and a scrub brush. The whole artillery of cleaning supplies. Atom watched him for a bit, then pointed with his toe and said,

'You missed a spot.'

Continued:

'We'd go out at night, we'd get close, we'd catch Russian soldiers. It had nothing to do with politics anymore. Our country was lost. It was a game. We'd catch them, then we'd tie them up. We'd boil water, then we'd lower them naked into the water and listen to them scream. Then we'd take them out and peel them like you'd peel a banana. Like you do with pigs. The skin would just slide right off. We'd leave them where the Russians would find them. It scared them shitless. That lemon stuff, the Lysol,' he said to Savan. 'Use that. It's in the storeroom.'

Tavit got up off his hands and knees, scarpered away.

'Just meat. You know what a man looks like when you skin him?'

He walked over to the hanging carcass of a skinned pig, slapped it a few times with the flat of his hand.

'Just like this. Just like a pig. It even feels like this.'

He slapped the pig a few more times, like he'd developed some sort of friendly attachment to it.

Tavit came back, tossed the Lysol around, scrubbed again.

'What are you,' he said to Tavit, 'a goddamn chambermaid? That's enough. Come here.'

Atom went over to the sheep's head.

'When I send you out there, when you work for me, you're not dealing with people, you're dealing with meat. Just chunks of meat. They don't have feelings, they don't think, they don't have souls. All they've got is my fucking dollars. That's all they are. Fucking chunks of meat holding on to my money.'

Atom lifted the head in both hands, held it up in front of the boys like he was making some kind of toast. Then he gouged out the sheep's eyes with his thumbs, a soft sucking sound.

Tavit started to retch again.

'I fucking send you out there to get my money, you come back with my money. You do what you've got to do to the meat, but you get me my money. Otherwise you have no function. Otherwise you're just meat too.'

He looked at Tavit. Tavit looked at Atom apologetically, turned, and was sick again.

'Somebody go back for the Lysol, will you?' said Uncle Atom. 'Jesus,' he said, shaking his head. He put the sheep's head back on the table where he'd found it and walked back into the office.

SIXTEEN

Maria, Anna's housekeeper, had set a table out by the pool. Crisp white tablecloth, candles, and the soft, surreal blue-green glow of the water. Roast chicken, salad, a white wine chilling in a clay container. Simple, relaxed, just what they needed. They'd been walking on eggshells with each other since the blow-up on the set. Spandau poured the wine. You could hear the traffic and the revelers outside the clubs on Sunset at the bottom of the hill. It was a cool night and they'd lit the space heater to envelope them in a warmish bubble, but every so often a short frigid blast swept across the table. Anna burrowed into her sweater. It was a ridiculous night for this kind of picnic and they both knew it. But it was romantic and they were alone and you could look up and see the stars. That had to count for something.

'Are you sure you don't want to go inside?' Spandau asked her.

'I'm fine,' she said. 'Not unless you do.'

'You're okay? You look like you're freezing.'

'I'm fine. Really. I like this. Don't you? If you don't like it we can go inside.'

Things felt off to a wrong start. They were trying too hard, and had already embarked on that frustrating waltz of trying to anticipate the other's desires, which invariably ended with nobody knowing what the hell anybody wanted. They were trying to converse in some neutral language neither was geared for – they were both naturally outspoken, and the effort wasn't to think of something to say, but to stop yourself from saying exactly what you did think. What made it worse is that they'd both been here before, in other relationships that had failed. This was the step before that final desperate weekend in Cabo or Maui or Tahoe, where you promised to revive the spark and patch things up, then came home reminded of how fucking hopeless it was after all. They sat there wanting to be close but struggling not to communicate. It was always impossible at the end. That's how you knew it was ending.

Anna picked up her wine, looked at it nervously, then sat it down again. She looked up at the stars. Spandau looked up at the stars. They both looked at the stars for a while. Then she said:

'I'm sorry about the other day. On the set.'

When in doubt apologize.

'No, I was out of line,' he said. 'You're right. This whole thing with Walter is just getting way out of hand. I've got to do something.'

'We've talked about this before. Walter is never going to get any better. I mean, I know you love him, but you're like his perfect enabler. He couldn't get away with any of this shit if you weren't around to cover for him. You're not doing him any favors either. Not really.'

'Jesus,' said Spandau. 'Now I'm an enabler. I suppose once I finally get in touch with my feelings I can give myself permission to feel what I feel and become integrated and then I can search for some closure.' He took a hefty gulp of wine. 'How did people manage to talk to each other before psychiatry?'

'Okay,' she said. 'Change of subject. I'm sorry I brought it up. I swore I wouldn't.'

'And what exactly is an enabler, anyway? Is it anything like allowing a grown-up in a democratic society to do what he wants with his own body, without foisting your own moral judgments on him?'

'Oh, come on. He's your friend but you're helping him kill himself and trying to pass it off as some deep philosophical decision you've made? Give me a break. You think he'd stay home hammered if he didn't know you were in the office covering for him? He's been running this company now for what, twenty-five or thirty years since his old man died, and he didn't do it before you started working for him. The business wouldn't have lasted fifteen minutes and you know it.'

'What is it you want,' Spandau said wearily.

'We've talked about this before. You need to get out. It's time you branched out on your own.'

'I'm not going to set myself up in competition with him.'

'You wouldn't be. No investigative work at all, strictly security. Personal security and security for film sets, performances, and so on. We both know there's a fortune to be made in it for somebody like you. I'll lend you the money. You can pay me back.'

'Ah god, Anna . . .'

'You've said it yourself. It's the investigative stuff that's killing you. All you ever see, all you deal with, is the worst side of people. It can't help but hurt you, mess up the way you see life. Why do you think Walter is this way? You keep talking about how you hate this place, how you hate the business, how you're looking for something to believe in. You're not going to find it where you are and you know it. This is killing you. So try something else.'

'I'll think about it,' he said.

'Yes of course. You think about it. You just think about it and get back to me in, say, a thousand years.'

'Have we moved onto accusations of passive-aggressive now?'

'You said it, not me.' She shivered. 'I'm going inside for a heavier sweater.'

'Are you sure you don't want to just move the whole thing indoors?'

'If you don't want to be out here,' she said, 'why don't you just say it?'

'I'm fine,' said Spandau, holding up his hands in mock surrender. 'I'm just swell.'

'Let's be nice,' she said. She kissed him. 'At least there are no fucking phones.'

She walked toward the house. When she was out of sight, Spandau pulled out his cell phone and checked the messages. Two texts and one voice mail from Pookie on the office number. He phoned her.

'Talk quick,' he said when she answered.

'She's gone to the little girl's room or something?'

'Exactly.'

'I won't say you're pathetic or anything, since I happen to be very low on the corporate scale, but . . .'

'Just give me the goddamn message, will you.'

'I've been hounding Rosenthal's office for days now and it's no go. He's not going to see you, and, frankly, I can't think of any reason he should. Can you?'

'Not really,' admitted Spandau.

'I suggest a rethink on your strategy.'

'Thank you, Carl von Clausewitz. If you come up with anything brilliant, you'll let me know, won't you. Look, for the rest of the

evening, if you need to talk to me just text. I can sneak glances
at the phone, I think.'

'There's one other thing.'

'Hurry up, will you? She's coming back.'

'Dee phoned. She wants to see you. She says it's important.'

'Ah, Jesus.'

'She said to tell you no one is sick or dying, because that's the
first thing you'd think. But she says it's important and wants you
to call her.'

'Right,' he said.

'You going to be okay?'

'I'm fine.'

'No you're not and I almost told her to leave you alone. You're
happy now and it's not fair, David, it just isn't.'

'I thought you always liked her.'

'I do like her. But I like you more.'

'I have to go.'

'You're not going to start drinking, are you?'

'No.'

'Promise?'

He heard Anna coming and shut off the phone and dropped it
in his pocket.

'You weren't on the phone, were you?'

'I was just admiring the stars,' he said.

She sat down as Spandau poured another glass of wine.

'I need a favor,' he said.

She put her elbow on the table and her chin in her hand. Looked
at him. Didn't ask what it was, didn't say sure why not, didn't
say anything. Waited.

'I need to talk to Mel Rosenthal.'

Again, nothing.

'You know him. I was wondering if you could help me out.'

'Everybody wants to talk to Mel,' she said. 'Nobody just waltzes
in, not even the A-list. Certainly not me. I'm not on anybody's
fucking list anymore. You forget, honey, I've been shunted back
to the minors.'

He studied her for a bit. She made a point of looking him
straight in the eye, as if challenging him to prove she was being
straight.

'Who called you?' Spandau asked her after a few moments. 'Was it him? What did he do, threaten me? Threaten you? You'll never work in this town again?'

This time her eyes broke away. She started to light a cigarette, then changed her mind on that as well. She leaned back in her seat, gaining some distance.

'Don't flatter yourself,' she said. 'Neither of us is important enough to threaten. And if you think Mel Rosenthal ever does his own dirty work, you seriously are naive. I had lunch yesterday with a mutual friend. Somewhere between the crab salad and the coffee, she said that Mel had related to her – in the strictest confidence, mind you – that your office kept calling to set up some sort of meeting, and that Mel was very sorry but he's very busy right now and he doesn't want to be rude especially since he knows you're my boyfriend but he wishes that you would stop. End of message.'

'And what did you say?'

'I told her you were a grown-up and anyway we had a kind of unspoken pact we'd never stick our noses in each other's work.'

'Why didn't you tell me?'

'I was hoping you wouldn't ask. It seems a little cheap to me.'

She was staring at him again. This time he couldn't meet her eyes, stared off at the lighted pool.

'You're right,' he said. 'I'm sorry. I'm having a week full of new lows.'

'Well, now that the cat is out of the bag,' she said, 'you need to stay the hell away from Mel Rosenthal. I mean it.'

'You're already in production and as far as I know he doesn't have a damn thing to do with it. He's not going make the effort of trying to shut you down just to get to me.'

She laughed and shook her head. 'Fuck you. You think it's career anxiety I'm worried about?'

She came forward, leaned on the table toward him.

'You're right about one thing. Mel is notorious for holding grudges, and yes, he probably can't touch this picture but it is likely I may have to kiss his ass sometime in the future. But if you think that's why I'm warning you, we really haven't got a goddamn thing to say to each other anymore.'

She got up to leave.

'Thank you,' she said, 'for a lovely romantic evening.'

'Look,' he said, 'don't go. Please. I'm sorry.'

'I don't want you to be sorry,' she said. 'I want you to be able to climb into bed with me at night with your head and major bones intact. Mel is a piece of work himself, but his friends are even nastier. He's not going to come after me. Too many people are looking and Mel just hates that kind of attention, which is why he's trying to warn you off. He's asking you in a very nice way, probably for my sake, to back down and leave him alone.'

She looked down at him. Suddenly the anger melted. She sighed and her shoulders fell and she seemed to grow older. She sat back down.

'For me,' she said. 'Just for me. For no other reason, other than I've asked you.'

'So what am I supposed to tell the client I'm working for? Sorry, my girlfriend says I can't work for you?'

'Yeah, why the fuck not. That will do for a start. Just walk away. Say, sorry, I'm not the right guy for you. Let somebody else do it. Let Walter send somebody else. Or better yet, let Walter rouse himself from his customary drunken stupor long enough to do his own shit work for a change.'

Spandau said nothing.

'Thank you,' she said. 'Thank you for sparing me your interminable and naive fucking lecture on why you should receive a knighthood. Those of us who live in the real world admit we have to back down every now and then. So few of us lesser mortals have the option of fucking up our lives in search of the Holy Grail.'

'Like the man said, you knew what you were signing on for.'

'Jesus,' she said. 'You know why I fell in love with you? Because you never used to say macho bullshit like that. What the fuck is happening to you?'

She left. Spandau drained his wine and smoked a cigarette. Then he drank another glass of wine and went down to the car and drove down Sunset toward the beach. When he hit the PCH at Malibu he pulled over and sat on the hood of his car and smoked and stared at the water. Then he called Dee.

'Hello, David,' she said.

His voice was soft, sad, and faraway. It was a moment before he could speak. Whatever it was he was going to say, he couldn't say it now.

'David?' she said.

'I got your message. Are you okay?'

'No,' she said. 'Charlie's missing. He's been gone for three days.'

'He hasn't called or anything? You don't know where he is?'

'He just disappeared and I haven't heard a word.'

'Was there a fight or something?'

'No,' she said. 'David, I can't call the police.'

'He'll turn up. He's what? Forty-five? Maybe midlife crisis has finally kicked in.'

She was quiet and he knew she was crying.

'It's been a year,' he said. 'Not a word. You didn't want to speak. Now you call me and tell me the guy you left me for has gone walkabout. I'm having a hard time searching for sympathy.'

'There's no one else I can call, David. He owes a lot of money. Some men came to the house. I don't know what to do.'

'What kind of money?'

'Gambling, apparently. It's a lot, we don't have this kind of money, he'll never be able to give it to them. Oh god, David, I hope they haven't hurt him.'

'When did they show up?'

'This afternoon. Three of them came to the door.'

'If they're looking for him, he's probably okay. It means he's dodged them so far.'

'I need to talk to you, David. Can you help me? There's nowhere else I can go, David. There's no one else I trust.'

'It's late,' he said. 'I can't see you now. Just stay by the phone and he'll probably call. Maybe it's nothing. Maybe it's just a misunderstanding and he'll turn up by morning.'

'You think so?'

'Sure,' he lied. 'This sort of thing happens all the time. He's got into a little trouble and he's panicked, thinking it's worse than it is.'

'You'll help, then? You'll find him for me?'

'Of course I will,' he said.

'Where are you now?' she asked. 'Can I see you?'

'The last thing you need is for me to be there when he walks in. Are you working tomorrow?'

'I'm taking some personal days. I've just been walking around the house, waiting.'

'We'll meet tomorrow,' he said. 'I'll call you in the morning and if he's not contacted you by then, I'll do what I can.'

'You'll find him? You'll make sure they don't hurt him?'

'I'm sure this is nothing. The bastard will probably stumble in pissed as a newt any time now. You can both have a big forgiveness hug.'

Silence. Then:

'I'm sorry I hurt you.'

'Try to get some sleep,' he said. 'If he shows up in the middle of the night, just send me a text or something.'

'Thank you,' she said.

'Yeah, sure. Just get some rest.'

He rang off, watched the waves a while longer. Thought. The message tone sounded on his phone. He looked at it. Anna.

Come home, it said.

SEVENTEEN

In the morning when he woke there was a text from Dee saying she'd heard nothing. He dressed and went down to the kitchen, where Anna was already at breakfast. Anna liked breakfast alone so it was always a simple affair unless one of them felt like frying eggs. Anna ate yogurt and fruit. Spandau sat across from her and poured a mug of black coffee and slathered some jam on toast.

She kept looking at him and smiled and then finally said:

'Why is makeup sex always the best?'

'You think it's the best?'

'I think it has something to do with the idea of guilt and forgiveness. When you come during makeup sex, you always feel as if you've really earned it.'

'You don't normally feel like you've earned an orgasm?'

'Not always.'

'This sounds like some deep insight into the female psyche I'm not sure I want to know about. Maybe you should discuss this with your therapist.'

'When I was in therapy all we talked about was sex. No – fucking. It was a male therapist and he felt it was somehow more liberal to call it fucking rather than sex or making love. I once pointed out to him that there was a difference between just having a casual bonk and making love. He rather curtly reminded me that one of the reasons I was in therapy in the first place was that I couldn't tell the difference. He said fucking was an umbrella term that covered all the variations.'

'It's 7 a.m.,' said Spandau, 'and you are telling me this why?'

'Because it was really great with you last night,' Anna said, 'and because with you it always is making love.'

When she talked like this he never knew what to say or how to react. It was one of the few things that could make him shy, one of the reasons she loved him. He looked down at the table but he was smiling.

'I was pissed off at you last night and I was hurt. I stewed about it but the longer I stewed the more I realized I just wanted you to make love to me. In a way I was glad you left because I'd have done you right there on the pool deck but I wouldn't have known why. By the time I texted you I'd figured it out.'

'You wanted to be forgiven?'

'No, fuck you. You were the one who was wrong and I still think you're an asshole about it.'

'This is going off in a whole new direction.'

'I just realized how scared I was,' she said. 'How scared I am lately sometimes. About us. I realized I was scared to death and all I wanted to do was draw you close to me again.'

'This explains those Kegel exercises you were doing?'

'Oh, honey,' she said, 'those weren't even voluntary, that's how hot it was.'

He laughed.

'You wait,' she said. 'I'll be able to peel a banana with it yet.'

'One of the things I love most about you,' he said, 'is how poetically sappy you get about sex.'

'I'm a Texas girl. My granny used to say that a true belle never underestimates the value of a tight snatch and a cocktail dress that'll hide your love handles. Oh shit,' she said, and went back into her office to retrieve her bag. She stood at the door and did the inventory: laptop, phone, cigarettes, scripts. Then came back and kissed him. Started out again but turned suddenly. 'We're okay, you and me, right?'

'This means I'm forgiven for last night? The pre-sex part, anyway.'

'Hell no. You're still an asshole about that. But I just want to establish that you're at least still *my* asshole.'

She batted her eyelashes at him then made a tight circle with her thumb and forefinger, which she kissed with a large smacking sound before she sailed out the door with a backward *ciao*. It might be said she had faults, Spandau thought, but not knowing how to make an exit was not one of them.

EIGHTEEN

He met her in the park at Malibu Lagoon, a mile down the road from where he'd been sitting last night. He pulled off the coast highway and parked in the lot. It was early and hers was the only other car there. He followed the path out to the guard station and the beach. She was standing at the edge of the water just beyond the reach of the surf, staring across the water at Santa Monica pier. He called her name, gently, careful of scaring her. She wasn't easily frightened, was Delia, but she hated surprises. She turned.

'This is a kind of ironic joke?' she said, as he trudged across the sand to her.

It was, of course. But he pretended he didn't catch her meaning.

'This is where you took me on our first date,' she said. 'Don't try to tell me that escaped you.'

'It didn't,' he said.

She opened her arms in a gesture of surrender. 'Well, here I am. You're angry, take your best shot. I left you, you want payback, now is great. You want me to screw you, I'll do that too. Whatever it takes, let's just get it over so I can find my husband.'

Oh that word husband. It hurt and she knew it would. It was just like her to set the terms, to get the hard part out of the way as quickly as possible. He went up to her anyway and kissed her softly on the cheek. Then she was in his arms. Neither was quite sure how that happened, her standing there crying with her head on his shoulder. He'd thought about something just like this for more than a year, ever since she'd left him. But she wasn't crying to come back, she wasn't crying for him. As much as he wanted to believe it was, he could feel in the taut curve of her back her refusal to let her body press too closely against him. It was not love she wanted, at least not that kind of love, and this small honest gesture hurt him more than anything else she could have said or done. She stepped back away from him, brushing at the tears with the tips of her fingers.

'I can't call the police,' she said, reading his mind. 'I don't know exactly what he's done.'

'If he's hiding from these bozos, it's probably not a great idea to have the cops looking for him anyway. They're not exactly discreet. All you're doing is fingering him for the bad guys. Anyway there's no law that says he has to come home. Are you sure it's gambling?'

'It can't be anything else.'

'He's done it before?'

Long pause. Too long.

'Yes, but not with me.' Later he remembered the look on her face and the weight of her voice when she said this, realizing what it must have cost her. 'Do you mind if we sit down? I haven't slept in a couple of days.'

It was three days, to be exact, and he'd find out she'd not eaten either. There was a lot she didn't tell him. There was a lot she never would. They sat down on a bench near the mouth of one of the lagoon trails.

'Nobody told me, you see. Charlie didn't, neither did his sister. There's a kind of weird solidarity there, even though they don't get along. I called her right after he went missing, told her about the three men. Then she told me. It's one of the things that ruined his first marriage, he'd been through therapy, GA, the whole thing. He was afraid to tell me, afraid of losing me. And everybody was sure he had it under control, his first wife was crazy, that's why he gambled, he was happy with me, I was his good-luck charm. It was all different now so why should they tell me.'

'And he's not gambled in the time you've been with him? Maybe some small stuff, amounts of money you might not notice?'

'No, nothing, I'm sure of it. All the accounts are shared. I'd know. That's how I found out how serious it is. He's emptied the savings account.'

'How much?'

'A little over thirty thousand. He took most of the checking too. I checked through the school and he's tried to get money out of the retirement account but he needs me for that. Nothing else seems to be gone. I mean we're teachers, for god's sake. There *is* nothing else.'

'No idea what he owes? These men didn't mention an amount?'

'They didn't mention numbers. Obviously more than thirty thousand.'

'He might be using the thirty grand to try and win the rest of it.'

'Oh god, you don't think he would?'

'Well, the smart thing would have been to give them the thirty grand to keep them sweet for a while, but clearly he's not done that. It's pretty common. You owe big money and you panic. In a way we should hope that's what he's doing. Everybody on the street will know by now he's hot so he'll have to hit the out-of-town casinos. If he's moving around there might be a trail. The trick is to find him before they do. Tell me about the men.'

'Dark. Middle Eastern looking. Late twenties, early thirties. One of them, the tall one, I think he was the boss. He did all the talking anyway. The other two just stood out in the yard. I remember one of them teasing the other, flicking him on the ear, things like that. Like kids. The one who came to the door was different. Very cold, very businesslike. He just asked to see Charlie and when I said he wasn't home he asked where he was. I said I didn't know. He asked when he'd be back and I said I didn't know that either. He just stared at me, as if he were trying to decide if I was lying. Then he gave me the bag and asked me to please give it to my husband when he returned.'

'What bag?'

'It was the strangest thing. It was just a little brown paper bag,

like a lunch bag. He handed it to me then they left. I looked inside
the bag but there was nothing except a small package wrapped in
butcher's paper. I opened it up and it was a pair of chicken legs,
raw chicken drumsticks. I couldn't image why on earth he'd give
me something like this. I didn't know whether to laugh or cry. I
went into the kitchen and just put them in the fridge, I couldn't
think of what else to do with them. I was so stupid, you know,
I just didn't get it. I kept thinking about them and after a while I
went in and took them out of the fridge and looked at them. Both
legs were bent at odd angles, broken, snapped right in half. That's
when I knew,' she said, 'that's when I knew my Charlie was in
trouble.'

She began to cry again. Spandau tried to touch her but she
shook him violently away and sat on the edge of the bench, bent
over and sobbing into her hands. Spandau watched her and felt
helpless but he was getting used to it.

NINETEEN

Spandau arrived at the office later that morning. Pookie was
at her desk looking crisp as usual with Leo hovering nearby
and resembling a lost calf. Spandau knew he'd be there and
sneaked up on the office door and entered quickly. Leo was caught
and attempted to look as if he were there for a good reason.

'I was just seeing if she got my account statements,' Leo said
quickly. 'You got my account statements, right?' he said to
Pookie.

'What account statements?' said Pookie. Making Leo miserable
was one of her favorite pastimes, and he made it so easy to do.

'The, um,' said Leo, who reddened and just went blank.

'Have you lost your mother, Leo?' Spandau asked him. 'Are
you looking to be adopted?'

'No, sir.'

'Then why do you keep circling this desk like a bottle fly at a
picnic? Why are you not at the public works office checking on
that utility connection date I asked you for?'

'I was just going,' he said, and went. He caught his jacket in the office door and had to make a humiliating re-entry to free it.

'I almost feel sorry for him,' Spandau said to Pookie when he'd gone.

'Don't,' she said. 'He showed up at my door unannounced last night and ruined a perfectly lovely date with Eric Winterbottom.'

'I thought Eric Winterbottom was gay.'

'He is but Leo doesn't know that. Eric was giving me a deep-tissue massage and Leo heard me moaning. I came to the door in a towel, too, just to get even. I thought he was going to break into tears. He's just spent the last half-hour trying to get me to assure him nothing happened.'

'Did you?'

'No,' she said. 'Of course not. He's so cute when he suffers.'

'You make me happy to be ancient and past all that,' he said.

'Oh you're not past anything,' said Pookie. 'Anna drops the occasional hint about your hi jinks.'

'Is there anything you don't have your nose into?'

'I have one of those faces that people talk to. I can't help it. It's a curse sometimes.'

'Well, maybe we can finally make it pay off. I have a job for you.'

'A job? You mean like a detective job? Really?' She practically squealed.

'You are not licensed by the state of California to perform any work of detection. However I do need you to snoop around a little, which is just letting you practice your favorite hobby.'

'An unofficial dick,' she said.

'Look, if you're going to go around saying things like that I'd just as soon have someone else do it.'

'No no, please. I'll be good. Promise.'

'It's more of a personal favor than anything else. Anna is not to know, Pook. I mean it.'

'What have you done?'

'Just calm down. I'm completely innocent of whatever vileness you have going through your mind right now. When Little Lord Fauntleroy comes back, I want to talk to both of you.'

'I'm working with Leo?'

'I don't want you doing this alone.'

'Do I get to be boss at least?'

'Yes, you get to be boss.'

'Boy, he'll hate that!' she said happily.

It was not the first time that Spandau suppressed an involuntary shiver at the way her mind worked. He almost felt sorry for Leo. And he would have, too, if he didn't have nearly as much fun tormenting Leo as she did.

TWENTY

Leo was back before noon. He opened the office door slowly and stuck his head in, as if worried someone might be throwing darts.

'You're safe,' Pookie told him. 'He's in the office on the phone.'

'It's nearly lunchtime. We could go somewhere.'

'I have my lunch, thank you, and I'm going to Maxfield to look at a dress.'

'I could drive you.'

'Buying a dress is too intimate to be shared with someone I know only on a casual basis. We are talking about clothing here. And there'd have to be several years of successful cohabitation before I could even think about taking you along for shoes.'

'I want to know you on more than a casual basis,' he said.

'Oh that is so sweet,' she said. 'But it would probably take a nuclear holocaust to shift the odds in your favor.'

'You don't have to enjoy being so cruel about it.'

'Well, I do enjoy it but that has nothing to do with the fact that emotionally you are a child and while this is not necessarily a turn-off it is a definite red flag.'

'What would I have to do. Just tell me.'

'Get rid of all that *Battlestar Galactica* stuff in your apartment. Trekkie stuff can be kind of retro-hip but the *BG* thing is just never going to fly. No one is ever going to have sex with you with Edward James Olmos staring down at them.'

'Are you saying that you'll have sex with me if I get rid of that poster in the bedroom?'

'I am not saying that at all. I'm saying that if you wish to ever procreate with another being of remotely your own kind – of which I am emphatically not, by the way – you will replace that signed photo of Tricia Helfer with a Miro lithograph or something.'

'You know what you are? You're a snob.'

'Of course I am. All the Rhode Island Vanderkamps are snobs. Otherwise we would be the Arkansas Vanderkamps or something. You really are the most juvenile thing.'

'That's it,' he said. He tossed some official-looking documents on the desk. 'Here, give him this. They're the stuff from public works he wanted. I'm going off to lunch by myself. I regret ever having fallen in love with you.'

'You really are in love with me?'

'Duh.'

'Well, oh god, I suppose I'll have to have lunch with you now. It would be unthinkably gauche if I didn't.'

'Don't strain yourself.'

'I have just offered up myself to lunch with you. If you are now having some kind of cris de coeur about it I would advise you to be sure. It is unlikely this will ever happen to you again.'

'I don't understand you,' he said flatly.

'No one would expect it of you. Anyway neither of us can go anywhere right now. He wanted to see us both when you got back.'

'Am I in trouble?'

'Just hold my hand and I'll walk you through it,' she said.

She buzzed and Spandau said to come in. Spandau was sitting behind the desk, the expensive cowboy boots perched precariously on the edge. He was leaning back in the chair and his hands were clasped behind his head.

'Dee's husband Charlie has done a runner,' said Spandau.

'You've been reading John Le Carré again, haven't you,' Pookie said to him.

'I have,' said Spandau. 'Anyway he's taken off.'

'Legged it,' offered Leo.

They both just looked at him.

'It's another British term,' Leo said weakly.

'Anyway,' said Spandau, 'he's gone. Dee thinks he's in hock for some gambling debts and is hiding. I think she's right. She's asked me to find him.'

'Ouch,' said Pookie.

'I'd rather you handle it. It means working closely with Dee and I don't think that's a good idea.'

'You mean you're giving us a case?' said Leo.

'Oh darling please shut up,' Pookie said to him. 'I will draw you little pictures later. Let me talk to the nice man now.'

'What I want you to do is go out and talk to her again. Pook, she knows you, that'll help.'

'Does she know you're having me – us – take over the case for you?'

'You're not actually taking over the case. All you're doing right now is some groundwork. Talk to her again and have her bring you up to speed. Then we'll compare versions and see if she's come up with anything new. Have her go over the bank accounts again and check the credit-card records for the last few months. Look especially at activities on both his and her cards over the last few days. What we're looking for is gas station, food and hotel receipts, especially around casinos.'

'If he's hiding, you think he's going to be dumb enough to leave a trail like that?' said Leo.

'It's not a matter of him being dumb,' said Spandau. 'He's got cash, but it's his gambling stake and if we're lucky he's not going to want to spend it. He also knows these guys don't have access to his card records so he's safe as far as they're concerned.'

'He has to know that Dee's going to check the cards,' said Pookie. 'What's to stop Dee from putting a hold on them? Maybe she should. How do we know he's not lying in a coma somewhere and somebody else is having a holiday with his cards?'

'The transactions themselves should tell you something. If it's Charlie, he's not going to be staying at the Ritz or eating gourmet or buying expensive lingerie. It'll be basic stuff like gas and food and motels. She could stop the cards, but I don't think she should. At that point we completely lose the trail and it's liable to throw him into a panic. Anyway, he's probably worried that's exactly what she's going to do. I wouldn't stop them unless Dee's worried about the amounts.'

'If she stops the cards, maybe it'll force him to call her,' said Leo.

'Maybe,' said Spandau. 'But he still has cash, and he's not out looking to make a summer vacation of this. If he's gambling at all – and I think he is – then he's going to want to make a quick score and give these guys enough to let him come back home. Sooner or later he knows he has to.'

'Or he could kill himself,' said Leo.

'Is he that type?' Pookie asked Spandau.

'I don't know,' said Spandau. 'I've managed to avoid meeting the guy. I have no idea how high-strung he is. This is not, by the way, something you should bring up to Dee, although I'm pretty sure that's one of the things she's worried about. Talk to the sister. And get a list of friends he might contact from both of them. We're assuming he's on the road, but he could just as easily be holed up with an old gambling buddy.'

'Or an old girlfriend,' said Leo.

'Only a man would think of that,' Pookie said to him.

'Nevertheless, he's right. See if you can get the sister to come up with some names.'

'What's the sister like?' asked Pookie.

'No idea,' said Spandau. 'This is why I'm giving this to you two. It's called beating the bushes. This is what we do in the gumshoe biz.'

'Shamus, gumshoe, private eye, dick,' said Leo.

'Sleuth,' said Pookie. 'That's my favorite.'

'Flatfoot?' said Leo.

'No,' said Pookie. 'That's just for cops.'

'Sherlock,' said Spandau, 'but we are wandering into the attention-deficit zone here. Talk to Dee and the sister. Do not, and I repeat do not, go wandering off and do anything else. Report back to me. And if you happen to come across these three bozos that are looking for him, run away, do not walk. Do not in any way make contact with these guys, I don't care if you have to leap out a five-story window to avoid them. The job is to find Charlie, not to sort out his personal problems for him.'

'Or to get coshed with a blackjack,' said Leo.

'Coshed,' repeated Pookie. 'Oh, I like that one. Coshed.'

Spandau gave her a look.

'Let's assume we find him,' Pookie said quickly. 'Then what? It doesn't resolve anything.'

'I'm not sure that we're in the resolve business,' said Spandau. 'Not yet anyway.'

'But this is what she wants,' said Pookie. 'She didn't come to you to find her husband. He'll eventually turn up one way or another. What she wants you to do is get him out of this.'

'This isn't what she asked.'

'Yeah, but you know this is what she wants.'

'Let's just see if we can find the bastard first,' said Spandau. 'I also want you to do a little background check on Jerry Margashack. Rumors, anything that could be used against him.'

'I appreciate your seeing me as the truly superior individual that I am,' said Pookie, 'but I'm not sure how I can do all this and hold the fort here as well.'

'Who was that friend of yours who subbed when you went on vacation? The cute little blonde?'

'You mean Tina?'

'Yeah, she was cute,' said Leo. Pookie pinched him and he gave out a short yelp.

'I'll call her. I don't think she's working now. Yale drama and she still can't find a job.'

'Meanwhile I've got this Margashack thing.'

'Is he as crazy as they say?' Leo asked.

'Look,' Spandau said to him, 'one of the first rules of this trade is that you don't go around gossiping about your clients. Got that?'

Leo reddened and nodded his head.

'But yeah,' said Spandau. 'Between you and me, he's as mad as a hatter.'

TWENTY-ONE

Meg Patterson took a sip of her martini and made a face. 'Jesus,' she said. 'I haven't had one of these things in years. It's like drinking cleaning fluid. But I mean that in the nicest possible way.'

'You want something else?' Spandau asked her. They were sitting in a booth at Musso and Franks. He'd asked her to lunch. She'd refused until he promised to take her somewhere decent for a change.

'Hell no,' she said. 'I love a martini. Two at the most.'

'With three I'm under the table,' said Spandau.

'With four I'm under my host,' she said, completing the poem. 'Don't you love Dorothy Parker? See, this is why I bother with you at all. You somehow manage to combine being strong and silent with an almost metrosexual understanding of the finer things in life.'

'Is that a compliment?'

'Why on earth would you think that? As my record will attest, I prefer men who are not particularly strong and only silent when they're trying to find out where I hide my silverware.'

The waiter came back.

'I'll have the New York steak, medium rare, the mashed potatoes, creamed spinach, and a tossed salad with Thousand Island dressing. And another martini.'

'Do I detect some unhappiness in your life?' Spandau asked her.

'Oh you mean because I'm eating like fifteen jackals on a downed wildebeest? You're buying, remember, and normally all you give me is a hot dog or something. I'm due for this. And you're about to hit me up for some other favor anyway.'

'I've seen you hoover up food pretty good before, thanks. I mean the martinis in the middle of the day. This is new. Is there something wrong at the paper?'

'Stuart left,' she said.

'And Stuart was . . .?'

'The musician. The oboe player. I swear to god I expected more out of an oboe player. It turns out they're just like everybody else. He called me a ball-buster. You don't think I'm a ball-buster, do you?'

Spandau put his forefinger and thumb about half an inch apart.

'Well, okay, they were tiny balls anyway. Men always have trouble with strong women.'

'I don't.'

'Oh yes you do. You're only happy with strong women when they get all gushy and icky around you. You never meet them as equals. You play off their weaknesses.'

'Jesus. Thank you. That's very sweet.'

'Don't take it personally, but I think all men should be castrated. I have this theory about all men subconsciously thinking of their dicks as a club.'

'I don't think this is really a new insight.'

'I never said it was new, I just said it was something I now firmly believe. Men have this dangly thing and they're like those monkeys at the beginning of Kubrick's *2001*. They've just got to beat something to death with it.'

'I can't wait to see where all this heads after the second martini.'

'What is the male equivalent of a ball-buster? See? There isn't one. Women have no word for men who try to desexualize them. This is because it's an accepted process throughout history.'

'If you're going to go all Andrea Dworkin on me,' said Spandau, 'then I'm going to have to get tanked as well. I recall we had this same conversation when Kenny left you. It was piña coladas then. Just before you threw up in the parking lot you were taking the line about all men being potential rapists.'

'All men are pigs,' she said. She raised her glass. 'To swine!'

'To swine.'

Spandau tapped her martini with his beer. They drank.

'I have to say you're a swine. One of the better ones, but a swine anyway.'

'Thank you.'

'I've always liked your eyes. They are good eyes for a swine. Decidedly unswinelike.'

'Mirror of an unswinish soul?'

'Maybe you're only half swine. There's a bloodhound in there somewhere. Kind of sad and tired and droopy eyed.'

There were tears forming in her eyes.

'Shit,' she said.

She got up and scurried back toward the restroom. She came back a few minutes later, her eyes dry but red.

'I don't see where an oboe player gets off calling anybody a ball-buster,' she said. 'A fucking oboe player. Maybe if he'd been a brass player. But the woodwinds are all pussified.'

'Pussified. Yes, I think I heard Aaron Copland mention that. The pussified woodwinds. You tell Stuart this?'

'Damn right.'

'And was this before or after the ball-buster remark? Jesus, Meg.'

'Do not make fun of me,' she said laughing. 'I'm in great personal anguish.'

'Didn't you once tell me that the suffering of others is our greatest source of comedy? I think you said that to me right after Dee left.'

'You were wallowing in self-pity.'

'Welcome to the pig pen.'

'You couldn't see it at the time, but she set you free. You were suffocating each other.'

'Oh, I don't feel much like discussing this, Margaret.'

'The trouble with men is that they'll just stare at a brick wall until it falls on them. Then they see the light on the other side.'

'I don't mind being called a swine or even a monkey beating things to death with my johnson. But if you are going to get all philosophical about my personal life, I'm grabbing the check now and going home.'

'You're so cute when your feelings are invaded. You do that thing with your mouth.'

'What thing with my mouth?'

'This thing. The spinster mouth. Your lips get all thin.'

She made the face.

'Even Anna's noticed it,' she said.

'For god's sake, is there anybody she doesn't talk to about our personal life?'

'It has nothing to do with you, but she's an Oscar-winner. She's one of the interesting creatures. Anyway, sweetheart, the time to worry is when a woman *stops* talking about you. Oh god.'

'What?'

'I just had this flash. I'd like to say I'm psychic but you are just such an open book. You're seeing Dee again, aren't you?'

'Charlie has gone missing. It looks like he's in hock to some shylocks. Dee's asked me to find him.'

'How convenient.'

'I thought you liked her.'

'I do like her. But she's just as capable of being manipulative as the rest of us. There are a thousand other people she could have picked and she chose you. Hm.'

'She knows me.'

'Yes indeed she does. She knows you're with Anna now too and she knows that it's working.'

'She didn't just make up this story about Charlie.'

'No, but Charlie's not the angel she thought he was, no pun

intended. So she comes to you. You asshole. Do not fuck this up with Anna.'

'It's not like that. She loves him. She just wants to make sure he's safe.'

'Look, I'm not saying you're an idiot, but you're an idiot.'

'Pookie and Leo are handling it. It's just a favor.'

'Right. You should take up the oboe, you know that? When you do your mouth like that it's perfect. You look just like Stuart.'

The food came. She may have been personally distraught but she tucked into it like a lumberjack. She was halfway through the steak before she spoke again.

'Okay,' she said. 'I'm being fed, we've exchanged the requisite personal shit. What do you want?'

'I need to see Mel Rosenthal.'

'Ha. You and the rest of the world. Ask Anna. She knows him.'

'I did. Somebody in his office warned her off.'

'Gosh you're off to a good start. You haven't even met the guy and already you're on his bad side. Which is not a great place to be, by the way. He's very friendly with the Boys.' She pushed her nose to one side. 'Anyway, why are you investigating Mel Rosenthal?'

'I'm not. I just want to talk to him.'

'Do not be coy with me. This is Auntie Meg. Give up the goods or I'm just going to eat and drink and puke on your cowboy boots again. Who is the client?'

'You know I'm not going to tell you that.'

'Jerry Margashack?'

'Jesus, Meg.'

'I read the papers too, you know. There's Oscar buzz all over the guy, then shit on him starts appearing in the media. Granted, it's a town full of imbeciles but even the brain-damaged can pick up on a smear campaign like this. It's not the first time Rosenthal has pulled this.'

'I'm not investigating Rosenthal, I'm not accusing Rosenthal of anything. I just want to ask him some questions but I can't get anywhere near him.'

'No shit. He'd just love to have you nosing into this.'

'This is where you come in. I want you to call him.'

'And ask about Margashack and rumors that Rosenthal may have released certain information.'

'Right.'

'You think this is going to drive him right into your arms?'

'You work for the *LA Times*. He'd sure as hell rather talk to me than you. I'm bound by confidentiality to my client.'

'Why talk to either one of us?'

'He's got a picture in the race too. He doesn't want this out there. If people think he's behind this it could screw up his own chances. You know as well as I do that it's like a politician running for office. They're going to want to contain this.'

'You think he's behind it?'

'That's what I'm trying to figure out.'

'So you're just going to walk up to him and ask him.'

'That's about the size of it.'

'And he's going to tell you the truth?'

'I have long ago given up on the idea that anyone ever tells me the truth,' said Spandau. 'Nowadays I just focus on the different ways people tell me lies. Anyway the truth is always the same, but you can tell a lot about a person by the way they con you.'

'Okay,' she said. 'Same deal as always. If the story breaks I get the exclusive.'

'If the story breaks. And it had better not break in front of me.'

'I thought you trusted me.'

'About as much as you trust me,' he said.

'We have both become bitter,' she said. 'You ever think of yourself as a kind of monster? I mean, it's a shitty world but we both really are pretty good at it.'

'Why don't we ask Dee and Stuart,' he said.

'Touché,' she said, and emptied her second martini.

TWENTY-TWO

Tina Belucci was beautiful by anybody's standards. She was a small blonde whose father had been an Italian Formula One driver and whose mother was a French actress. She had her father's olive skin and her mother's hair. She got her cheerful disposition and intelligence from them both, along with a personality that made her seem like she was flirting even when she wasn't. This made her popular with men in ways she didn't particularly like, and unpopular with women in ways that were worse. Anna didn't like her, for instance, and referred to her as 'that horny little Italian runt'.

Spandau had to admit it was hard to take your eyes off her, and she had this way of looking up and gazing while you spoke. Spandau had never thought much about the difference between a simple look and a gaze. After Tina, his conclusion was that a look was just a look, but a gaze made you want to sit on the edge of the desk and talk about your childhood. This was distracting but by no means a bad talent to have in a detective agency. Tina was smart, as well, and was reliable and had a mind that could juggle a dozen things at once, which is what the job called for.

When Spandau came into the office she said:

'Mr Rosenthal's assistant called. Lena Swift. Would you call her back at your convenience.'

She handed him the number and smiled. This was accompanied by a gaze, in which Spandau noted how long her eyelashes were, and that somehow he had come to roost on the edge of her desk. He got up.

'Should I ring her for you?'

'No no, I'll just make the call from my office. Walter's office.'

'I don't mind,' she said, gazing.

She rang the number. Spandau looked at her hands and noted there was no wedding or engagement ring. He wondered how many times a day other men did the same thing.

'David Spandau returning Lena Swift's call . . . Yes, thank you.'

She handed him the phone.

'Mr Spandau?' said the voice. 'I'm Lena Swift, one of Mel's assistants. Mel would like to meet with you. If it's convenient.'

'Please thank Mr Rosenthal. When would he like to meet?'

'He has a busy day and there won't be much time. What about half an hour?'

'Sure. What is the address?'

'We'll send a car for you.'

'I can drive.'

'Mel would prefer that you didn't. At your office in say twenty minutes?'

'Great. Should I pack a lunch?'

'As I say, Mel has a busy day and we'll have you back at a reasonable time. Would you like the driver to bring you a sandwich?'

'I'll try to stick it out,' he said, and she hung up. 'I'm going on a journey,' he said to Tina. 'There's a car picking me up in twenty minutes. Just buzz me, will you? I'm going to go curl my sideburns.'

She giggled. It was very hard to resist a giggle and a gaze. Spandau suppressed the urge to sit back on the desk and tell her about a pet rabbit he had as a kid. Instead he went into the office and called Meg at the newspaper.

'He bit,' he said.

'When do you meet him?'

'In half an hour. He's sending a car for me.'

'A car? Look, leave a trail of breadcrumbs. If they take you to a house in the woods made of gingerbread, run like a bastard.'

The car arrived exactly twenty minutes later. The driver was standing by the car and blocking a hefty section of Sunset Boulevard. He didn't seem to mind. He opened the door for Spandau, closed it, and casually strolled around the car to the driver's seat. If the honking bothered him he didn't show it.

'No bag over my head?' Spandau said to the driver once they were in traffic.

'Sir?'

'They seemed reluctant to give me the address. I could have driven myself.'

'Oh, Mr Rosenthal moves around a lot. Busy man. Half the time even he doesn't know where he's supposed to be.'

'Then can I ask where you're taking me?'

'To the beach house. Unless somebody calls and says different. That happens all the time too.'

And if Spandau didn't know where he was going, neither would his office or anybody else. He'd heard Rosenthal was a control-freak and liked all the bases covered. This was a subtle way of making sure nobody else showed up unannounced. It was a little Gestapo-like, but effective if you wanted your visitor with the shit scared out of him.

TWENTY-THREE

They drove to the Malibu colony. The driver deposited him at a large house that backed up to the ocean. Before Spandau could ring the bell the door was opened by a big man in a dark suit.

'Hello, Louis,' said Spandau. 'How's it hanging these days?'

Louis scowled, but then Spandau had never seen him when he wasn't. Spandau followed him up a short flight of stairs and through the living room out onto the deck. Salvatore Locatelli stood leaning against the wooden railing, smoking a cigar and looking down on a fashion model being photographed on the beach below. She was half naked and trying not to freeze to death in eight inches of cold Pacific.

Locatelli was an elegant man with graying hair, impeccable manners, and a well-clipped mustache. He was small but grew considerably taller when you remembered he controlled nearly every crooked racket between Tijuana and San Luis Obispo, and only stopped there because, until you got to San Francisco, there wasn't enough money to make it worthwhile. Anyway his cousin Angelo owned San Francisco.

'I've got to get one of these,' Locatelli said.

'You mean the model or the beach house?'

'The beach house,' said Locatelli. 'I've sworn off models. If I'm going to have another mistress, which is questionable I might add, I'd prefer someone less self-absorbed. They are wonderful to look at though. What do they call it? Eye candy?'

'Don't wait too long,' said Spandau. 'Pretty soon it's going to be like trying to shoot pool with a rope.'

Locatelli laughed. 'George Burns said that. You didn't think I'd catch it, did you? It's true though. We're all getting old, Texas. We have to face up to it.'

'You face up to it. I'm going to stay in denial a while longer if you don't mind.'

'Ah, yeah, that's right. You're with that actress now. She's still a beauty okay. Which one is she again?'

'You know damned well who she is. You were in Cannes with us when all that shit with Perec and Special came down. You also published that self-serving piece-of-crap book he wrote about it.'

'And don't forget the film. We're making a bundle on that one too. *The Princess and the Pimp*. You have to admit it's a good story. Anyway, what are you complaining about? You came out looking okay. You're a star now too.'

Louis came out carrying a tray of sandwiches and beer.

'Somebody told me you were hungry,' Locatelli said. 'Come on, Texas. Tell me you're surprised to see me.'

'I'd be surprised if Mel Rosenthal was hiding behind the sofa,' Spandau said, taking a sandwich. 'Is this picnic just for us or do I actually get to talk to him?'

'Mel will be along directly. I just felt it would be a good time for you and me to get reacquainted.'

'I'm touched and all,' Spandau said, 'but if you're going to threaten me, why bring me all the way out here? Why have me meet Rosenthal at all?'

'You think you're being threatened? If you were being threatened, Texas, your meeting with Louis at the door would have been less than cordial. Look, he made you sandwiches.'

'Louis will make somebody a swell nanny. You want to tell me what the hell is going on?'

'First of all,' said Locatelli, 'you have to stop seeing enemies where there are none. If I wanted you harmed, there's not a damned thing you could do about it, and you and I both know it. This is one of those occasions where I can actually do you some good. We can both do each other some good.'

'Sorry. Honorable monkey no scratchee back. Can somebody drive me home or do I have to call a cab?'

'You want your ex-wife's husband found, I can help you do it. And I can tell you who's looking for him too.'

'And in return what? I sell out my client?'

'Texas, you have the most misguided set of loyalties I have ever come across. You're not working for Jerry Margashack, because Jerry Margashack doesn't want you working for him. You're working for Frank Jurado, and it's no secret around town that you hate each other's guts and when he finds some way of pushing you under a truck he'll do it. Exactly whose interests are being served here? Be that as it may, I don't really care, but I'd like to assure you that right now I'm probably the closest friend you've got.'

'What sort of deal are you trying to make?'

'Just talk to Mel. You get that end of it straightened out, then we'll talk.'

As if on cue the door opened downstairs. Mel Rosenthal trudged up the steps followed by Lena Swift. He said something to Lena and she nodded and then went downstairs. Rosenthal sauntered on out to the deck.

'Mr Spandau?'

'That's right.'

'Sal tells me you can be a real pain in the ass when you feel like it.'

They shook hands.

'He's a real kidder, our Sal,' said Spandau. 'He gets a few in him and he's liable to wear a lampshade and dance on the table.'

'Did you actually hit Frank Jurado?'

'It was an accident. I was reaching for my milkshake and he got in the way.'

'Somebody should club the oily bastard to death,' said Rosenthal. 'Everybody hates him, but he doesn't give a shit. You have to respect that.'

'Is this the part where you tell me that being a sociopath is actually an attribute in our business?'

'That's one way of looking at it,' said Rosenthal. 'Anyway, this thing you think I'm doing, I'm not doing it.'

'And exactly what thing is it that I think you're doing that you're not doing?' said Spandau. To Locatelli he said, 'Did I get that right?'

'I'm not trying to smear Jerry Margashack. I don't need to. *Wet Eye* is a good film but our film is better, and Jurado is a clever fucker but he's never got an Oscar and I've got a dozen of them. He doesn't know how to get there and I do. If I needed the extra leverage, I'd smear his ass all over the place, but in this case I don't. I don't need it and it's not worth the risk. If you knew anything about Academy Award politics you wouldn't even have to ask.'

'You don't think *Wet Eye* is competition?'

'Everything nominated is competition. *Wet Eye* isn't *serious* competition. Jurado has fucked around with reshooting and the editing and he's getting a late start. He's second-guessed his director and everybody knows it and that in itself is like pouring blood into shark-filled waters. People haven't got a fucking idea now who they're giving the award to. Besides, he's in trouble financially and he hasn't got the bread to back a serious campaign, even if he did know how to do it. This is not a crap shoot, my friend, this is science. There are little rivalries everywhere. It's a popularity contest just like everything else. You sell a film to the Oscars the same way you sell it to the rest of the world.'

Inside the house Lena Swift came up the steps followed by the model, now huddled into a thick terrycloth robe. Spandau finally recognized her. She had long black hair and icy blue eyes, and the sort of delicate face you saw carved on Victorian lockets. You'd have to spend a while getting used to those before you ever started worrying about what was under the robe.

'Toni, Toni, Toni,' said Rosenthal. 'Get your ass out here.'

'There are icicles hanging from my tits,' Toni said. 'There's no way in hell I'm coming out there again.'

'Toni is staying here while she's in town,' said Rosenthal. 'When do you go to Milan?' he asked her.

'Next week,' she said. 'Come in here and talk to me. And close the door.'

They went inside. Rosenthal walked over and kissed Toni very lightly on the lips. 'When do I finally get tongue?' Rosenthal said to nobody in particular.

She grabbed a handful of middle-aged belly and pinched it. 'Lose some of this and maybe you'll get the whole enchilada one of these days.'

'I'll make you a star,' said Rosenthal.

'Both of us know I can't act worth a damn,' she said.

'When has that ever made any difference?'

'I did that Italian thing and even you laughed at it.'

'Wrong casting, honey,' he said. 'You look like an Italian social worker the way I look like a Chippendale.'

She shrugged, sat down on the sofa, and reached for a packet of cigarettes and a lighter on the coffee table. She lit it and looked at Spandau through the smoke.

'I need to talk to you,' Rosenthal said to Locatelli. Locatelli and Lena Swift followed him out of the room.

'That was subtle,' Toni said to Spandau. 'I'm supposed to seduce you, or haven't you figured that out.'

'How far are you prepared to go?'

'Not very far,' she said. She opened the robe and flashed lots of skin and little bikini. 'Are you swooning?'

'There's a definite weakness at the knees,' he said, and sat in a chair across from her. He took out one of his own cigarettes and she reached across the table to light it for him. She saw the appreciative look on his face and smiled.

'You're living with Anna Mayhew,' she said.

'Sorta kinda,' he said. 'I still have my place and she has hers.'

'Is that a hint?'

'No. Just a statement of fact. I was married and I'm still a little gun shy about cohabitation.'

'You're the faithful type. You look it, you know. Jesus, don't look so hurt. I meant it as a compliment. You were practically any other guy, I'd be feeling your eyes all over me. It's not always so nice.'

'So I've been told.'

'She's beautiful, your Anna. I bet she's got enough of that in her time.'

'Still does.'

'You ever get jealous?'

'A little, every now and then,' he said. 'At the end of the day you have to figure she's with me because she wants to be, not because she doesn't have other choices. I can't say I always understand her reasons, but I don't have to. They're her reasons, not mine, and they seem to work for her.'

'You're not half bad,' she said. 'If I changed my mind about seducing you, how far do you think I'd get?'

'I could tell you about this pet rabbit I had as a kid,' he said.

'If I had a nickel for every time somebody has tried that line on me,' she said. They laughed. 'Lucky woman,' she said.

'Now I am swooning.'

Louis appeared at the top of the stairs. He stood there looking at Spandau until Spandau finally got up and went over to him.

'Mr Rosenthal has gone,' Louis whispered, 'and Mr Locatelli would like to know if you are going or staying.'

'Tell Mr Locatelli that I will be going.'

'You're sure?' said Louis.

'Reasonably,' said Spandau.

Louis turned and left. Spandau looked over at Toni, who was standing next to the sofa smiling at him.

'Nothing but class, these guys,' she said. 'They know how to treat a woman, right?'

'It was nice meeting you,' he said. 'Maybe we'll meet again in less awkward circumstances.'

'I'm here until next week,' she said. 'In case you have a change of heart.' She slid the robe off her shoulders and let it fall to the floor. 'Not bad, right?'

'Not bad at all,' he said, and meant every word of it.

TWENTY-FOUR

'I tried to tell him it wouldn't work,' Locatelli said when Spandau climbed into the waiting Lincoln. 'Mel thinks everybody in the world is motivated by the same things he is. She's not bad, though. Maybe I should reconsider this ban on models.'

'Leave her alone, for chrissake,' said Spandau. 'I'm sure she enjoys getting passed around like a plate of hors d'oeuvres. She's not a bad kid.'

'This is what I mean about you and your misplaced sympathies,' Locatelli said. 'She would eat both of us alive.'

'I'd give you an argument,' Spandau said, 'but lecturing you on human morality is about the biggest waste of breath I can think of.'

'Don't push your luck, Texas,' Locatelli said in a cold voice. 'I live by a different set of rules than you do, and maybe you don't see that, but it doesn't mean I don't have them. You sitting here now proves that. There are a lot of savages out there, and every day it's like the fucking barbarian hordes are hammering at the gates, a lot of animals with no rules at all. Your friend Charlie has managed to fall into a nest of them.'

'Are you going to do a fan dance all the way back to Santa Monica, or are you going to tell me what you want to tell me?'

'Your pal Charlie,' said Locatelli, 'owes eighty-five thousand dollars to an Armenian fucking lunatic named Atom Baldessarian. Uncle Atom, he owns a butcher shop in Los Feliz down by the 101. Butcher is a good name for him.'

'The Armenian mafia?'

'There is no such thing as the mafia,' said Locatelli. 'How many times have I got to tell you this? They're a gang of fucking hoodlums is all they are, crazy fucking animals who have no sense and are giving me a pain in the ass. Their idea of collecting on a debt is to hack off an arm or something. That's about as subtle as they get. Every time they pull this shit it makes life harder for me. In addition to several other badly run little operations, he's got this scam where he hangs around private clubs and casinos and pops up offering a loan to some loser on the spot. The fucking vigorish is impossible and I can't imagine what his collection rate is like. It doesn't make any sense to me. I mean, you want the marks to pay, right, so hacking off an arm and crippling the poor fuckers doesn't make any sense. I'm not even sure he wants to collect, you know? It's like he just hates people and has got it in for the entire human race. Sick crazy, this guy. All I know is that various arms and legs and other body parts have been cropping up all over LA and I'm getting tired of trying to explain it isn't any of my boys. Who thinks about fucking Armenians? There used to be like three of them in LA and now they're all over the fucking place.'

'He's got three guys who collect for him?'

'You mean the Chipmunks.'

'The what?'

'His nephews. It's an Armenian thing, you know, the guy who invented Alvin and the Chipmunks was Armenian or something. No wonder they have a hard time collecting with a tag like that. Anyway, two of them are idiots but the oldest is a pretty cool character. He's scared shitless of his uncle – they all are – but I could probably deal with him if I could get Atom out of the way. It's not a bad little operation if it wasn't run by a psychopath.'

'How do I come into this?'

'You keep looking for Charlie and you are going to cross their path at some point, I assure you. When you do, I want you to talk to the oldest nephew for me. I want to see if we can make some

sort of deal. I can't send any of my boys around without sending
up a fucking signal flare and having Atom go apeshit like a fucking
Ubangi with a machete. Nobody is looking at you.'

'Thanks for the info, but finding Charlie is no great shakes. I'd
find him anyway sooner or later.'

'If he steps into any gambling establishment in the United States
I can finger him in about ten minutes, whereas you're sniffing the
ground like Tonto and hoping you'll get lucky and nab him before
he's as limbless as a twenty-pound sack of potatoes. Even if you
find him, what the hell are you going to do? He's still into Atom
for the eighty-five big ones. You get to the nephew and maybe we
can negotiate something. Charlie gets to keep his arms and legs
and you're a big hero to your ex-old lady.'

'What about this campaign against Jerry Margashack? That is
the reason I trooped all the way out here.'

'Well, here's where it gets really amusing. It seems Jerry's into
Atom too. Not for a lot, but enough to put Uncle Atom at the top
of your must-do list.'

'Why would Atom want to smear Jerry?'

'Don't be stupid. Atom has nothing to do with that. But considering he's your client, I'd think keeping him in one piece might
be of interest to you.'

'And Mel?'

'You know as well as I do that Mel has nothing to do with any
of this. You heard what he said. There's no percentage in it for
him. Even you with your limited abilities should be able to see
this.'

'So what happens if I don't manage to cross paths with these
Chipmunks?'

'Oh, you keep nosing around, you'll run into them okay. Trust
me on this. And when you do, you are going to be looking around
for a friendly face.'

'What's to keep me from just backing away from the whole
damned thing?'

'That's what I'd do. Except you won't do it. Like it or not, Texas,
you've got two lives dumped into your lap. I know you, Texas. You're
fucking Gary Cooper. Everything is fucking *High Noon* with you.
I'd walk away and not think twice but you can't do it and we both
know it. Everybody knows it. You're as predictable as a clock, which

is why people dump this stuff on you in the first place. Sooner or later this is going to get you killed, and I will miss our little jokes when you are gone, but your stupidity about such things is not my problem.'

Locatelli clipped a Cuban cigar and lit it, filling the back of the car with a fug of smoke.

'It's not too late to turn around and go back to the beach house,' he said. 'She doesn't leave for Milan until next week. You lay up and act out every fantasy you've ever had, and by the time you stick you head out again it will all be over. Just say the word. Come on, Texas. Surprise me.'

'Don't you ever get tired of playing Mephistopheles?'

'With you, Texas? Never. You're one of the few things in life that never disappoint me. I always know right where you are if I happen to need you. That's very comforting to a man like me.'

Locatelli almost sounded as if he meant it. When Spandau realized that he did, and in what way, it made the hairs stand up on his neck.

TWENTY-FIVE

Pookie sat on the terrace of a hip cafe on Melrose looking glamorous in her sunglasses and a Hermès scarf draped over her head. Spandau was inside getting the coffees. Pookie watched the young and beautiful come and go. After a while Spandau came out with two cups and wound his way toward her with an irritated look on his face.

'Can you explain to me why you can order a double shot of orgasmic foot-crushed Kahuna bean and Nubian goat's milk latte and they get that right, but I order a lousy cup of black coffee and that confuses them?'

'Would you go to La Tour d'Argent and ask for a hamburger?'

'If I did,' said Spandau, 'I would at least expect them to look at me as if they knew what it was. We could have gone to Starbucks.'

'Not with me you couldn't.'

'Don't you think you're taking this "my life is a work of art" thing a bit too far?'

'First Starbucks, then Arby's. It all ends in a trailer park with the Schlitz cans piling up outside the window. It's a slippery road.' She took a sip of her latte. 'It's a bit coolish, but I can live.'

'Thank god,' said Spandau. 'I'd hate to try committing hara-kiri with a spork.'

'Your pal Margashack is an interesting character. Tina did a web search and I had her email you some old articles. He was out of the news for a long time, until *Wet Eye* and now this.'

'Anything incriminating?'

'Oh my yes. Lots. Just nothing that wasn't already public knowledge. He's never been very discreet, has he, your Jerry?'

'You say that like I've taken him for a pet.'

'He's another cowboy. You'll be like Randolph Scott and Joel McCrea in *Ride the High Country*. Two aging cowpokes. You can go shootin' and stuff together. Except I don't think he's a very nice man, your Jerry. Not very nice to women.'

'What did you find?'

'A lot of booze, a lot of drugs. It was always like Keith Richards sitting in a director's chair. He did half his films drunk or high, rumors of excess that makes Led Zeppelin and their fish episode seem like *Sesame Street*. Worked with a lot of great actors and it was either love or hate, never a middle ground. He wasn't exactly the darling of completion bond companies, since everybody expected to see him kack at any minute. Came close though on his last studio film, collapsed on set and they called in another director to finish. The suits claimed it was drugs but Jerry says it was exhaustion, he'd pissed them off and they were trying to break him. That did it for our Jerry in Tinseltown. He's done some low-budget features and a couple of documentaries to keep afloat. Supposedly he's cleaned up but one does begin to doubt.'

'What about him lifting that script?'

'Finally settled through arbitration with the Writer's Guild and the studio. Money exchanged hands, hush papers were signed. The other guy made a good enough buck off of it.'

'But is it true?'

'Nobody knows. I could ask around but we've all got our hands full right now and I don't think it would do any good. All we'd get are conflicting rumors at this point.'

'You don't much like him.'

'No,' she said. 'I don't, not much.'

'Why?'

'He's not very nice to women.'

'You know better than to believe what you read in the papers. Women seem to like him well enough.'

'He has a rather aggressive libido when he's stoned. He drinks and gropes. I talked to some people who'd worked with him. They finally had to stop hiring female production assistants on his sets. He seemed to think that doing it doggie style in the trailer was part of their job description.'

'Doggie style?'

'Well, I admit that part is my own contribution. Doggie style would give a man like that a sense of empowerment. He's probably into gagging too.'

'Damn, Pookie,' said Spandau, 'where do you come up with this shit?'

'Just because I went to a good school doesn't mean I'm naive,' she said. 'I also like watching you turn red. It's so cute.'

'He married a couple of his actresses.'

'And oh, didn't that work out well for everybody. One he gave a broken jaw and another claims he tried to cut her throat while she slept.'

'Tried?'

'Apparently she woke up when he climbed into bed with the knife or something.'

'At least half this sounds like the usual Hollywood bullshit and you know it. If *Wet Eye* gets an Oscar for Best Director the same people who said this stuff will be ringing his phone off the hook and trying to nominate him for Pope.'

'I don't like the fact that you like him.'

'Would any of this have to do with you being worried about me drinking again?'

'There's a lot I'm worried about,' she said. 'Walter, I worry about him, he's killing himself but there's nothing anybody can do, it's as if he's beyond redemption. And I get mad at him for what he does to you. I know Walter loves you but he can't help destroying the things he cares about most. I was glad when Anna showed up, she's turned everything around for you, you're different since you met her, you're even strong enough to stand up to Walter's efforts at Armageddon. I don't want to see you screw this up, David. You've got a shot at being happy finally. And now this thing with Dee.'

'I thought you liked Dee.'

'I do like Dee. She's a wonderful woman but just not for you. There, I finally said it. There's no question that Dee is a saint but you are a poor flawed truly human bastard and it's painful watching you kill yourself trying to live up to her exalted standards. Anna is no angel but she's human, just like you, which is what you need.'

Spandau was quiet.

'Am I fired?' she said.

'I'm thinking,' he said.

'Well fine if I am fired I don't care,' she said in one breath. 'Walter is lost and I can't bear watching you get lost again too. I just can't.'

'Pook . . .'

'This is where you very sweetly thank me for my concern but to mind my own goddamned business.'

'Right, Pook, except maybe not so sweetly, okay?'

'I bet you think I'm going to cry now, huh? Shows you how much you know about women, buster. I do however have this thing in my eye that urgently needs removing,' she said, hopping up from the table and walking quickly towards the restroom.

Spandau sighed, got out his cell phone, and read the notes that Pookie had sent him. When she came back, still dabbing at her red eyes, she said:

'I wasn't crying so don't flatter yourself.'

'And still nothing from Charlie?'

'He's not using the cards, at least not yet anyway. No more activity on the bank accounts, and he hasn't phoned.'

'This means he's eating into his stash, so he isn't going to wander too far from home.'

'Unless he's winning,' she said.

'He's a gambling junkie. If the cards are running well he's not going to walk away on his luck. Either way he won't go far. Just far enough away to feel safe from Atom and the Chipmunks.'

'Atom and the Chipmunks,' she repeated.

'It's a long story,' said Spandau. 'Get a list of friends from Dee and the sister. Press the sister for a list of old girlfriends – there must be some around. Follow up on that. My guess is that he hasn't gone far and is laying up with somebody. Do not let Dee know that we're following up this ex-girlfriend thing. It's ugly enough already. Stop looking at me that way.'

'You really do love her.'

'This is enough of you getting all gooey on me. At least start pretending you have a smidgeon of professional objectivity, or I'm going to remove your petite Ivy League buttocks from this case before it has a chance to start it. Are you reading me?'

'Yes, yes.'

'Meanwhile I go on with this Jerry thing. How fresh are these addresses?'

'Wives one and three are out of state, one in Louisiana and the other in New York. Wife two is currently in San Diego, Escondido to be exact. An ex-soft porn actress who now sells real estate. Just your type. How'd you like the photo? Those breasts aren't real, by the way.'

'Do I detect a hint of jealousy?'

'Not on your life. Anybody can buy a set of plastic jugs. It's working with what you've got that makes the woman.'

TWENTY-SIX

The trick of driving from LA to San Diego is simply refusing to do it. It took two hours to make the trip one way, so, given the traffic patterns on the roads between, you were bound to get snarled in traffic either coming or going. There was no way around it. He got to Escondido just after four in the afternoon, one jump ahead of the wave of traffic that would surely engulf him on the way back. Oh joy.

In the few instances Escondido is mentioned in the travel guides, it is referred to as a sleepy, working-class suburb. Working class it is, but not so much sleepy as already comatose. Vicky Rawlins lived at the end of a short cul-de-sac lined by stubby palm trees and oversize pickup trucks. Between her house and the neighbors there was a lovely unimpeded view of a freeway. Maybe it was southern California but for all you could tell it could have been Oshkosh. Spandau rang the bell, which apparently didn't work. He knocked and that didn't work either, so he peered in through the living-room window to catch a large, well-built man attempting to initiate sex with a girl maybe one third his age. She seemed fairly practiced at pushing his hands away and appeared more bored than terrified, but she was getting tired and both of them knew it was only a matter of time. Spandau banged on the window. The man pulled his hand out of her blouse and let her go, drifting toward the back of the house. The girl straightened her clothing and came to greet Spandau.

When she opened the door she was even younger than he thought, fourteen or fifteen, and was nearly past that weird stage when baby fat struggles to morph into the lush body of a young woman. Her eyes were red and a bit unfocused, as if she'd been crying, but her languid voice and the smell of pot wafting out of the door gave it away.

'You the detective guy?' She stood there surveying him, one hand on the door knob and the other on her hip.

'That's right. I'm David Spandau. Mrs Rawlins said to meet her here.'

'She called and said she'd be a little late. I'm supposed to keep you entertained. Whatever the fuck that means.'

'You'd be her daughter, right?'

'Yup.'

She didn't invite him in but stood aside. Inside the smell of dope was stronger. The big muscled guy came out of a back room toking on a joint. He stopped for a moment, glared at Spandau, then went on into the kitchen and out of a door to the garage. Spandau heard a big-engined car and the opening of the garage door. A Mustang Cobra backed roughly out of the drive and tore off down the street. Both Spandau and the girl watched the car through the front windows. She turned to Spandau and said,

'Asshole.'

She went into the kitchen and opened the fridge.

'You want something to drink? Like a beer?'

'Nothing, thanks.'

The girl took out a beer and popped it open. She walked into the living room and flopped down cross-legged in a chair. She drank the beer and made an effort to look bored. She stared at Spandau and waited for him to say something. He didn't.

'You can sit down if you want,' she said finally.

Spandau sat on the sofa across from her.

'That guy a friend of yours?'

'You are joking, right? Don't make me puke. He's my mom's old man. Why? Did you recognize him?'

Spandau shook his head. 'Am I supposed to?'

The girl took a roach from an ashtray on the coffee table. She lit it, took a few hits, offered it to Spandau. He shook his head.

'He's supposed to be famous or something,' she said in that squeaky I-don't-want-to-waste-the-dope voice. Then she exhaled. 'He's some kind of porn star. Carl "Hogsleg" Hogg. His thing is huge. Maybe when he comes back he'll show it to you. You probably won't be able to stop him.'

'He often come on to you like that?'

'Oh, you mean just now? Yeah. Old Carl is pretty persistent okay.'

'He ever, ah . . .'

'No! God, yuck, no way. I mean he wants to, he's like pushing that thing up against me all the time, you know, like I'm supposed to be all worked up by it. It's ugly. I mean, I'm not like an expert or something but that doesn't look anywhere like normal. Ugh.'

'You told your mom any of this?'

'Are you kidding? First time one of her boyfriends tried this shit I was, what, maybe ten, and she chewed my ass out all over the place, said it was me having a filthy mind and trying to flirt with him. I was fucking ten, for chrissake. How freaking sad is that, this thirtysome-year-old woman with tits is jealous of her ten-year-old daughter. I tell her any of this shit now and it's just not worth the hassle it'll bring down. It's just easier to let Carl grab my boobs every now and then.'

'How much longer you think you can fend him off?'

'He's starting to get bored with her, you know. Greener pastures. They never stay that long. She's just too, like, fucking needy. He will be gone like the others in a week or two. I mean, that's the pattern, right? They get fucking tired of her and then they start really coming on to me. I fucking hate men. Fucking pigs. I'd rather do it with a girl. That shock you?'

'No. Frankly, after what you've told me I think it's a wise decision.'

She laughed. 'You are so funny. It doesn't turn you on a little, two teenage chicks getting it on?'

'I was wounded in the war,' he said. 'One day you'll read Hemingway and you'll understand.'

'Jake Barnes!' she shouted.

'Wow, now I am impressed.'

'I read it this summer. This guy in college I was seeing, he said there's this weird famous book they were making him read for Freshman Lit about a guy who got his balls blown off but otherwise goes around acting perfectly normal, like it didn't bother him very much. So I thought, wow, that's kind of cool, like, what would a guy do if he lost his nuts. So I read it and I actually thought it was a pretty cool book, I liked that Brett babe, but I could never figure out if Jake was really worried about losing his balls or what.'

'He wasn't a happy camper, I'm pretty sure about this.'

'And was it his balls or what? They never really said. That bugged me.'

'Now you get to join in with eight bazillion other literary critics and draw your own conclusion.'

'It was symbolic, right?'

'It probably was to Hemingway,' Spandau said, 'but not to Jake.'

'Cool,' she said.

Another car pulled into the driveway.

'I want you to do me a favor,' Spandau said. He took out his business card and handed it to her. 'I'm sure you have the situation well under control and all, but, let's say old Carl is getting a little too persistent, you can give me a call.'

'What are you going to do, beat him up for me? How much will it cost?'

'I'm not going to beat anybody up. I'm the quiet type. I'll just talk to him. And there's no charge for a fellow Hemingway fan.'

She stared at him for a moment, as if trying to figure out what he was up to. Then she shrugged and tucked the card out of sight into her bra just as her mother came in through the front door.

'Sorry to keep you waiting,' she said. 'A last-minute looker. The market is so lousy right now, I can't afford to let any get away.'

She tossed her purse on a table by the front door, took off her jacket and hung it in the closet. 'Will you get me a beer, hon?' she said to her daughter, and sat down heavily in the chair where the girl had been. 'Where's Carl?'

'How the hell should I know,' said the girl. 'I hope he drives into a telephone pole and burns to death.'

'You got any kids?' Vicky asked Spandau.

'Nope.'

'You ever have any, kill them when they're small and defenseless, that's my advice.'

The girl brought over the beer and handed it to her mother. When she crossed behind her she made a face at the back of her mother's head and gave Spandau a big smile.

'What kind of trouble is the crazy son of a bitch in now?' Vicky asked Spandau.

'Someone is releasing all his dirty little secrets to the media.'

'He's got a few of them. They blackmailing him?'

'Not so far. It looks more like somebody's just trying to hurt him.'

'The Oscar thing?'

'Yeah, that seems to be it, given the timing. Nobody's asking for money, so it's personal. And somebody close to him. Or was close at one point.'

'And you think maybe it's me because I wrote that book.'

'You said some harsh things about him. It wasn't a pretty picture.'

'The truth is I've regretted the hell out of that damned book ever since I wrote it. And anyway I didn't write it, not really. The publishers hired some asshole to ghost it. I just answered whatever questions he asked me and took the money. The ink on the divorce papers hadn't dried and I was still hurt and angry. I said a lot of things I shouldn't.'

'Such as?'

'That whole broken-jaw thing. I mean, he hit me, yeah. But I

damn near killed him with a heavy glass ashtray. And he didn't
break my jaw. That writer son of a bitch, he put that in there, I
kept trying to tell him but once I signed the contract they just
glad-handed me and wrote whatever the hell they wanted. Jerry
was no picnic but I don't hate him and I don't want to hurt him
anymore.' She smiled. 'Leastways not enough to do it for free.'
She took a swig of the beer. To the girl she said, 'Carl say when
he'd be back?'

'Jeez, get a life, will you,' said the girl.

'So if you don't want to hurt him, who does?'

'Three ex-wives, a few hundred women he's shit on over the
years, any producer he's ever worked for. Jerry's got this knack
for polarizing people. I mean, you either love him or you hate
him, and sooner or later everybody gets their fair share of both.
He can be the sweetest guy on the face of the earth, and then the
next minute it's like some switch goes off and he turns mean. He
still drinking?'

'There's usually a bottle nearby.'

'Let me tell you something. He's like a child. That tough-guy
routine, he's the thinnest-skinned human being I ever met. You
know how many times I've seen him cry? And I mean about stupid
crap, just some tiny slight or something. He'd stand up to the
studio bastards, god he fought with them like a junkyard dog every
picture, but that never bothered him, not really. I mean it took its
toll. But it was the small stuff that killed him, like somebody
forgetting his birthday, or not getting invited to dinner, or him just
being convinced somebody was mad at him whether they were or
not. He told me once, he said the only things in the world that
scared him were the people he loved. Everything else he could
deal with.'

Spandau sighed. Vicky laughed.

'I wish I had a dime for every time I've seen him cause that
face you just made. Welcome to the club. Nobody understands the
bastard, he's got us all confused. But he gets under your skin,
doesn't he? It's amazing, absolutely amazing. You sure you won't
have a beer?'

'Yeah, sure. Why not.'

Vicky signaled to her daughter, who brought Spandau a beer.
'I think his movies suck,' the girl said. 'All this sick macho

blood and gore shit. It's all like this suppressed homo wet-dream stuff.'

'Gay is one thing Jerry isn't, I'm here to tell you,' said Vicky. 'Oh my.'

'I do not want to hear this,' said the girl. 'The very thought of all you old people having sex turns my stomach.'

'Look, honey, a woman hits her sexual peak at forty-two.'

'Yeah, right, just in time to be tripping over her own tits. This "sexual peak" stuff is just a code word for desperate. Own it, Mother.'

'I'm doing just fine, sweetheart, thank you.'

'You mean your scuzzy tripod boyfriend? Oh, puh-leez. It's like this ridiculous dildo carrying this human-shaped thing around.'

'And just how would you know?'

'We get cable, Mother. Every third channel is showing porn. I've seen him. Not much in the way of creativity, is he? And doesn't it just remotely bother you what he's been doing with that thing all day?'

'Look, it's just business. Why is this any different than if he was a proctologist?'

'God, Mother, that is the most desperate thing I have ever heard, even from you.'

'I'm campaigning for a new California law,' Vicky said to Spandau, 'in favor of retroactive abortion. I should be able to kill her now with the state on my side. I'm sorry you get to witness this.'

'I bet he loves it,' said the girl. 'Men just love catfights. It gets them hot. Are you getting hot?'

'Jesus god,' said Vicky.

'This is all very entertaining,' Spandau said to the girl, 'and just like a Eugene O'Neill play. The problem is I've got this attention deficit disorder that only lets me concentrate on one thing at a time. If you're still playing by Friday I can come back for the matinee, but for now all I can think about is Jerry Margashack.'

From the kitchen, the girl hit him in the back of the head with a scouring pad, thankfully dry. 'And I was just beginning to think you weren't really one of the old farts,' she said. 'I'm going to my room and leave this place to the geezers.'

'I'm telling you,' said Vicky. 'Kill them while they're still babies. You want another beer?'

'None of this makes sense,' said Spandau.

'That would be Jerry all over. Now try to imagine living with this twenty-four-seven and you begin to see what my life was like.'

Spandau drank his beer and thought for a while. 'What do you know about his life before you met him? His hometown?'

'Somebody from Cheney come back to haunt him?'

'He's still got family there, right? Any long-term feuds you can remember?'

'Both parents dead. His sister took over the ranch and then sold it and moved off fifteen years back. There are some cousins around I think, but nobody he was close to, except maybe the priest. I don't know about him having any enemies there. The general opinion is that he didn't really turn into a crazy pain in the ass until after he left and started making movies. Though his sister was a cold-hearted bitch too. It's hard to know how much to blame on genetics and how much to blame on Hollywood. He refuses to help, huh?'

'It's like investigating a murder while the corpse is sitting up laughing at you.'

'You might want to talk to Lewis Tollund.'

'The actor?'

'They did a bunch of films together, were real close for a long time. Then something happened – with Jerry it always does – and they stopped talking. But he and Lewis were tight. Lewis was as close to a brother as I ever saw Jerry have.'

'You know where the sister is?'

She shook her head. "We never liked each other.'

'What about this priest?'

'Father something or other. Father Michael. Yeah, I think that's it. Cheney is small, there were maybe three or four other Catholic families around where Jerry grew up. It was Father Mike's parish.'

'Jerry a good Catholic?'

'Jerry? Ha! He was an atheist when I knew him. I dunno, maybe he's found Jesus since but it doesn't sound that way. I don't think he was ever religious, he used to make fun of the whole thing. Father Mike was just more of a mentor than anything else. Look, nobody in Jerry's family ever read a book or gave a damn about movies or anything except beer and barbecue. Just regular old Americans. Father Mike used to talk to him about books and movies. Jerry felt like he owed the guy. We used to have fights about it.'

'Why?'

'Jerry would send him money. I don't know how much, but it was always regular, or at least whenever Jerry had some, which was never that often. You know Jerry and his fiscal sense, which is zero. I always figured that Jerry thought money was dirty somehow and just wanted to get it out of his hands as fast as possible. Anyway Jerry used to send money to the parish. We'd be nearly flat broke and in a panic and I'd find out Jerry had sent off a chunk of change to the priest.'

'How much?'

'A few hundred at a time, when I knew him. Never more than a thousand, I don't think. I mean, these are just the ones I caught. There might have been more. Probably were. Jerry is an asshole in a lot of ways, but when he cares he's got this weird sort of loyalty.'

'He's a hard guy to figure out.'

'When you do, let me know how it turns out, will you? I was married to the guy for five years and every goddamn time I thought I knew who he was, he turned out to be somebody else.'

They heard the sound of Carl's Mustang pulling in and the garage door opening.

'Excuse me,' said Vicky, and went out there. In a moment voices were raised. The girl came back into the room.

Carl shouted: 'I don't have to answer to you, you stupid goddamned cunt.'

Carl shouted: 'I'll fuck half of southern fucking California if I want to.'

Carl shouted: 'Take your fucking baggy tits and flabby ass and get inside and leave me alone. You're goddamn lucky I fuck you at all, nobody else would.'

Vicky begging, crying.

'Great show, huh?' said the girl. There were tears in her eyes.

Vicky came back in, passed through to the back of the house without saying a word, shielding her face with her hand. A door slammed.

'I think your interview is over,' said the girl.

Spandau stood up. 'Thank you for the beer and the conversation. And please thank your mother for me, she's been a lot of help.'

'So maybe the day isn't a total fucking waste, huh.'

'I gave you my card. I'm David. You never told me your name.'

'Joy,' she said. 'My name is Joy. What a hoot, ain't it?'

'My old man used to beat us,' Spandau said to her. 'I can't remember thirty happy seconds when that guy was anywhere within a mile of us. But there are good things and good people out there. You can find them, and then you hang on to them for dear life, because they're what get you by. One day you get control of your own life, you get to say who you want in and out of it. Things get better, I promise. The hard part is not letting the bad shit ruin you before all the good comes rolling along.'

Joy nodded and then burst into tears. She ran over and put her arms around Spandau, hid her face among the buttons of his shirt. He let her stay like that for a very few moments and then touched her hair and gently pushed her away.

'You hang in there, kiddo, okay? You got my number if you need it.'

When Spandau came out the garage door was open and Carl was inside cleaning the windows of his car. Spandau started toward his own car then stopped and turned around and looked at Carl.

'What the fuck is your problem,' Carl said to him. They stared at each other and then Carl gave this contemptuous laugh and turned his back on Spandau and went back to washing his car.

Spandau walked quickly over and kicked Carl behind the right knee. Carl buckled and slid down the side of the car to the garage floor. Carl was big and muscular but it was all for show, built for nothing but to look good on the screen. A broken nose would send Carl into a month of unemployment. Carl was no problem.

'What the fuck is wrong with you?' said Carl.

'I've decided I don't like you,' Spandau said to him. He got out his cell phone and turned on the camera. 'If you have any sense at all you will just sit there and shut up and not move.'

Spandau took several photos of Carl, then took photos of the Mustang and the license plate.

'What are these for?' Carl started to climb to his feet.

'Tell me you're getting up,' said Spandau. 'Please tell me this is what you're doing.'

Carl sat back down.

'The girl has my telephone number,' said Spandau. 'All she has to do is make one call and you will find two or three short-tempered cops knocking on your door. I know several personally who get tired of seeing vile bastards like you walking around loose, and you would be a great way to work out their frustrations. And these photos will also go to every cop and social worker I can think of, along with a sworn statement of what I saw through that window. The only reason you are not being force-fed a tire iron is because of that kid. Her life is confused enough already. Never touch her again. Or better yet, get the fuck out of her life. Get the fuck out of both their lives. I mean it.'

Spandau wanted to kick him again but thought better of it. He got into his car and drove away.

TWENTY-SEVEN

Araz was dressing when his mother, Kadarine, called up the stairs.

'Araz!'

'Yes, mayr.'

'Are you going out?'

'Yes, mayr.'

'Can you stop by the Ralph's on the way home for bread and milk? We don't have any bread and milk.'

'Yes, mayr.'

A pause.

'Will you be late?'

'Probably.'

'The Ralph's may not be open.'

'Mayr, I think the Ralph's is always open. I think it's open twenty-four hours.'

'Are you sure?'

'Yes,' he said, even though he wasn't.

'Are you going out with Anush?'

'Yes, mayr.'

'Tell her mother I said hello.'

'Okay.'

'Tell Anush I said hello as well. She's a nice girl.'

'I'll tell her.'

'Don't forget to tell her mother. She'll be mad at me if you don't. That woman, she takes offense at everything. She drives me crazy.'

'I know what it's like,' said Araz.

'What?' said his mother.

'I said I know, I'll be sure to tell her if she's home.'

Pause.

'Why wouldn't she be home?' she said. 'Where would she be at night in the middle of the week?'

Pause.

'Be sure to say goodbye to your father.'

This finally irritated him. When the fuck have I not ever said goodbye to my father? Like I'd ever walk out and never say goodbye, like it has ever happened.

He dressed and went downstairs to the living room. His mother sat in a chair watching TV. His father's bed was in the corner, where it had been ever since the stroke. His father was sixty, not an old man, but he'd had a stroke the previous year and barely walked or spoke. He understood most things or at least they thought he did. Anyway he cried sometimes, usually at very small things, like not saying goodbye when you left the house.

Araz kissed his mother, went over and kissed his father. His father looked up at him with dark, damp eyes. He smiled and laid his hand on his son's chest.

'Stay out of trouble, Pop,' he said.

The old man's smile widened. He doesn't understand what I'm saying, thought Araz, I'm sure he doesn't. It's just the voice, he must recognize something about the voice. Araz's mother was convinced her husband understood every word, and discussed TV shows with him as they watched.

'My god, Garo, did you see that, she's killed her husband. Had her lover put the body in the car and bury it. It was the DNA that did it for her, Garo, it's amazing how they do that stuff now. Used to be all we had were fingerprints and you couldn't get fingerprints off a body, Garo, at least not in the old days. I think they can now. Araz?'

'What, mayr?'

'Can they get fingerprints off bodies now?'

'I think so,' he said, though he wasn't sure.

'Did you hear that, Garo? Fingerprints off everything. Amazing. Be careful and don't forget the bread and milk.'

This last part for Araz. You had to listen carefully, she'd never take her eyes off the TV, sometimes you never knew who the hell she was talking to.

TWENTY-EIGHT

A raz pulled into the driveway of the Salopian family's home. He started to get out of the car but the front door flew open and Anush came scuttling out.

'What's wrong?' said Araz, half in, half out of the car.

'Get in get in get in!' she said, hurrying to the passenger side and jumping in. 'Let's go! Go!'

'What the hell is wrong?'

Mrs Salopian came out the door.

'Slut!' she yelled.

'Go go go, for fuck's sake,' said Anush, whose name means 'sweet' in Armenian. She gave her mother the finger as the car began to back out.

'Whore!' cried her mother.

Araz rolled down the window. 'My mother says to say hello, Mrs Salopian!'

Mrs Salopian came rushing at the car. Araz backed out quickly into the street and he and Anush drove away laughing.

'What have you done this time?' Araz asked Anush.

'Do you think this is cheap,' she said, and unbuttoned her sweater. The dress she wore underneath was short and cut remarkably low.

'That's like something Sharon Stone would wear to the Oscars,' he said.

'You see? She doesn't know what she's talking about.'

'No,' said Araz, 'it means I can almost see your nipples. In fact I think I can see a little brown there.'

'You don't like it? I wore it for you. I thought it would steam you up a little while we dance.'

'It will steam everybody up a little,' he said.

'This is what I love about you,' she said. 'You're not the jealous type. Other guys I've dated, it's like there's always a problem, it's suffocating, you go out and some guy talks to you, there's all this shit, like I don't have any fucking control over what asshole comes up to me, am I supposed to put out his eye with a toothpick or something? You, you're so sweet, you don't have all these male insecurities, you know who you are. I love that.'

'What are you going to do while we're dancing and your breast falls out?'

'It's just a tit, for chrissake,' she said. 'Look!'

She opened the front of her dress to expose her boobs. Some guys in the car next to them honked and shouted. Anush flashed them again, laughing. Araz sped up. The other car followed them, trying to stay apace. Araz pressed down on the accelerator, changed lanes, darted in front of another car, and floored it.

'Are they still following?' he asked her.

'Yeah,' she said.

'Why the fuck do you want to cause so much trouble,' he said. 'I should just pull over and give you to them.'

He was going nearly a hundred. When he couldn't see them in the mirror, he changed lanes, slowed quickly, and exited the freeway.

'That made me all hot,' she said. 'Come on, didn't it get you hot?'

She reached over, felt his crotch.

'Oh yeah,' she said. 'Pull over.'

'Are you crazy? Not here.'

She began to unzip his fly.

'You want to keep driving, that's okay, but I'm not wasting this.'

He pulled over and parked across the street from a Starbucks.

She blew him as he watched people drink their coffees. When she'd finished, she said,

'Are you going to fuck me later?'

'No,' he said.

TWENTY-NINE

L ewis Tollund lived in Encino behind a high wrought-iron fence in a house that was a very limp stone's throw from the street. You might be tempted to infer from this that the grounds were not large, but you would be mistaken. Once you were allowed through the front door and passed into the house, you confronted a living room with a soaring cathedral ceiling and an acre of clear window that showed an immaculate Zen rock garden and beyond that another landscaped garden and beyond that a pool and a tennis court.

'There's a stable somewhere,' said Lewis Tollund, 'but I haven't been out there in years. I screwed up my back about ten years ago and had to stop riding. Got rid of the horses. I miss 'em, god knows, but it's cruel to just let them sit there and not ride them. A bit like a woman,' he said, and flashed that famous smile.

'Thank you for seeing me,' Spandau said.

'I confess it had less to do with helping you than just hearing about Margashack. I haven't seen the crazy bastard in a long time. I know he must be in some kind of trouble – hell, he always was, and most of it he stirred up himself out of sheer boredom, I think. I miss him.'

'How long since you've seen him?'

'Five, six years. Ran into him at the Farmer's Market in West Hollywood, of all places. Said hello, gave me one of his bear hugs. He's a great hugger, our Jerry. I hadn't seen him for a couple of years before that. Made the usual promises to stay in touch but of course we didn't. Well, he tried. To my great shame I blew him off.'

'Why?'

'It's hard to explain. I think age has something to do with it. I just woke up one day and realized I'd gotten old, it wasn't even middle age anymore. And Jerry didn't. Jerry is the eternal child, the eternal puckish kid who sticks his finger in the cake icing simply because you told him not to, just to watch you blow up at him. Jerry's this existentialist Peter Pan, he creates chaos to remind himself he still exists. And there was that mystic streak. I used to call him my Mad Monk. You can see it in the movies, there's very much that samurai ethic that runs through all of them. That's why we clicked. We understood each other that way. I did zazen, Jerry drank. He used to call it hitting the liquid satori. We had some good fights together, with each other and side by side against the philistines. I kept giving him malas, I even taught him a chant once. Useless. Somebody did tell me he's taken to carrying around a rosary, of all things. Maybe he's found God.' The thought seemed to amuse him.

'You think that's likely with him? I mean, does he strike you as the sort that would?'

'Jerry's problem is that Jerry is a bad Catholic. Always was.'

'You mean he believes but doesn't practice?'

'No, no,' he said. 'You have to remember we're talking about Jerry here, and not some normal human being whose actions stand at least a chance of making sense. Jerry moveth in ways mysterious to know. Jerry the mad monk, the dark mystic. Jerry is a guy who doesn't believe in God, doesn't believe in Heaven, doesn't subscribe to a single Christian belief other than the scourging presence of guilt, and guilt without redemption at that. Again, man, look at the films. They're these great macho epics, but every one of them is about guys who are trying somehow to redeem themselves.'

'But redeem themselves to who?'

'That's the trick, see. Jerry is like the guy who thinks he's committed some heinous crime and is desperately looking around for a cop to surrender to but can't find one. The dangerous thing about Jerry is that he does shit so he *can* be punished. If you can grasp this, you've got the key to Jerry Margashack, lock, stock, and barrel. It's exhausting. Sad and exhausting. I never minded marching alongside Jerry into righteous battle, but he'd stir up shit out of that black need of his, and you'd find yourself mired in some bloody crusade and realize there was no point to it, other than Jerry's need to taste blood, his own and somebody else's. I got tired of watching it happen. He's got this charisma, our Jerry. People follow him into battle and then they waste their lives.'

'You felt that was happening to you?'

'To an extent. I mean, you feel used. It was the same with Jerry and women. Probably still is. He'd latch on to a woman, fall madly in love, and for a while it was like the heavens opened and the angels sang. Up until he turned, and, man, he always turned. He'd pick them up by the ankles and use them like a cat o' nine tails to beat himself. Jerry could take it, they couldn't. By the time he finished there wasn't much left. You talked to Vicky. God, there was a woman who loved to be punished. That whole relationship was based on it. It was touch and go as to who'd kill who first. She was tough, man. The best favor Jerry ever did her was finding that Asian broad and walking out. I hope her taste has improved since.'

'History repeats itself,' said Spandau.

'I'm sorry to hear that. People fall back on what they know. We're all doomed to keep playing the same roles over and over. We just change stages. That, my friend, is the human comedy.'

'So you decided to break the connection.'

'It's not as simple as that. Nothing ever is with Jerry. Let me see if I can explain this.' Tollund paused, considered what he was about to say, then plunged into it. 'There was Jerry. Jerry Margashack, he's a genius, no doubt about it. He's got charisma, he's bigger than life, you walk with Jerry and you're walking through opera. *La Bohème* every minute of the day. It's great, if you're an actor, if you like artists, if you're into bigger than life. You love him or you hate him right away. But if you love him, man, you're hooked. Jerry could be like a drug. It's amazing.

'So you go racing through the woods with Jerry, you're high – literally and figuratively, most of the time – on whatever drug he's happy to share. Then, boom, there comes this fork in the road, and here there are the two Jerrys. You want to go on with Jerry, you go one road if you're a man, and if you're a woman you take the other one. You don't get a choice. You can turn back but nobody ever does.

'Jerry with guys and Jerry with women, oh man, these are entirely different worlds. Jerry with women . . . Jerry's one of those guys who loves women, he needs women, but at the same time he resents the hell out of needing them. So Jerry with women, he sooner or later becomes a monster and things get ugly.

'There was this girl . . .'

Tollund stopped. He reached into a humidor, pulled out a cigar. Offered one to Spandau, who shook his head. Tollund took his time about lighting the cigar. Took several experimental puffs. When he was satisfied the cigar was going well, he sat back, stared out the window at the Zen garden, then said:

'I've heard about you. That job you did for Anna Mayhew in France. You're supposed to be a straight-shooter. Is that right?'

'I like to think so.'

'Then you'll be a gentleman and keep what I'm about to tell you between ourselves, right?'

'I can agree to that as long as it doesn't interfere with my duty to my client.'

'Which would be Jerry.'

'That's a good question, since Jerry isn't the one hiring me. But, yeah, as far as I'm concerned my primary duty is to Jerry.'

Tollund laughed. 'I begin to sense that you are a complicated man.'

'Not complicated,' said Spandau. 'Just middling confused like everybody else.'

'I broke with Jerry not because of anything he did to me, but because of something he did to a friend of mine. A girl. No,' said Tollund, 'I know the conclusion you're jumping to. She wasn't a lover, Jerry didn't steal some doll away from me – although he did a few times. We both did.' Tollund smiled. 'Actually I didn't even know the girl that well. She was just this sweet, funny kid, from Kentucky. She had that southern twang in her voice. Cute as a bug's ear, and sexy as hell in a kind of innocent way. Like everybody else she came out here to act, ended up as a production assistant on a few films. That's how I met her. She had a brother who'd died, and I became a kind of substitute. Between films she'd help me out with stuff, I'd put her on the payroll until another film came along. She was just one of those people you liked having around. Hell, everybody liked having her around.

'Jerry was here one day, he'd come over to talk about a part he had for me, we were going over the script. The girl – let's call her Susie, which is not her name – had been out doing some errands for me. A grocery run. I heard her come in and then she popped up in the doorway here to let me know she was back, ask if I needed anything else. I introduced her to Jerry, the single act for which I may forever burn in hell. When she left Jerry turned to me and rolled his eyes and asked who she was. I told him and he asked if I was nailing her. I told him no, and to banish any thoughts of his own, she was a good kid and the town would eat her up soon enough without either of us rushing the process.

'Jerry didn't mention it again and we went back to work. A while later Jerry got up to go to the head. He was gone a while but I was concentrating on the script, I didn't think about it. Then he came back and we worked for the rest of the afternoon and then he left. He didn't say another word about her.

'Everything is fine, she's working around the house, running errands, whatever, for a few weeks. She's her usual happy self, singing, humming. She was like that.

'Then one day she doesn't show up. No call, nothing. This is not like her. We call her number, no answer. One day, two days, three days. We call around. Nobody has heard from her, seen her. A bad love affair. Maybe the city has just gotten to her, she's back in the hills of Kentucky. It happens. Sometimes the place just sneaks up on you and that's it, baby, something snaps and you get in the car and just keep driving. Happens all the time.

'Until one night, after she'd been missing four or five days. She shows up here, alone. She looked like hell, man. I'm telling you, she was in this trauma, this look in her eyes like some frightened animal. Hair was greasy, she hadn't bathed, face all puffy from crying. Shaking, falling apart but struggling to keep just under control, not to fly off in all directions. You want to see what crazy looks like, this is it, I remember thinking. This is what the ante-room to madness looks like.

'I bring her in, sit her down, right there where you're sitting. Offer her a drink, a Valium, whatever she needs. She says no, she doesn't want anything, she just sits there. I ask what's happened. She says she's sorry, she apologizes over and over for coming here, for not showing up for work, for not calling, she's sorry, she's sorry. I tell her not to worry, that whatever happened she's safe now, just tell me and maybe I can help. And then she tells me. She gets quiet, and then she explains the whole story in this weird monotone, as if she'd suddenly become someone else who knew the story.

'Jerry of course had hit on her that day he was here. Made a fucking beeline into the kitchen where she was, wasted no time getting her phone number. Made a point of asking her not to mention it. He seemed like such a nice guy, she said. Was so funny and was so complimentary. He made her laugh right off the bat. That's why she liked him.

'So they go out a few times. And of course Jerry makes a pass. She's used to this, grew up fending off guys back in Kentucky, it's no big deal. She likes Jerry but she's not in love. Yes, hard to believe, but even in California there are still beautiful women who will fuck only for love. They go out a few more times, Jerry is a little more persistent, but he stops when she says stop.

'One night Jerry picks her up, says let's go to this great Mexican restaurant in San Diego. It's the best Mexican restaurant in the world, he says. You'll love it.

'They drive to San Diego and it is indeed a very nice restaurant. Jerry seems to know everybody there, they treat him like Prince Edward the Second. She's impressed, it's a great evening. Jerry is very sweet, very happy. This is our Jerry, all is fine until he starts drinking. And even then he can knock them back all night and nothing happens, he's got this continual glow on. Other times it can be one or two drinks, he starts out happy as hell and then it's like some black cloak descends on him. At that point you never know where things are going to go.

'They were fine, she said, until they left the restaurant. He'd been drinking a lot but he didn't seem drunk, seemed under control so she wasn't so worried about him driving. Except he got quiet. Bad sign for our Jerry. If he's not rattling on, be careful. They're driving along and Jerry says, look, I'm tired, it's a long drive, there's this great hotel on the beach in La Jolla, why don't we go there. No, she says, she has to be at work in the morning. Call in sick, says Jerry, I'll get someone to cover for you, whatever. No, she says. I'll treat you like a princess, he says. She repeated this several times when she told it to me. I'll treat you like a princess, he said.

'No, thank you, I need to go home. He starts to argue. No, she says, I need to go home, please take me home. He drives for a bit longer and he's quiet and then she sees that he's crying. She can see the tears on his cheeks when the headlights pass. What's wrong? she says. What's the matter? She feels like she's done something wrong, she's hurt him somehow. Can we talk, he says. Can we please just stop and talk?

'Jerry pulls off the road, pulls down toward the beach. Stops the car. She waits for him to talk, asks him again what's wrong, has she done something. He doesn't say anything for a while, then says, you're so beautiful. He moves toward her and she pushes him away. Then he hits her and starts calling her names and that's when it happens.'

Tollund stopped. Spandau could see it wasn't for dramatic effect this time. Tollund stared out the window and Spandau could see the muscles in his jaw and neck tighten and release, tighten and release. Tollund said:

'I didn't ask for details.' He puffed on the cigar, ground it out angrily in the ashtray. 'It gets better though.' He stood up. 'You want a cognac?'

'Yeah, thanks.'

Tollund crossed the room to the bar. He poured two snifters of cognac. 'I don't normally drink this early in the day, but let's make an exception, shall we?' He brought them over and handed one to Spandau. He said:

'She was a bit drunk herself, and Jerry had slapped her around a little. He seemed to realize what he'd done and said oh god oh god a few times and pulled away from her and huddled up on his side of the car and didn't bother to stop her when she got out of the car and wandered up toward the highway. No purse, no money, no cell phone. Confused, in shock. She gets up to the highway and starts walking along. She hopes Jerry won't follow her, she hopes he'll just let her go, let her go on home.

'She doesn't know how far she walks along the highway. People stare but nobody stops. She's not even sure if she wants them to, said she didn't know what she would tell them. Finally somebody does stop, they pull over, tell her to get in. She does. It's three or four white guys in a van, maybe college kids. So she gets in. At this point she'd do anything anybody tells her. And guess what?'

'Jesus,' said Spandau.

Tollund drained about half his cognac. Coughed. Gathered himself.

'By the time they'd had their fun they were already in Manhattan Beach. They pulled over and gently deposited her beneath an underpass on the 405 and drove away. She wandered into a 7-Eleven and borrowed a phone from the guy behind the counter to call a friend to come and pick her up.

'Wouldn't tell her friend what happened, wouldn't tell a soul. Just wanted it to go away. But it wouldn't, she kept reliving it over and over, and didn't leave her apartment for three days, couldn't bring herself to go outside, to see anyone. I offered to take her to a doctor, to contact the police, whatever she wanted. She said all she wanted was just to go away, to leave, to go away and never look back. She asked if I would help her. I said sure, anything, tell me where you want to go, I'll contact your family, get you a plane ticket, a shrink, anything she wanted. She just wanted to get away, she said. Could I lend her just enough money to get away. So I did. I gave her all the cash I had, a few hundred in the house, and wrote her a check for ten grand. I said look, stay here for a while until you can think straight, until she had a plan. No, she said, she had to leave. She knew what she had to do. I tried to stop her. I think I grabbed her arm at one point, trying to get her to listen to reason, but she turned and began screaming at the top of her lungs. So I let her go. There was nothing I could do.

'I went to see Jerry the next day. I was furious, I was going to tear his head off. I was ready to go to the cops, whatever, I wanted the bastard to suffer. But something told me to hear his side of it first.

'So I got to see him and I tell him what happened and the son of a bitch starts laughing. I ask him what the fuck is so funny, and he says she laid close to the same rap on him that same evening, except it was me who tried to rape her but couldn't get it up and sent her out into the streets, that I'd threatened her life and she had to get away. Then he asked me how much I'd given her. I said ten grand. He said he'd given her three and started cackling like a madman. He said he wondered how many times she'd pulled this that one day, and anyway thirteen thousand dollars was a good day's wages for a Kentucky hillbilly.

'I asked him if he'd believed her and he said shit no, not a word of it. He admitted going out with her a few times but she had all these wild tales, guys always abusing her and then her getting back at them in some tricky way. Some of the stories sounded pretty outlandish. He could see what she was like and anyway it was worth three grand for the remarkably detailed and entertaining story about how my shriveled old dick wouldn't work.'

A long beat while Spandau let it all sink in. 'You ever hear from her again?'

'Nope. Nobody has, as far as I know, and I've asked around.'

'Anybody else come up with a tale like this? People who knew her?'

'Nothing. But a couple of people did remember her telling stories about guys she's gotten revenge on.'

'She cash the check?'

'First thing the next morning at my bank.'

Spandau couldn't find anything to say.

'Welcome to Jerry's World,' said Tollund.

Finally Spandau said:

'So the million-dollar question is, which story do you believe?'

Tollund thought.

'I don't know,' he said. 'I've gone over this a million times and I honestly don't know.'

'If it's true, it's a damned good reason somebody might want to hurt him.'

'True. But there are enough of those anyway.'

'You won't tell me her name, then?'

'Nope,' said Tollund. 'And if I find you've been asking around, it would put you very high on my shit list. If it's true, then she needs to be protected, and if it's not true, then it's dangerous for Jerry.'

'Why tell me at all?'

'Just to let you know what you're in for. And because you hit me at a moment when I finally felt like telling it to somebody. Who knows? Maybe you'll stumble across the truth and you can come back and put me out of my misery. Either way though somebody I trusted turns out to be a shit ass. This is never something that makes you happy.'

'Gut feeling?'

Tollund finished his brandy.

'Oh, he did it, the miserable cocksucker. I can feel it. I'd just rather that I didn't.'

THIRTY

S avan said,

'This homo goes into a pet store, wants to buy a parrot, right?'

'Why a parrot?' asks Tavit.

They were in the van, driving to a sushi place on Western to fuck up the Jap who owned it. The Jap was new and had ratted them out to the cops after they'd pressed him for insurance money. Atom wanted to make an example of him. Atom liked examples.

'Shut the fuck up and don't bust my balls,' Savan said. 'This is a faggot joke, something you can relate to. Anyway, the homo goes up to this one parrot, says, "Polly want a cracker?" and the parrot says, "Fuck that shit, I talk better than you do. Buy me and I'll talk your fucking ears off. I'm cheap too, because I don't have any claws. Look." The homo looks closer and sees the parrot doesn't have any fucking legs, he's just wrapped around the branch by his dick.

'The homo buys the parrot for like ten bucks – he's a defective parrot, right? – and takes him home to his gay lover. "Oh looky looky," he says to his gay pal, "I've just bought this adorable parrot." But one thing leads to another and they start ass-fucking each other and the fag forgets to tell his lover that the parrot can talk.'

'Is this going to be a long fucking joke?' asks Tavit.

'Why? All this talk about fags making you too excited?'

'It fucking takes you forever.'

'It takes me as long as I need, asswipe,' Savan said, giving Tavit a sharp flick on the ear. Tavit yelped. Savan continued.

'So the fag goes to work—'

'Which fag?' asks Tavit.

'The fag who bought the parrot, moron. The fag goes to work, leaves his boyfriend at home—'

'The boyfriend doesn't work?' said Tavit, looking for trouble.

'He's a fucking stay at home faggot, okay?' said Savan. 'When he gets home that evening, he walks in the door, the parrot waves him over and whispers, "I got something to tell you."'

'Faggot goes over and the parrot says, "Not long after you left, there's a knock at the door, and your boyfriend lets this other guy in."

'The fag is interested. He says, "Go on." The parrot says, "Then they kiss." The fag says, "And then?" And the parrot says, "Then your boyfriend unbuttons the guy's pants." "And?" says the fag. "Well, your friend pulls down the guy's pants." "And?" says the fag, getting excited. "And?" "Then your pal gets down on his knees . . ." "And?" says the fag, getting real excited, "And? And?" "And," says the parrot, "I dunno what happened next, I popped a boner and I fell off my fucking perch."'

Savan cracked up. Tavit laughed in spite of himself. Araz said,

'So we just slap him around a little, right?'

'The guy fucking tried to rat us to the cops,' Savan said. 'For that you get fucked up. Atom said he wanted to make an example of him. Asshole thinks the police are going to do him some good. Fucking foreigners.'

'We're fucking foreigners,' said Araz.

'The hell we are,' said Savan. 'I was born here. Do I look like a fucking slope or a wetback to you?'

'So how come Atom gave the instructions to you instead of me?'

'How the hell do I know? You weren't there, he told me instead.'

'Fucking testing me,' said Araz. 'He's mad about that fucking gambling debt.'

'Don't get all paranoid,' said Savan. 'You didn't like the joke?'

'Yeah,' said Araz. 'It was funny.'

They pulled up in front of the sushi place. It was 3 p.m., nobody was in there. Araz turned off the engine. He said,

'You're in a gay bar, suddenly this condom goes flying across the room. What does everybody say?'

'I dunno,' said Savan.

'Who farted?' said Araz.

They laughed.

'That's a good one,' said Savan.

There was nobody in the restaurant. When they walked in Tavit locked the door. The owner was in the kitchen. His wife came out.

'What you want?' she said, crossing her arms defiantly.

Savan grabbed her by the hair and dragged her back into the kitchen, threw her at her husband's feet.

'No violence!' said the man. 'No violence!'

'Too fucking late for that,' said Savan. 'You should have thought about that before you went yakking to the fucking cops.'

'I no go police!' said the man.

'Fucking lying Toyota motherfucker,' said Savan, and picked up a metal soup ladle and swung it and caught the man on the side of the head. The man staggered back. The woman came forward. Tavit grabbed her. She was screaming.

'Shut her up,' Savan said to Tavit. Tavit hit her in the mouth. She stopped.

'You went to the police?' the man said in Japanese to his wife. 'I told you not to!'

'You're a coward!' she said. 'Someone had to!'

'You've killed me,' said the man.

'Stop that fucking jabbering,' said Savan.

'She no understand!' said the man.

Savan was looking around. He spotted the deep-fat fryer.

'Come here,' he said to the man.

The man had followed Savan's eyes and made a run for the dining room. Araz hit him and threw him back toward Savan. Savan grabbed him and the man struggled.

'Fucking help me,' Savan said to Araz.

Araz went over and grabbed the little man around the neck, bending one of his arms high up behind his back. Savan grabbed the other arm. The little man struggled, shouted. Still gripping the man's wrist Savan picked up a plate and hit him repeatedly across the bridge of the nose until the nose dissolved in a mass of blood and the man stopped.

'Hold him,' said Savan, and submerged the man's hand into the roiling fat. The man screamed, flopped. The woman screamed too. Tavit clouted her again.

It was a job to hang on to the little fellow. The grease popped and splattered. Savan released him and both he and Araz jumped back as the man danced around, swinging the arm and flinging bits of hot flesh and crying.

'Mother fuck,' said Savan, who'd burned his own hand a little. He went over and turned on the cold-water tap and held it beneath the stream. 'This fucking hurts.'

The man had gone to his wife who held him as they both cried and the man stuck his peeling and deep-fried arm uselessly in the air away from them. Savan watched this as he bathed his hand, but it angered him to watch them comforting each other and he went over and kicked them for a while then went back to bathing his hand.

'Was that worth it?' Araz asked him when they were back in the van.

'What do you mean, was it fucking worth it?' Savan snapped at him. 'We did what we were fucking told to do. At least I did anyway. What the fuck is it with you, just standing around like you're waiting for a fucking bus. Goddamn this hurts.'

'You think we're going to collect anything now? The guy can't cook, he'll be lucky he keeps the fucking hand. They'll close down the business. Where's the profit in that?'

'Fuck the profit,' said Savan. 'We made an example out of him.'

'All we had to do was smack him around a little,' Araz said. 'He'd have paid.'

'That's not the point.'

'What is the point exactly? I've lost track. I thought we were supposed to be making money. Do you see any money? Are we walking away with any fucking money?'

'Atom is right, there's something fucking wrong with you.'

'That's what Atom said?'

'Talk to Atom.'

'Maybe I will,' Araz said. 'This whole operation has gone fucking nuts. We're supposed to be making fucking money, not getting revenge on the fucking whole of humanity. None of this makes any sense. It's just fucking crazy, that's all.'

'You tell Uncle Atom he's crazy,' Tavit said laughing. 'I want to be there.'

'Shut up, you fucking needle dick,' Savan said to him. To Savan he said, 'Can we stop and get some fucking Neosporin or something?'

Tavit started to recommend something else, but Savan told him to shut the fuck up again so he did.

THIRTY-ONE

Spandau had phoned Walter off and on for two days now and finally decided to go by the house. He rang the bell and to his surprise Rosa answered.

'I thought he fired you,' Spandau said.

'He fire me all the time,' Rosa said in her Salvadorean accent, 'but I never listen. I tell him I come even if he don't pay me, so he give up and I come and he pay me. Same as always.'

'I've been calling for two days. I got worried.'

'He tell me not to answer the phone. You know what he like sometime.'

'How is he?'

'You go see for yourself.'

Walter was in his study. The walls were lined with books and photos of Walter with various distinguished people. Walter had a talent for cultivating people who were important, which was the key to his success. Of the books, there was not a single work of fiction among them. Books on history and law and psychology and forensics. Walter thought fiction was a waste of time.

The room was half dark. Soft jazz came piped in from an expensive system hidden in a hall closet. Walter lay on his back on the leather sofa, a thin blanket pulled up to his chest. Spandau thought he might be asleep and started to leave.

'Don't you ever call first,' Walter said. 'I don't remember issuing an invitation.'

'I did call. You gave orders not to answer the phone.'

'That in itself might tell you something.'

'I was worried. If you're in one of your moods I'd just as soon go anyway. I've got a touch of the red ass myself and my patience is thin.'

'You're becoming a fucking prima donna, sport.'

'I'm not the self-indulgent lush curled up in a dark room in a fetal position in the middle of the day.'

Walter gave a short laugh. 'Ouch.'

'I want you to get up off your ass and let me take you back to the desert to dry out.'

'I don't think so, sport.'

'You intend to spend the rest of your days doing this?'

'That's pretty much the idea. You want to drop this now, because you're getting to be a real fucking bore about this. Why don't you mind your own goddamned business. You want to nag my ass about shit of which you know absolutely nothing, you know where the door is. Otherwise Rosa is no fucking Lillian Hellman and I could use the conversation.'

Spandau sat down.

'Go ahead and get it out of your system,' said Walter. 'You're just dying to tell me I look like shit.'

'You look like shit.'

'Great, thank you,' Walter said. 'How is the Margashack thing coming?'

'I feel like a hamster on one of those plastic wheels. I'm not going anywhere.'

'Nobody's talking?'

'Oh, people are talking okay. It's just the more they talk the more confused I get. I've never seen a case with so many leads that are certain to go absolutely nowhere.'

'Follow the enemies, sport. That's the way it works.'

'Yeah, but with Margashack, all the enemies and all the friends turn out to be the same people.' Pause. 'I'm thinking about dropping the case.'

'Well goodness, sport, why in the hell would you want to do that?' Walter pushed aside the blanket and sat up on the couch. Spandau noticed that it caused him pain.

'You need to go to the doctor.'

'You need to stop being such a pussy,' said Walter. 'I leave you for five minutes and you go all wimpy on me. You've never dropped a case before. Next thing you know you'll be telling me you've turned into a goddamn Buddhist or something.'

'Turns out he may have raped a girl. I don't want to work for the guy.'

'How'd you find this out?'

'A friend of his told me.'

'And he knows this for a fact?'

'The girl told him.'

'You talk to Margashack about it? He own up to it?'

'I haven't seen him yet.'

'Is there a police report?'

'It was never reported.'

'Let me see if I have this straight,' Walter said. 'You interview a bunch of people but you can't figure out which ones love him and which ones hate him, although it's likely that one of them might be trying to stick a knife in his back. I have this correct so far?'

'Yeah.'

'Then you tell me that one of these people – who may or may not hate his guts – tells you a story that he says he heard from someone else. A story, I might add, which is completely unsubstantiated by any sort of facts. And on the basis of this you are willing to decide that the bastard is guilty and your finer sensibili ties won't let you defend him? Am I still on the beam here?'

'It could be true,' said Spandau. 'Maybe it's true.'

'You think he did it?'

'I don't know.'

'Do you have a brain tumor, sport? Are unresolved sexual and emotional conflicts being stirred up and haunting you, clouding your mind? Has Jesus or at least one of the Apostles tapped you on the shoulder and given you the exclusive lowdown on the soul of Man?'

'I'm allowed to make a moral choice.'

'No you're not,' said Walter. 'Who in hell put that idea into your head? Grow up, for god's sake. We're not in the moral-choice business, we're in the do the fuck what we said we'd do business. Somebody hire you to find out if this girl was raped?'

Spandau got up to leave.

'Sit your ass down,' said Walter.

'I'm not prepared to argue this with you, Walter.'

'Me either. Which is fine, because this isn't an argument, it's a goddamned lecture. You are going to sit your ass back down and listen to me.'

Spandau was angry, wanted to leave. But Walter looked up at him and Spandau could see that Walter wasn't angry, just concerned.

'It doesn't work this way,' Walter said.

'Meaning what? The customer is always right even if he destroys some innocent girl's life?'

'You've got him tried and convicted already, when there's no proof that he did it. And even if he did, it doesn't matter. Not now. Not after you've taken the case.'

'I can't believe I'm hearing you say this. You can be a callous shit much of the time, but this is a new low.'

'We're hired to do a job, not to pass moral sentence. I'll tell you the same thing a defense attorney told me once, after I asked him if he'd ever defended anyone he was convinced was guilty. He said sure, all the time. Then I asked him how he could do it. And he said, I'm not defending the guy in the dock, I'm defending his rights, and what happens to him after that doesn't concern me one way or another. That's not my job, he said, and if he allowed himself to look at it any other way he'd be so crippled by moral confusion that he couldn't function at all.'

'I'm not Jerry Margashack's attorney.'

'No you're not. Nobody hired you to defend him or convict him. That has nothing to do with you. That's for somebody else to work out. You were hired to do one thing, to find out who's releasing this information. There's no moral element to this. There rarely is, and what worries me is that if you keep thinking this way, you're not going to be able to function either. You're not even working for Jerry Margashack, you're working for Frank Jurado's production company, and Jurado is a man you actually know to be a shit, but you took the job anyway. I'm interested in how you square this in your tight little moral universe.'

'You're right, I should never have taken the case.'

'What I'm trying to say, sport, is that you keep doing all the right things for all the wrong reasons. So far it seems to be working for you, but sooner or later you're going to get your tit caught in the wringer. One day you're going to get on your crusader's high horse and make one of your emotional calls and it's going to be the wrong one and somebody is going to get hurt. Life's not that simple. You just do your job, you follow the only clear path. Sometimes the job seems like shit and you feel bad at the end of it but you have to tell yourself it was never your call to begin with. Just do your job.'

'You and Eichmann and the banality of evil, right?'

'You are a fucking child, David,' said Walter. 'You're starting to sound like Dee. The world isn't that simple. And by the way I'd appreciate it if my employees didn't take such an active interest in my personal life.'

'Pookie's just worried about you.'

'It's not just Pookie I'm talking about.' Walter shifted painfully on the couch. 'When you can see clear to come down off of your cloud, I'd suggest you follow the fucking trail to that priest. Something doesn't sound right. God keeps cropping up too fucking often for my satisfaction. You might want to go north.'

Spandau got up to leave.

'By the way,' said Walter, 'I know about this crap with Dee's husband.'

'I've already set it up to pay for it out of my own pocket.'

'Good, because it's unprofessional as hell, not to mention emotionally stupid. I guess it's too late now. Just don't let it interfere with anything else. You've got Pookie and Leo on it?'

'We didn't have anything much for Leo and we'd both talked about giving Pookie a shot at street work. This seemed a fairly harmless way to begin.'

'Sometimes I think you forget who it was that taught you how to bullshit,' Walter said. 'Just don't let them get hurt.'

'You need anything?'

'Yeah, I need you to run my agency like you know what you're doing. Can you do that?'

'I don't hear the toilet flushing yet.'

'Good. Now get the fuck out of my face and go make some money.'

THIRTY-TWO

To get into the Glendale game room – number three of six Atom had running across town – you went into a barber shop, then out the back door into an alley. The alley had been sealed at both ends with locked covered gates. You walked across the alley and through a door that led into a former upholstery shop now brightened by a bar and half a dozen tables with card games going on and a couple of tables shooting craps. The place wasn't packed but it did steady business and it was the middle of the afternoon. Araz did a sweep around the place, his usual check, then went back into the office to count the day's take. While he was in there one of the girls at the bar came and told him Joey was up front. Araz counted out some money, put it in an envelope, and made a note of it in the account book he carried.

Joey Vernors was sitting back in the barber's chair when Araz came in. Oracio the barber was wrapping a cloth around him. Joey always got a free haircut, shave, mustache trim, and ear, eyebrow, and nasal-hair prune. He was an ex-cop and knew what his rights were.

'Araz, my man,' Joey said.

'How's it going, Joey.'

They shook hands. They always shook hands. Araz pulled his away. Joey's remained extended. Araz put the envelope into it, and it disappeared beneath the barber's cloth. They did this every week.

'Do what you can with the bald spot,' Joey said to Oracio. This too he did every week. 'How's business?' he said to Araz.

'Not bad.'

'Would you tell me?'

'Jesus, Joey, why would I lie to you?'

'Maybe the envelope ought to be a little thicker.'

'Come back and look, Joey. It's going to look the same fucking way it did this time last week and the week before. Business is steady but the economy sucks.'

'This ain't a BMW dealership.'

'People can't spend what they don't have.'

'Of course they can. They're fucking card junkies.'

'I let somebody lose more than they have and then I have to figure out some way to collect. It's a pain in the ass. You know how it works.'

'Like that fucking Jap you tempuraed.'

'You heard about that?'

'That was stupid. It doesn't sound like you. I told that to the boys when I heard it. I said that's not Araz, that's crazy fucking Uncle Atom.'

'Well,' said Araz.

'I'm supposed to remind you,' Joey said, 'that's not your turf.'

'Atom know that?'

'He knows that.'

Araz shrugged. 'I just do what I'm told.'

'Watch yourself. Benny Bono's got the contract on that street from Locatelli and he's gone back bitching that you guys have now fucked him out of a couple of grand a month and this isn't the first time.'

'You mean the Jap was already paying Benny Bono?'

'That's right.'

'Atom know this?'

'Fucking straight Atom knows it. If he didn't tell you he's yanking your chain for some reason. You're lucky Benny didn't show up. Talk to your uncle. Atom's never been the sanest fucker out there but you guys are pushing the envelope here. Unless you're ready for a turf war with Benny Bono, which you are not, you'd better get your uncle to start using his head.'

'I'll find a more diplomatic way of saying it.'

Joey laughed. 'You're a good kid. You understand I'm not picking favorites here. The boys in blue don't want to see things get ugly any more than you do. They just asked me to mention this.'

'Okay, Joey. Thanks.'

'Don't mention it, kid. And watch your ass. Not just from the guineas, either, if you know what I mean.'

Araz nodded. Joey leaned back and closed his eyes and Oracio shoved a small electric trimmer up his nose.

THIRTY-THREE

S pandau caught a flight from Burbank to Sacramento, had hoped to rent something nice and roomy but ended up with a smaller Nissan and driving north toward Redding with his knees up around his ears. He'd spent time rodeoing up here and it always felt good to be back. He liked this part of the state and couldn't think why he didn't come more often. But this was the sort of thing everybody says, as if people actually ran their own lives.

As he drove there were long stretches where it was still possible to imagine a time when genuine cowboys worked ranches that extended farther than the eye could see. What agribusiness hadn't ruined the real-estate developers had, and neither of them had much use for a breed of men who wouldn't or couldn't conform. The irony is that you couldn't drive three miles without seeing an ad for some cowboy-themed restaurant, motel, or tourist spot. They'd taken the American West and shrunk it too small for the real people.

Spandau stopped in Redding and had a steak and a beer in a restaurant decorated with posters of Crazy Horse and Geronimo. You could get a Cochise Burger with avocado and jalapeño Jack cheese, keeping with the natural progression of everything in America to become Disneyland in the end. We do the same thing to culture that Jivaro tribesmen do to heads. He found a country-western station on the car radio but switched it off when he realized once again that C&W nowadays is nothing but pop songs rendered through the nose.

Cheney was fifty miles east of Redding, wedged in a valley between two national forests at the feet of the Sierra Madres. Before leaving LA he called a friend who often fished in the area, asked him if he knew anything about Cheney. He said yes, it's the gateway to Burney. There were less than fifteen hundred inhabitants and one main street. Spandau didn't think it would take long to find the Catholic church. He stopped at a mom and pop diner, got a slice of cherry pie and a cup of coffee. The waitress was a friendly woman in her forties who wore a uniform three sizes too small for her expansive cleavage. She scratched a mosquito bite on her freckled left boob and pointed out the window and down the street. Spandau grossly overtipped her. She reminded him of the older woman, a friend of his mother's, who took his virginity all those years ago in Flagstaff. He thought he could still smell the Woolworth's perfume.

The Cheney Catholic church was a small redwood frame building at the end of the main street. There was no steeple or tower but there was a cross on the outside wall and a statue of St Francis of Assisi preaching to a small patch of winter-sleeping roses. Spandau walked up the steps and went into the church. It was dark and cool and smelled vaguely of cedar and was as stark as anything you'd find in a Bergman film. Spandau half expected to see Gunnar Björnstand but instead found a blond priest of about thirty squatting near the altar and ineptly trying to fix a broken electrical outlet. He'd not turned off the power, got zapped when he touched the hot wire and yelped and said, 'Shit!' before he realized he'd done it. When Spandau came up the priest looked up at him with a look of utter despair. He had short hair and a cowlick that made him look like Opie Taylor had been called to the cloth.

The priest apologized for swearing, then said,

'You wouldn't happen to know how to change one of these things, would you? Somebody broke it and it's the outlet we use for the electric organ. The electrician wanted to charge me sixty dollars just to come and look at it. He's a Methodist, wouldn't you know. If he'd been a Catholic I might have had some leverage.'

'You have the new outlet?'

The priest held up the box.

'You know where the fuse box is?' Spandau asked.

'I think so. Why?'

'First you have to turn off the electricity. Otherwise you get shocked.'

'Why didn't I know that? God has given me a few talents but a mechanical sense isn't one of them. I excel at the less strenuous sports, like book-keeping.'

The priest went through a side door into a small kitchen. He opened a closet.

'Is this it?'

Spandau nodded and opened the circuit box. He found the breaker and shut it off. Most of the lights around the altar went off as well.

'Oh Lord,' said the priest, 'what have you done?'

'Everything on that circuit gets shut off too. They'll all be back on in a minute.'

'You're sure you know what you're doing?'

'More or less. But if I happen to burst into flames, don't try to put me out with water, okay?'

He nodded, not realizing it was a joke. Spandau took the screwdriver from the priest and set about changing the outlet.

'You're not Father Michael,' Spandau said.

'Oh heavens no. I'm Father Paul. Father Michael looks like John Wayne and is probably the one who installed all this wiring in the first place. He's retiring this year and I'm taking over for him.'

'Is he around?'

'I'd say right about now he's on the river catching the evening rise or whatever they call it. He's quite the fly-fisherman. It's a wonder he doesn't step on a rattlesnake. The things are all over the place up here.'

'I take it you didn't grow up here.'

'I'm from Columbus, Ohio. The 'burbs, where the most you had to worry about was an angry raccoon. People see bears here. Bears, I ask you. What do I do if I run into a bear? Ask him if he wants to confess?'

'It's hard if you don't grow up in these places.'

'Did you?'

'Some place like it. I grew up on my uncle's ranch just outside of Flagstaff. There's not a lot to do.'

'I suppose it's easier now with the internet and all. I'd go crazy without email and blogging and Netflix. Do you do Facebook?'

'No.'

'I've got contacts all over the world. It's amazing. I've put this church online. We have a website and a blog and everything. Our parishioners are scattered all over the place. It's a wonderful way of keeping the parish informed, keeping everyone together. You ought to check it out.'

'I will, thanks.'

Spandau connected the wires to the new outlet and screwed it into place, then the wall plate. He handed the screwdriver back to Father Paul and went into the kitchen and flipped on the breaker. The lights came back on. The priest looked greatly relieved.

'It should work now,' Spandau said. 'If you could point me in the direction of Father Michael.'

'I can tell you where he is, but he can be rather ill-tempered when he's fishing.'

'I'll have to risk it.'

'Maybe I could be of help.'

'I'm a researcher for HBO. We're planning a bio of Jerry Margashack and they've sent me up to look around. I understand he grew up around here. Did you know him?'

'A little before my time, I'm afraid. I've only been here a year. Father Michael is definitely your man, then. He and Jerry have always been close.'

'Jerry was a good Catholic?'

'Well, that's not exactly my understanding. They've been friends a long time. I don't think it's so much a priestly thing as a kind of father–son relationship. I knew Jerry didn't get along with his father, didn't really get along with anybody in his family. It was Father Michael who used to bail him out of things.'

'So they still see each other?'

'I don't think they've actually seen each other in years. Certainly not since I've been here. Mainly emails and letters.'

'Snail mail? Don't you think that's odd? I mean, why write letters when you have email?'

'I don't think they're letters exactly.'

'A check maybe? A contribution to the parish?'

'I wouldn't know. You'd have to take that up with Father Michael.'

'How can I find him?'

'I'll draw you a map. He's got a small trailer about five miles out of town, right across the road from the creek. It looks like a bait shop inside. He's moving the whole thing up to Oregon in a few months when he retires. He goes up there all the time. People joke he's got a woman up there, but, oh Lord, you can't say that around him, can you, he'll tear your head off. Apparently he has friends up near Ashland where they're going to let him put his trailer. Near the river again. I know Our Lord liked fishermen but frankly I can't see the point.'

THIRTY-FOUR

Father Paul didn't have much of a talent for cartography either, but Spandau found the place, tucked away in some trees across the road from the river. He knocked on the door of the trailer and got no answer. He crossed the road and picked his way through the rocks down to the water, making more than enough noise to warn any rattlers. There was a path along the bank and Spandau followed it round a bend and saw Father Michael up ahead and a few yards out in the water. He was an odd sight in waders and a dog collar but he knew what he was doing and Spandau stood for a bit and watched the old man cast the line upstream over and over in an effortless gentle roll. The line stretched itself out on the water without ripple and floated almost invisible down the current until he swept it from the water and into the air to cast again.

'Having any luck?' Spandau said as he approached.

'Not if you're going to stomp around in those rocks like a damned Clydesdale,' said the old man. 'These trout are catch and release and are probably better educated at this point than either of us. Regardless of what people think, they're not entirely stupid. If all you did all day long, day in and day out your entire life, was look for the right bugs to eat, you'd get pretty good at it, wouldn't you? What do you want with me?'

'You knew I was coming?'

'I'm old but I can still read the text on my cell phone. Paul knows better than to let you sneak up on me. I'd've had his head in a basket. I don't like surprises.'

'I wanted to talk to you about Jerry Margashack.'

'So I understand,' said the priest. He looked around. The light was fading. 'If you can just hold your water I've got time for a couple of more casts.'

Spandau watched the old priest make his casts until neither of them could see the fly and the priest reeled in his line.

'A Parachute Adams,' said the priest, dangling the tiny fly so

Spandau could see it. 'See the little white tuft of hair on top? That's why they call it a parachute. You tie them with that part sticking up so that old farts like me can see them. It seems like cheating but that's what happens when you get old. You have to cheat. It's the only way we can even the game with you youngsters.'

He clipped off the tie and hooked it to the wool pad on his vest.

'You tie them yourself?' Spandau asked.

'Something to do winter evenings while I watch TV.'

'It is my understanding that trout season up here doesn't start until May.'

'Really?' said the priest. He cranked the line onto the reel and broke down the fly rod. 'I'll have to ask the warden when he comes to mass on Sunday.'

The priest turned and headed up the bank still in his waders. 'You better follow me unless you want to break an ankle,' he said to Spandau over his shoulder.

Spandau followed him up to the road. He was a tall man, still taller than Spandau's six-two, and walked with a determined stride. He didn't wait for Spandau or look back to see if he followed. Spandau shuffled along just behind him, dogging him back down the road to the trailer. The old priest pulled off his waders outside the door and hung them from a clothesline to dry. He went into the trailer and let the screen door nearly take Spandau's nose off. Spandau pulled it open again and went in.

It didn't actually look like a bait shop but it didn't leave any doubt what the old man's enthusiasms were. Rods in one corner, the better ones on a rack on the wall. A makeshift fly-tying table beneath a window. Lots of photos, mainly fish-related, Father Michael holding up a prize catch.

'There's whisky on the shelf over there,' said the priest, and went into the bathroom.

Spandau went over and poured two glasses of Macallan's. Directly he could hear the old man grunting behind the door. Spandau took a sip of the scotch and sat the old man's glass on a beat-up coffee table. There weren't many photos of people, a few obviously long-dead relatives. Several photos of a tired-looking but smiling woman maybe in her late thirties or early forties. She had been pretty once but now the smile looked as if it took some work. There were a couple more of her and a boy with Down's syndrome, taken a few years apart. There was one photo of the three of them together, and one of Father Michael and the boy, taken maybe five years ago, with the boy smiling brightly and holding up his own rainbow.

Father Michael came out of the bathroom, saw Spandau looking at the photos. 'Now you want to tell me who the hell you are and what you want?'

He sat down on the sofa and picked up his glass, stared at Spandau.

'I do research for HBO. We're thinking of doing a documentary on Jerry Margashack and I'm interviewing people who knew him.'

'Uh huh.'

'I understand you used to be his priest.'

'You understand wrongly. I was a friend of his but I was never his priest. If you knew anything about Jerry Margashack you'd know he's never had much truck with such things.'

'But you knew him well?'

'Do they give you some sort of card, these HBO people?'

'No.'

'So what you're telling me is that you might just be anybody, maybe even somebody Jerry owes money to, maybe somebody looking to hurt him?'

'I'm not looking to hurt him.'

'But you are a liar. You don't listen to confessions for thirty years and not learn to spot a bold-faced lie from half a mile away. You're not too good at it either. Anybody ever tell you that?'

'What was it? My innocent-looking face?'

'It's your ego. You don't want it bad enough. You're embarrassed at having to lie and there's this hitch in your attitude that can't help telling me you don't give a damn if I believe you or not. Would that be about right?'

'I should introduce you to my boss. The two of you would get along.'

'This is not to say I appreciate being lied to. I never did get used to it. You still don't care, do you?'

'Not really.'

'Well,' said the priest, 'finish your drink and then I'm going to throw you out of here on your head.'

'Jerry's in trouble and I've been hired to help him out.'

'Then you got your hands full, son, because I've never known Jerry Margashack when he wasn't in trouble of some sort.'

'You ever see any of his films?'

'I think I saw one of them once. A lot of sex and foul language and violence. I'm not prudish but I didn't see the point. You could imagine Jerry making it though. He always did like to shock people. Most of us grow out of that sort of thing.'

'You keep up with him. I imagine you know the shape his career's been in the last few years.'

'His career is none of my business.'

'I thought you were friends?'

'I can tell you don't know much about human relations. Not everything is so conveniently defined, and I gave up worrying about it a long time ago. I just do what God calls me to do and leave the worrying to Him.'

'Jerry's broke and struggling. This new movie he's done has a shot at the Oscars, which would turn his life around, but somebody is trying to ruin it for him. Somebody who knows him, knows his private life, is releasing information about his indiscretions.'

'And you've been hired to stop them?'

'That's right.'

'Are they lies, this information they're putting out?'

'I don't know.'

'Well that puts you in a kind of morally ambiguous area, doesn't it? What if they're true?'

'That's not for me to decide.'

'Aha,' said the priest. 'I could rummage around in my head for about a dozen biblical quotes that say you're wrong, but they'd be wasted on you. You've already got everything figured out.'

'What about "judge not lest ye be judged" and all that.'

'"For with what judgment ye judge, ye shall be judged: and with what measure ye mete, it shall be measured to you again". That would be Matthew 7,' the priest quoted automatically. 'People are always half-assing this verse. Are you really stupid enough to argue scripture with a Catholic priest?'

Father Michael took another sip of scotch and leaned forward and looked Spandau in the eyes.

'If you look at it – and I assure you that once or twice I have

– it is not the moral loophole that everybody seems to think it is. What it is actually is the Golden Rule all over again. Treat others as you'd like to be treated. It doesn't say a thing about not judging people. It just says that when you do pass verdict on somebody, use the same standards you'd want them to use on you. Try to be fair, in other words.'

The priest released a discreet belch, shook his head incredulously, and went on.

'You want the easy way. You want not to be judged at all, you want a get out of jail free card,' he said. 'It doesn't exist. Like it or not it's a moral universe. Some points can be debated but most not. Not the big ones. We all know the difference between right and wrong, most of us are just too damned lazy to apply it. Like everybody else, you're just scared shitless somebody is going to call you on your choices. And you know what? They will. You're going to be judged no matter what you do. Some will seem fair, some won't, but you're going to have to learn to live with it and that's what kills you, doesn't it? You have to have the balls to live with your choices. In the end, buddy, it's just you and God and my advice is try to shut up and listen.'

Father Michael drained his scotch. He stood up and removed the half-filled glass from Spandau's hand.

'I'm throwing you out now,' he said. 'Go back to the City of Lost Angels and give everybody a break. And don't go bothering Father Paul, he won't talk to you again. Anyway the poor man can't find his ass with both hands. I wouldn't put much value in whatever he told you.'

The priest unlatched the door and held it open for Spandau. A cool early winter darkness had settled outside and you could hear the river across the road and trucks passing on the highway. Spandau suddenly felt lonely and reluctant to leave the cramped little trailer. The old priest knew what he was doing. Even his timing was impeccable. The old bastard had control from the beginning. He worked in his lecture and when Spandau was off balance he dumped his ass out into the snow. Spandau wondered if they taught that kind of nifty psychology at the seminary. Spandau felt like a fool now but he admired the old guy. He'd been manipulated, but on the other hand the old bastard hadn't said anything Spandau wasn't already bothered about.

Spandau went down the cinderblock steps into the yard, then turned and said, 'Thank you for your help.'

The priest laughed. 'Do you always make a habit of saying things you don't believe?' Spandau started to open his mouth again but Father Michael said, 'It was a rhetorical question. Don't bother trying to answer it. I doubt you even know the answer yourself.'

Father Michael stepped back and let the thin door slam shut. Then the light by the door went out and Spandau stood in the yard for a moment, lighting a cigarette and listening to the old priest moving around inside. Spandau wanted to knock on the door and argue with the priest to claim his rights as an honest man, a good man, a man to be trusted. Spandau didn't owe the old bastard anything and couldn't see why he needed the old man's approval. This did piss him off. He was tempted to knock on the door but instead turned and walked to the car because the truth was that the priest was right. In regard to his being a good man – whatever the hell that was supposed to be – Spandau no longer knew.

THIRTY-FIVE

There was a motel he'd seen on Highway 299 coming into town that afternoon. He drove through Cheney – it was just past 7 p.m. and already the streets had rolled up. Most of the shops had closed on the main street. The diner and the convenience store and the supermarket were still open. As he drove past houses he could smell the smoke from the fireplaces and look through the windows at families having dinner. How long had it been since he'd sat down to a dinner with his family, with anybody's family? It was with Dee and her parents just before her father Beau died. Thanksgiving on Beau and Mary Macaulay's ranch near Ojai. Married nearly forty years and somehow still hugged and kissed like teenagers. Dee had grown up in a nest of love, had never known what it was like to live without it. Then came Spandau.

Spandau had married the boss's daughter. He'd come out of the army with no prospects but a half-hearted dream of making a living on the rodeo circuit. Two years in Germany without even seeing a horse left him ill-prepared for staying on top of an angry one. By the time he'd worked his riding and roping skills back up to speed, he recalled what had driven him into the army in the first place. He wasn't that good. He was okay, every now and then he won something. But it was never going to be enough to make even the months of travel worthwhile, much less pay for the broken bones.

Beau Macaulay was the stunt coordinator for a Western being filmed in Flagstaff. Somebody told Spandau they were looking for extras who could stay on a horse and come in sober on consecutive days.

Spandau showed up at a local ranch where they were casting the extras. In one corral they had gathered some of the local horses they were going to use in the film. There were a lot of people and trucks and film equipment being shuffled around and the horses were nervous. Spandau stood and watched the horses for a while. He noticed a big redheaded man watching him. Spandau was six foot two but this guy was four inches taller.

Spandau went over to him and asked if he knew how you went about getting a job as an extra. The big man looked him up and down and then pointed to a horse tethered to a fence post. The horse looked tired and irritable and shifted around uneasily.

'You ever do any riding?' the man asked him.

'Rodeo here and there,' said Spandau.

'You any good?'

Spandau laughed. 'Not much,' he said.

'You reckon you could run up on that horse over there and leap up over his hindquarters onto the saddle?'

'You mean like Roy Rogers?'

The man nodded.

'Well,' said Spandau, 'I can't see any reason anybody would ever want to do that. But if I did, and you don't hobble that horse, he's more than likely going to kick the shit out of me when I grab his ass.'

'It never made any sense to me either,' said Big Beau Macaulay. He pointed to a woman with a clipboard standing near the table where extras were lined up to be interviewed. 'You go over to that scary looking woman right there and tell her Beau says you're hired. If she starts giving you any shit tell her to come and see me.'

The woman did indeed start giving Spandau shit. Spandau listened to her for a while and then started to leave.

'Where you going?' Beau asked him.

'She told me I didn't look right.'

'Did she say why?'

'She said I looked more like a New Jersey club bouncer than a cowboy.'

Beau looked at him for a few moments, then stared at the ground and huffed and shook his head. 'You stay right here,' he said to Spandau and went over to a tall man sweating behind a pair of expensive sunglasses. It turned out to be the producer.

'Dino,' Beau said to the man, 'I want you to watch something.'

Beau went over to where a tall, striking auburn-haired woman and two young and athletic but unruly looking men were sitting and talking under a marquee. One of them was tall and the other was a little shorter. Both looked slightly crazy and no one you'd like to mess with in a fight.

'Who wants to be a goddamn cow?' said Beau, and the taller man laughed and got up.

Beau picked up a lariat and walked over and handed it to Spandau. 'I want you to get on that horse yonder – the right way – and when this poor ugly sumbitch,' he put his hand on the young man's shoulder, 'takes off running I want you to rope him before he reaches the other side of that paddock.'

'Neck or feet?' asked Spandau.

'Whatever you feel like. Just don't kill him because, stupid as he is, I need him.'

Dino said, 'If there's anybody from the fucking bond company walking around, they will ram a power drill up my ass.'

'Goddamn it, Dino,' said Beau, 'it's a cowboy picture, ain't it? Let's pretend we're not all a bunch of Santa Monica pansies.'

Spandau took the rope and got up onto the horse. He moved him around a little, saw how he reacted to the reins touching his neck and the shift of Spandau's weight. He was a good horse. Spandau let out a loop of rope and nodded to Beau.

Beau said to the temporary cow, 'Don't make it easy for him, we want a little show,' and sent the man off at a dead run. He waited until the man had a more than fair head start and then gave Spandau the high sign. Spandau kicked the horse and flew through the open paddock gate. The man looked over his shoulder at Spandau coming down on him and began to bob and weave. Cows don't bob and weave quite so much as a man and Spandau was worried more than anything else about the guy accidentally running under the horse. He gave the man just enough space to where he could throw the loop and have it fall no lower than the waist. As it was when Spandau reined the horse the rope cinched on the still running man and yanked him sharply backwards onto his ass. Spandau jumped off the horse fearing busted ribs or a snapped back.

The guy lay there but looked up at Spandau and said a little breathless, 'Well shit, you're not going to pig me, are you?' Some of the buttons had snapped off his shirt but he looked fine. The man got up and waved toward Beau. Suddenly there was all this cheering and clapping. Spandau had forgotten the whole place was watching. The human cow, whose name turned out to be Rodney, shook Spandau's hand and they walked together back to where Beau and the producer stood at the gate.

'Moo, goddammit,' Rodney said to Beau as they approached.

'At least I found something you're good for,' Beau said to him. 'Hamburger.'

'Next time you want a cow,' Rodney said rubbing his midriff, 'find a cow.'

'Can you fall off a horse?' asked the producer.

'I do it all the time,' said Spandau. 'I guess I could figure out how to do it on purpose for a change.'

Beau and Rodney walked Spandau past the sour casting assistant over to the marquee. She didn't look at either Beau or Spandau but you could see the muscles in her neck tightened like cables. Beau didn't smile until he'd passed her and she couldn't see it. That was the sort of man he was. Beau never rubbed your nose in it but he never told you a third time either.

The young woman and two men stopped laughing as Rodney came up.

'Looks like you might have damaged one of your udders there, Bessie,' the girl said seriously.

'It does my heart good to see a little doggie run free like that,' said the shorter man. 'Reminds me of my days on the plains with Buffalo Bill. Anybody ever tell you you got that heifer's trot down to a tee, that cute little sway in your hips?' and started singing 'Don't Fence Me In'. Everybody joined the serenade.

'Kiss my ass,' said Rodney, climbing up onto the table and lying down.

The girl reached into a cooler and pulled out a can of beer and slid it into a sleeve that looked like Coca-Cola. She sat it on Rodney's chest, then bent over and kissed him gently on the lips. She went back to the cooler and brought faux sodas to Spandau and Beau.

'You proud of yourself?' the girl said to Beau. 'You'd have looked like a damn fool if he hadn't roped him, wouldn't you?'

Beau popped the cap on his beer.

'He didn't think he could do it, he wouldn't have got on that horse. Anyway you know I never make mistakes, even if I'm not always right.'

'You've pissed off old Miss Sunbeam anyway, which is all you wanted.'

'I just eased that stick out of her bunghole an inch or two,' he said. 'Now maybe she'll quit crossing me. Fresh out of some back east drama school, not knowing shit from Shinola about a goddamned thing, much less who is and who ain't looking like a cowboy.'

'Don't get worked up.'

'I ain't getting worked up,' he said. 'You call your mother and ask if they got my truck fixed yet?'

'You can pick it up this afternoon. You could quit being a cheap old Scots codger and just buy a new truck.'

'I have owned this truck since 1965. I restored it and have replaced two engines and just about every nut and bolt with my bare hands. I'd be doing it again right now if I wasn't stuck out here in the middle of God's Country or wherever the hell we are. Anyway it was your mother that broke the goddamn axle. I keep telling her it ain't no jeep.'

'Isn't it about time to go home?' Rodney said from the table. 'That hotel's got a hot tub and I'm going to get a bottle of wine and soak until the rest of my body is as wrinkled as my scrotum.'

'That is quite an image and I for one do not thank you for it,' said the other man. 'I was thinking about a steak but now I don't know if I could keep it down.'

Beau pulled out a railroad watch and checked the time. 'Pack it up,' he said.

Beau picked up his battered briefcase. Rodney and the other man, whose name turned out to be Dale, gathered up their belongings and each grabbed a handle of the cooler, heading for the parking lot.

'Does this mean I'm hired?' Spandau asked, standing there lost with the beer can still unopened in his hand.

'Lord help me,' said Beau to himself as he walked off, 'another dumb one.'

The girl picked up several empty cans and fast-food wrappers and carried them to a trash bin. She came back and checked around to see nothing important remained. You could see she was used to doing this. Finally she looked at Spandau and smiled.

'Be here in the morning at seven,' she said and walked away.

Tall with auburn hair and the bluest clearest eyes Spandau had ever seen.

Delilah.

Dee.

He didn't know it yet, but that peculiar feeling worming its way through his chest was love.

THIRTY-SIX

As he drove out of town onto the highway he noticed that he'd picked up a sheriff's car. There were no lights and they kept back a way but they were there. Spandau pulled into the motel parking lot and the car went on past. Probably nothing. He was a stranger in town and likely they were just running his plates.

He pushed the buzzer outside the motel office. In a minute a sleepy middle-aged man in a bathrobe came to the door.

'Didn't mean to wake you up,' said Spandau.

'Fell asleep watching TV with the cat in my lap. Happens every time,' he said. 'No matter.'

He let Spandau into the office and allowed him to pay with a credit card. He gave Spandau the key and told him where the room was and no, sorry, they didn't have that internet thing.

'And if you want to smoke,' said the man, 'you either got to go outside or hang your head out the window.'

Spandau reparked the car outside his room. Still no sign of the sheriff's car. He went in and tossed his suitcase and his computer bag onto the bed. He was hungry and thinking about where he might eat, but called Pookie on his cell phone.

'Where are you?' he said when she answered. 'Is Leo with you?'

'The answer to the first part of your question is that I'm home and soaking in a hot bath surrounded by aroma-therapeutic candles. I feel no changes but they cost a fortune and I think I've been hoodwinked,' she said. 'This sleuthing business is hard work and I'm going to have to wear flats, how boring. The answer to the second part is that yes, Leo is here, but he's safely on the other side of a locked door reading *Paris Match* and waiting to take me out to dinner. By the way I'm fine, thank you.'

'How's Dee?'

'She's holding up pretty well. We've got a nice list of people and places. Tomorrow we talk to the sister. Still no news from Charlie but we didn't really expect it, did we.'

A few dead moments.

'No,' said Pookie, 'we didn't talk about you. She didn't mention it and I didn't bring it up.'

'Things are complicated enough as they are,' he said.

'I'd feel so much better if your voice weren't all syrupy with disappointment. Anna loves you too and I'm afraid you're going to screw this up. Yes yes, none of my business. The zipping of the mouth. Umf.'

'Listen, before you drag Leo out and spend all his money, I want him to use some of those computer smarts we're supposed to be paying him for. I'm texting you the name of a website. It's for the Catholic church here. I want him to scan it and check any references to a Father Michael and places in Oregon. I'm looking for family friends, fishing spots, whatever. Then I want him to call me back.'

'He'll have to use my laptop,' she said lamely.

'So what?'

'I don't want him nosing through my computer,' she said. 'My diary is on there and there's my Facebook stuff with all my friends.'

'Humor me,' said Spandau. 'I'm up here at the Bates Motel waiting for Anthony Perkins to show up in a wig.'

'Okay,' she said, 'but if he ends up stalking all my girlfriends on your head be it.'

'Oh come on. Leo is a boy scout.'

'Nevertheless, he's been prowling around outside the door and I've had to stick tissue in the keyhole.'

'He's probably just worried about you going up in a blaze of aromatic wax,' he said. 'What's he doing in your apartment in the first place?'

'I told you, he's taking me out to dinner. He's been completely dull about it all day. I had to say yes just to shut him up and anyway it's that new French place on La Cienega. He had to stop and buy a sports jacket. Thank god I was with him.'

'Don't you feel just the slightest bit sympathetic?'

'Of course I do,' Pookie said. 'I'm taking this huge chance that people will actually see us together.'

Spandau rang off and was putting on his jacket to go out to forage through Cheney for dinner. There was a loud and firm knock. Three large sheriff's deputies filled the doorway.

'I'm sorry to bother you, sir, but may I see your driver's license?'

Spandau actually started to ask why, but he knew why, and it wouldn't have done any good anyway. He took out his wallet, handed over the license.

'Is this your license, sir?'

'Uh huh.'

'And your name is David R. Spandau?'

'Uh huh.'

'And you are a California resident?'

'Yup.'

'And is this your correct address? Is the information on this license correct and up to date?'

'That's right. Okay, I'm going to bite and ask why you're here, like I don't already know.'

'Would you mind telling us your profession, sir?'

'I'm a turkey-sexer.'

'Pardon me, sir?'

'I sex turkeys. You know, I hold up the turkeys and I check to see if it's a girl turkey or a boy turkey. Most people don't know how specialized this is. It's often very hard to tell.'

'It has come to our attention that you've been representing yourself as a –' he checked a small notebook – 'researcher for HBO.'

'Actually I do both. When I'm on the road for HBO I try to take advantage of any turkey farms in the area, just to keep my hand in. So to speak.'

'Would you mind coming with us, Mr Spandau?'

'I would in fact. I'm tired and I haven't had dinner yet and I will be leaving town first thing in the morning, so all this is pointless.'

'We'd still like to talk to you, Mr Spandau, so if you wouldn't mind . . .'

Spandau followed them outside. He was pulling on his coat when one of them took it away from him and another slammed him forward against the police car.

'Put your hands on the hood there, Mr Spandau. You know how to do this. Take a step back and spread your feet apart.'

They frisked him quickly and roughly, then pulled his hands behind him and cuffed them.

'Why don't we call Father Michael now and tell him I get the point.'

'I have no idea who you are referring to, sir, we are only civic officers in pursuit of our duty. We have no real idea who you are, sir, and as a stranger in our community there is some question as to your identity and your motives. We have a right to hold you for up to twenty-four hours, sir, while we attempt to verify your real identity.'

'You been having trouble with jewel thieves in this area lately?'

'That is an odd question to ask, sir, and it is overtly suspicious that you should mention it.'

Overtly, thought Spandau. I love that.

They pushed him into the car. One of them sat in back next to him. They were all smiling. Three of them in one patrol car meant this whole thing wasn't official, and the guy sitting next to him wasn't wearing a piece. Spandau also noticed they were heading out of town.

'Would it be overtly insulting if I pointed out that you're driving in the wrong direction?'

'No, sir, it would not.'

They drove about five miles out of town, then pulled off onto a dirt road and drove another quarter of a mile deep into the trees. They pulled over and dragged Spandau from the car. One of them opened the trunk and took out a canvas duffel bag.

'You've had your fun,' said Spandau. 'Either take me to the station or take me home because anything else is kidnapping. Get me back to town before the diner closes and maybe I'll be sympathetic when they start to throw your asses in prison.'

They led Spandau into the woods.

'Let's see. I haven't done anything serious enough to justify murder, and it'll be hard to explain showing up in a few hours with the crap beaten out of me. It's too early in the year to look for mushrooms and I'm really hoping you don't have any amorous intentions. Otherwise I'm at a loss to figure out why the hell we're here.'

'You ever been on a snipe hunt, Mr Spandau?'

'Oh come on. Even you guys aren't hick enough to still be doing that.'

One of them kicked out and swept Spandau's feet from under him. He fell into the earth and wet leaves. The deputy with the duffel bag opened it and took out ten feet of lightweight logging chain. He swung it around a three-foot-diameter tree, catching the other end, then clamped it together with a padlock.

'I don't know how you fancy dudes in the big city do it, but up here in Oregon' (he pronounced it OR-ee-gon) 'we have a game of snipe that we save just for smart sons of bitches from out of town who cause trouble and try to make us look like assholes.'

The guy with the duffel bag pulled out a plastic tarp and spread it on the ground at the foot of the tree. Then he took out a cheap sleeping bag and a blanket and set them down on the tarp.

Spandau looked at the setup.

'You're kidding. Come on guys.'

'Right now I am going to uncuff one of your hands, Mr Spandau, and I assure you that if you take a swing or try to run we are going to stomp all over you and you will be sitting on your ass on the cold wet ground until we feel like coming to get you. Now play nice.'

They uncuffed one of his hands, then attached the empty cuff loosely to the chain.

'Now see there, you can go anywhere you like as long as it

ain't more than about three feet away from this tree. There's a slight slope down that a way, so unless you don't mind sitting in it all night I suggest you shit or pee on the downward side.'

The guy with the duffel bag upended it onto the tarp, spilling several bottles of water, a bunch of granola power bars, and a roll of toilet paper.

'We are civilized people, Mr Spandau, and believe it or not we are concerned with your welfare. We want you to be comfortable, but not so comfortable that you're ever going to show your sorry Ralph Lauren Polo-wearing Spago-sitting arrogant big-city ass in this county again.'

'Would it help to swear I've learned my lesson?'

'Nope. It won't help to yell either, because there's nobody for a couple of miles. Now listen, Mr Spandau, here are the rules. You just sit right here under this tree, and if you see a snipe, then you yell "snipe" and we'll run right back out here and pick you up. You got that? It's real simple.'

'Did I mention my asthma and my heart condition and how I forgot my meds?'

'That reminds me. You want to toss me your cell phone? We'll give it back to you in the morning.'

He relinquished the phone.

'Snakes you don't have to worry about. I've seen wild pigs but if they come it'll be for the power bars and not you, so throw the damn things as far away as you can. Same thing for bears. You see a bear, I suggest you use that LA charm of yours. Or better yet, tell him you're with Showtime and you want to do a documentary on him. Frigging bears will believe anything.'

THIRTY-SEVEN

He managed one-handed to wrap the blanket around him and slide himself into the sleeping bag. He was still damned cold but he wouldn't freeze. He ate all the power bars but went light on the water since he didn't want to climb out to pee. There were no bears or wild pigs but small animals did move invisibly in the brush. Their frequent slaughter of the fish in his backyard pond gave him a distaste for raccoons, the vicious bastards.

He was actually asleep when a truck pulled up off the road and stopped a few yards away, blinding him in the headlights. A man got out. He didn't recognize the lead deputy until he came over and unlocked the chain and handcuffs. Spandau looked at his watch.

'It's just eleven,' Spandau said. 'Don't tell me you got soft-hearted all of a sudden.'

He gave Spandau back his cell phone. 'You got some messages you probably ought to look at.'

The deputy began gathering the snipe gear. Spandau checked his phone. Nearly a dozen texts all saying more or less the same thing. Walter dead. Where are you. And then the phone messages, Pookie's anguished voice, sobbing, doing her best to give Spandau the ugly details.

'Man, I'm sorry,' said the deputy. 'We were just trying . . . Well, you know, it wasn't like . . .'

Spandau tried to dial but there was no fucking reception anyway.

'I'm sorry,' the deputy repeated. 'I hope it wasn't anybody family.'

'Just get me back to my fucking car, will you? Can you manage that?'

THIRTY-EIGHT

'Oh baby, oh baby don't stop.'

Araz pumped harder. They were both bathed in sweat.

'This what you want?' Araz said. 'This what you've been wanting?'

'Yes oh yes.'

'You want me to stop? You want me to stop fucking you?'

'No don't stop.'

'Say it, cunt,' said Araz. 'Beg me to fuck you.'

'Don't stop. Please. Fuck me.'

Araz thrust angrily a few more times then came and collapsed onto the flesh beneath him.

'Oh god,' said Mitchell.

'Was it good?' asked Araz when he could get his breath. He kissed Mitchell between the shoulders.

'Are you taking vitamins or something? What is it with you, getting all Joe Dalessandro on me? It's like an Andy Warhol porn film.' Araz started to pull away but Mitchell said, 'Don't move, just stay there for a little longer.'

Araz lay his head on the damp back. 'What do you say in a gay bar when a condom goes flying across the room?'

'Who farted,' said Mitchell. 'I told you that one. What a time to think of it.'

'What about the parrot with no legs?'

'You've ruined the moment,' said Mitchell. 'You romantic fool you.'

Araz pulled out. The condom remained in his lover's ass. Araz gently removed it, then rolled off Mitchell and went to the bathroom to throw the condom away.

'I'm not fucking around,' said Mitchell, 'and if you're not then we don't need that.'

Araz climbed back into bed but didn't reply. Mitchell said,

'We could get tested, if that would make you feel better.'

'Great,' said Araz. 'That's just all I need. We could also wear matching "I'm Queer!" T-shirts. My uncle would love that.'

'Fuck your uncle.'

'My uncle saw us like this he'd kill us both. I mean that literally.'

'You're such a drama queen. Who cares what he thinks.'

'I keep telling you, you don't fucking understand. I mean it. He'd kill us both. You have to understand this. You don't know how big a deal this is. He finds out, we're both dead. I don't know how I can make that any clearer.'

'I think you're exaggerating.'

'You haven't said anything, right? No one knows?'

'Calm down. No, I haven't told anybody. Not that I don't want to. How long is this supposed to go on?'

'I don't know. Always. Or until he dies. Maybe when he dies.'

'So you're my fucking ghost lover until your fucking uncle dies? This makes me so happy, Araz, to hear how much you love me.'

'Who said I love you?' Araz puts his arms around him, pulled him close.

'You did, about a hundred times last night, until you got what you wanted.'

'You didn't like it?'

Mitchell laughed. 'I'd rather you were less In and more Out.'

'You don't start taking this whole thing seriously,' Araz said, 'and maybe the best thing I can do is get us buried together. Would that make you happy?'

He got out of bed, started dressing.

'Where are you going?' asked Mitchell. 'Don't you want a shower?'

'I have to see my uncle first thing.'

'I'm sorry I don't smell like cunt,' said Mitchell. 'Some little eau de snatch for you to wear around all day. Would Uncle Atom recognize dried semen on your shirt collar?'

'Don't even joke about it,' said Araz. He went over to kiss Mitchell, who tried to pull him back into bed. Araz broke free.

'Asshole,' said Mitchell.

'Cunt,' said Araz, who blew a kiss and left.

THIRTY-NINE

Uncle Atom sat at his desk. The archaic adding machine was turned upside down in front of him. He was poking at it with a screwdriver.

'This fucking machine,' said Atom. 'You know anything about this?'

'You mean adding machines?' said Araz.

'No,' said Atom, 'fucking atomic physics.'

Atom prodded a bit, tossed the screwdriver down onto the desk. He looked up at Araz and considered him for a moment. Said,

'You hear anything about the debt you're owed? Any news?'

'I'm sorry,' said Araz. 'Didn't you understand what I just said?'

Uncle Atom was sitting behind the desk. He got up, walked around to Araz, then backhanded him across the face.

'Don't you ever talk to me like that again.'

'I'm sorry,' said Araz automatically, rubbing his cheek. 'I just, I just thought it was important.'

'You do? You think it's important?'

'We don't want to go to war with Locatelli, right?'

'Why not,' said Uncle Atom.

'Because they're bigger and stronger than we are. They'll wipe us out.'

Uncle Atom shrugged.

'Maybe,' he said. 'But nobody is going to war with anybody. Maybe one day, but not yet. And when it happens, my friend, it won't be over a fucking Jap sushi parlor. You're being manipulated. It worries me you can't see this. We give Joey Vernors money to keep the cops in that neighborhood off our back. Locatelli gives him more. Which of us do you think he'd rather keep doing business with? You've got to stop being stupid.'

'He says they're upset about the Jap.'

Atom raised his voice.

'I'm telling you nobody gives a shit about the Jap! Are you hearing me, you little prick? I don't care about the Jap, Benny Bono doesn't care about the Jap, Joey Vernors sure as shit doesn't care about the Jap. The only fucking asshole who seems to care about the Jap is you, for reasons that escape me. Joey Vernors collects twice for the same turf. Salvatore Locatelli could drop a nuclear bomb on us and Joey Vernors doesn't care except he loses the envelope every week. It's not convenient for Mr Joey Vernors for anything to happen to us yet, you moron.'

Uncle Atom belched.

'Stupidity upsets my stomach,' he said. He went over to a small fridge, took out a can of Diet Coke, popped it, took a swig, belched heartily again. He sat back down. 'What is it with you and this Jap?'

'Nothing,' said Araz.

'Then what the hell do you care what happens to him?'

'I just thought it was, you know, over the top. We fried his fucking hand. He can't work. That seems kind of self-defeating. He can't work, he can't pay.'

'Over the top,' said Uncle Atom.

'You know,' said Araz, 'overkill.'

'Over the top,' said Uncle Atom. 'Overkill. How about when your fucking paycheck is over, how about that, hah? I'll give you over.'

'I just meant—'

'I'm talking to you, I'm standing right here, I can hear you. I know what you meant. Look me in the eye.'

Araz looked at him.

'I never want to hear about Savan doing your job for you again, you hear me?'

'You gave the orders to Savan.'

'What is this, your feelings are hurt? I told Savan and Savan told you and you're the one in fucking charge. You're the eldest, you're the one who I'm supposed to depend on to carry out the orders. Not Tavit, not Savan. You.'

'I'm sorry.'

'You're weak,' Atom said. 'You're like your father. Savan isn't.'

'Savan doesn't use his head.'

'And that's the only damned reason you've still got a job,' said Atom. 'But I don't need a goddamned intellectual out here for me. I need a tiger. Can you be a tiger?'

'Yes.'

'We'll see. Now get out of my face.'

Araz started to leave.

'I mean it about that money,' said Atom. 'You don't retrieve it, it comes out of your pocket.'

Araz nodded.

Atom belched. Picked up the screwdriver, prodded the carcass of the adding machine.

'Piece of shit,' he said.

Araz left.

FORTY

Lieutenant Luis Ramirez of the LAPD stared at the shot of whiskey and the glass of beer on the bar in front of him. He shook his head, picked up the shot and knocked it back, reached quickly for the beer and took a pull to counteract the bourbon as it hit his guts.

'Fucking crazy bastard,' he said, shaking his head again, 'but a class act. A pain in the fucking ass, but a class act anyway.'

He rapped on the bar to get Pancho's attention and Pancho brought over another shot and sat it in front of him.

'You want another too? On the house this evening,' he said to Spandau, who sat next to Ramirez. There were just the three of them in the place.

'Sure,' said Spandau. 'Why not?'

They were in Pancho's Mexican Bar and Grill on Olympia. Frank 'Pancho' Obeler was an ex-cop and in the good old bad old days before Anna, Walter and Spandau used to come in here to do their serious drinking, Walter had loaned Pancho the money to start the bar and in turn Pancho provided a safe place for Walter to get smashed. Walter couldn't just get drunk anywhere, he had a certain reputation to keep up for his elite clientele, couldn't just get blotto in front of the crowd at the Polo Lounge then expect them to sit across your desk and trust you with their dirty little secrets. Walter Coren always said the key to the success of Coren Security and Investigations was giving the appearance that you were gentleman enough to trust but amoral enough to get the job done. They need to feel you were 'one of them', a member of the club, though it was important you both realized you were there only on sufferance, only there because you provided a service they needed and couldn't trust to anybody else. It was an odd juggling act and Walter did it beautifully.

Ramirez said, 'Are you sure you want to hear this?'

Spandau nodded.

'He goes into the Beverly Wilshire,' said Ramirez. 'He gets a suite on the top floor, big fucking rooms, like he's going to throw a goddamn party or something. He's dead sober but he's tipping like a goddamn sailor in a Filipino whorehouse. Handing out c-notes all over the place. Smiling like a bastard, happy as hell, they say. He's got a small briefcase, no other luggage, but nobody is suspicious because people rent these places all the time just to throw a shindig, impress clients, that sort of thing.'

He guzzled down a third of his beer, wiped his mouth with the back of a hairy paw the size of a catcher's mitt. Ramirez was six-four and ugly with dark hair shaved to marine buzz cut. When he was thinking or nervous, like now, he put his hand to his head and the tips of his fingers rode back and forth on a four-inch scar somebody once made with a broken wine bottle.

'They take him up to his room. Yes Mr Coren, no Mr Coren, they can't do enough for him. He orders a huge meal. Oysters, steak, champagne. Are you expecting guests, Mr Coren? No, he says politely, it's just me. But if a Mr Gabriel shows up, send him directly up, will you?'

Spandau and Ramirez and Pancho all laugh. It's such a fucking Walter thing to say. Walter in that smartass way is telling them exactly what's about to happen and they don't even know.

'An hour later somebody hears the noise. Like somebody set off a fucking firecracker. They call the desk, the manager and the house dick come running up. They both know Walter, they know he drinks, they know he can be a bastard if he feels like it, maybe he's tanked and dropping firecrackers out the window to scare the shit out of people by the pool.

'They knock, knock, no answer. They unlock the door, go in, and the house dick, another ex-cop, knows exactly what's happened the second he steps in. Maybe he smells the cordite, or maybe it's just that after you've been around it enough you can feel death still circling around.

'They go in the bathroom, there's Walter. He's in the shower. He's got that old military .45 of his still in his hand. There's a clear plastic bag over his head, full of what's left of Walter's head. He did it through the plastic bag, so's not to make too much of a mess. He's left an envelope with a thousand dollars to the cleaning staff and a note with a little happy face that says, Sorry. In his jacket pocket, also in a plastic bag, is an instruction that his attorney should be contacted immediately.'

'Nothing else? No note?'

'Nothing else. Except, well, apparently just before he did it he called the credit-card company and said some bastard had stole his card and was impersonating him at the Beverly Wilshire Hotel. They stopped payment on the tab.'

Pancho and Spandau both looked at each other and laughed.

'What's so funny?' asked Ramirez.

'Walter hated the Beverly Wilshire,' Pancho said. 'I can't

remember what it was they did to him, but Walter could hold a grudge.'

'You're telling me he killed himself to piss off the Beverly Wilshire?'

'No,' said Pancho, 'but if Walter could kill two birds with one stone – so to speak – he could be real efficient that way.'

'His second wife,' said Spandau.

'What?' said Pancho.

'Walter's second wife. What was her name, Antonia, Alicia, something like that. Brazilian. Big tall dark girl, beautiful but crazy as a bedbug. You remember?'

'I remember,' said Pancho. 'Wasn't she the one that liked to drink and take off her clothes?'

'That's the one.'

'Damn, yeah,' said Pancho. 'She was something.'

'They had their honeymoon at the Beverly Wilshire . . .'

'Ah,' said Pancho.

'. . . And she got stewed and naked and went for a stroll. Walter caught her just before she got into the elevator headed to the lobby. He was dragging her back to the room laughing his ass off and she was kicking and screaming and fighting like a bobcat. Doors opened and the Sultan of Brunei or somebody and his mother see old Walter carrying this big fucking butt-nekkid Brazilian Amazon over his shoulder. About the time they reach the sultan and his old lady, Antonia or Alicia or whoever lets out this enormous endless fart and then both Antonia and Walter just fall down in the middle of the hallway laughing. Apparently the sultan's mom found this offensive.'

'Imagine that,' said Ramirez.

'The hotel asked them to leave. Walter was civil after that but he always swore he'd get even.'

Pancho wiped his eyes. 'Damn, that's a story. I'm going to miss the old bastard. I never had a better friend or a customer who was a bigger pain in the ass.'

'No idea why he did it?' Ramirez asked.

'The drinking just got worse and worse,' said Pancho. 'Hell, David, you know what he was like. At the best of times you could never figure out what was going on in his head. Then he'd drink and it would take him away that much farther. I think he just finally gave up and went on to where he was headed anyway.'

'Where does that leave you?' Ramirez asked Spandau. 'You out of a job now?'

'I don't know,' said Spandau. 'Most likely. I'm supposed to meet the lawyer tomorrow and I guess he'll lay everything out. Anna's been on me to start my own outfit and I suppose this is it. Maybe I can bring Pookie along. Jesus, this has about killed her. She was a little in love with him. Hell, he was a little in love with her too. Walter had a way of confusing the shit out of everything and then he'd just back off and see how people coped. This is no different.'

'Hard not to be angry when somebody does this shit,' Ramirez said.

'Yeah,' said Spandau, 'I'm angry. He was my best friend and the bastard shot himself and if he hadn't done that he'd have drunk himself to death inside a couple of months. In the end you realize I didn't understand him any better than anybody else. In the end the sonofabitch just locked me out the same as he did everybody.'

Spandau downed the shot, made a face.

'There going to be a service or what?' asked Ramirez.

'I don't know,' said Spandau. 'I guess the lawyer will tell us all that, I'm sure Walter made some sort of arrangements. Maybe he's rented St Paul's and will hide whoopee cushions in every seat. Right now I got Pookie and Leo and a bunch of nervous clients to worry about.'

Spandau slid off the barstool.

'You leaving?' asked Pancho.

'I'm past drinking, and I got all of Walter's shit to clean up, just the way it's always been.'

'He loved you,' said Pancho.

'Walter Coren was a selfish fuck who died just the way he lived, alone and laughing at everybody who ever gave a damn about him. He blows his fucking brains out but makes sure it's nothing but a final joke. Walter got his last laugh but it's not much of a memorial, is it?'

'You know,' said Pancho, 'I never felt the need to hit you but I'm about to now. He was my friend and he was your friend and I know you're grieved but you can't talk about him this way, not here, not in my place, not after all he's done for me and you too, you ungrateful slob. So you say another word and I swear to god I'm coming over this bar with this fucking Louisville Slugger under here.'

Pancho was red-faced and murderous and when a customer walked in Pancho said, 'Beat it, we're closed.'

'What the hell,' said the startled customer. 'Is this a fucking funeral or something?'

'That's exactly what it is,' said Pancho, 'and it'll be yours too if you don't get your ass back out that door.'

FORTY-ONE

I t was 11 a.m. and Savan was in the Salopian living room, looking down Anush's cleavage and laying out several lines of cocaine on the back of Mrs Salopian's best silver coffee tray. They were in the house alone.

'So where is your sister?'

'Why,' said Anush.

'I came by to see her.'

'Sure you did,' said Anush.

'Why else would I come by?'

'You know my parents are working and Lilit is in class and today is my day off. You just happen to show up with a gram of coke knowing Lilit is like queen of the fucking holy rollers when it comes to dope.'

He cut the lines using a credit card and rolled a twenty-dollar bill to snort with. They each did a couple of lines.

'Aren't you supposed to be, like, working for Uncle Atom or something?' she said. 'You appropriated some of this, did you? Testing the merchandise?'

Savan smiled. He rubbed her knee. She moved his hand away.

'I miss fucking you,' he said.

'You had a good thing going,' she said, 'and you blew it.'

'I've settled down now. I'm a different guy.'

'Sure you are.'

'Araz still doesn't know?'

'Nobody knows,' she said. 'It's not like I was proud of you or something. Getting banged by you is no great honor. You'll fuck anything.'

He put his hand back on her knee. This time she let it stay.

'How can you stand that guy touching you.'

'Araz is okay. He treats me like a lady.'

'You didn't used to fuck like no lady,' he said.

'Not everything is about sex.'

Savan pulled back. Stared at her.

'He's not fucking you!' he said, laughing.

'I think he's shy,' she said.

'Fucking shy my ass,' said Savan. 'You and him don't do anything?'

'I've blown him a couple of times,' she said, 'and he's fingered me. I just can't get him to stick it in.'

'I knew it,' said Savan. 'I knew there was something wrong with this guy.'

'His cock is bigger than yours,' she said.

'It don't do you much good if he won't use it, huh. You're not doing anybody else?'

'Araz is a good catch and I'm not going to mess it up,' she said. 'Anyway he's going to be your boss one day.'

'We'll see,' said Savan.

Anush leaned forward and did two more lines, sat back rubbing her nose. 'Whoa, that's good.'

'You've got to be missing it,' he said to her.

She smiled. 'A little.'

Savan slid his hand up her skirt.

'This doesn't count,' she said, opening her thighs. 'I'm stoned and you're fucking taking advantage of me.'

'Whatever,' he said, and removed her panties.

FORTY-TWO

He'd called Tina and asked that she, Pookie, and Leo meet him at the office. Pookie was crying and put her arms around him the moment he came into the room.

'The bastard,' she said.

'The way he was going, I don't think any of us should be surprised,' Spandau said. 'For the time being we're just going to carry on, business as usual. I know it's going to be hard, but Walter had all this planned out and I'm sure he's left some sort of arrangements. I'm meeting with his lawyer in the morning and I'm sure he'll tell us what happens next. Meanwhile until we get all this figured out, we act like professionals. There are still clients who depend on us.'

'Do we close down the company or what?' asked Leo. Pookie gave him a deadly glare. 'Look, we have to know. People are asking.'

'We do what we've been doing until somebody tells us to stop,' said Spandau. 'Everything will be fine. The important thing is to make sure everybody gets the impression it's all under control, we're not dropping the ball. Got it? Anybody asks, it's business as usual. We all have a job to do, so I suggest we do it. Until further notice we all still work for Walter, and you know how he'd feel about this.'

'Get our asses to work,' said Leo.

'Exactly,' said Spandau. 'Pookie, Leo, get back on the Charlie thing, I want reports at the end of each day, I don't want to read them like you're writing a novel in monthly installments. Tina, we're going to start returning calls and holding hands. We'll start at the top of the list and just work through them.'

'What about the press?' asked Tina. 'They've been ringing all day.'

'The official word is that we have no idea as to Mr Coren's state of mind or the reason for his death. As for Coren Investigations, business continues as usual.'

'Until further notice?' added Tina.

'Just say business as usual. We still have open cases and private client files. What we don't want right now is everybody we've ever worked for showing up to clean out our cupboards. The truth is that we have no idea what plans Walter made, we just can't tell them that.' To Tina he said, 'Give me a few minutes and we'll start returning calls.'

Spandau went into the office and dialed Anna on his cell phone. She'd left for the set by the time he arrived back from Cheney late that morning and he'd only spoken to her briefly, just enough to assure her he was holding up. She'd started off on an array of apologies for the things she'd said about Walter, she hadn't meant them personally, etc., etc. and Spandau frankly hadn't been in the mood to hear it.

'Where are you?' she said.

'At the office.'

'How is it there?'

'About like you'd expect. Everybody wants to sit around and blubber but we still have to act like we know what we're doing. The vultures are already circling.'

'I'm sorry, David.'

'It was never about Walter, it's just that I've always wanted the best for you. The best for us.'

'I know.'

'Did you talk to Ramirez?'

'Yeah, he told me the whole story, as much as anybody knows. It's just too ugly, Anna, and we'll talk about it later. The press will get a sanitized version of it but even then I can't say anything until I've spoken to the lawyer.'

'And you still don't know why?'

'Jesus, Anna, he was drinking himself to death anyway. He just got fucking tired of doing it in the slow lane, okay? People keep asking this like he was the fucking Dalai Lama or something. He fucking hated himself and everybody else and he just stopped it, end of story.'

'Do you want me to come home?'

'We both have work to do. I've got all these fires to put out, and I'd just as soon stay busy instead of sit around and think about it.'

'Call me if you need me.'

'Sure.'

There was a knock at the office door. Leo popped his head in.

'I just wanted to tell you, I scoped out the webpage of that Catholic church,' he said. 'I got some interesting results. I could show you if you've got time. Just a couple of minutes.'

Leo came over and logged onto his own account using the computer on the desk. He showed Spandau the website and the archives, then showed a separate text file where he'd listed all cross-references to Father Michael and Oregon.

'There are a few references to Father Michael going fishing in Oregon, then Father Michael visiting some friends up around Medford.'

'But nothing closer than that? No addresses or specifics? No names?'

'No names, nothing mentioned specifically. But look. Here in the blog for this past June.'

There was a photo of Father Michael on a river, holding up another goddamned fish.

'Yeah, great, but this doesn't help me.'

'Wait,' said Leo.

Up pops another photo, of Father Michael standing with his arm around the same woman he'd seen in the priest's trailer.

'Is there a name?' asked Spandau. 'An address?'

'No name, no address,' said Leo.

'Then why are you showing me this?'

'Because look.'

Leo returned to the first photo, clicked on it, typed a few keys, and a map showed up with a small arrow.

'This is where the photo was taken,' said Leo. 'Most people don't know it, but every time they post a photo on the internet there's a code that logs exactly where the photo was taken. You can find it on a map. It's accurate to like a couple of hundred feet most of the time.'

'You're serious?'

'Dead serious. It's great. People are always posting these photos of their kids and stuff, but they have no idea you can track every one of them. You might as well be giving perverts a list of where you take your kids. But it's also wonderful for people like us.'

He clicked on the photo of Father Michael and the woman, then got the map.

'See here? It's no more than a mile or two from where the river photo is taken, about fifteen miles outside of Medford.'

'How close can you zoom in?'

'Watch,' said Leo.

The map zoomed in until the names of highways were clear, and the name of the street where the photo was taken.

'Damn,' said Spandau.

'And this,' said Leo.

He switched from map to terrain and there was a photo of the house and its surroundings.

'Satellite,' said Leo. 'Jesus, you got to love Google.'

'Can you get me an address? And a name,' said Spandau. 'I want a name.'

'No problem,' said Leo, beaming. 'Give me a few minutes. I'll work on Tina's computer.' Before he left he said, 'So you'll admit I'm not entirely useless.'

'Who told you that?'

'Pookie said that you said it.'

'I never said you were entirely useless,' Spandau said. 'Just mainly.'

Spandau's cell phone buzzed. A text from Dee. She'd already left several texts and a couple of phone messages. This one said, 'Come and see me. Please.'

As Leo went out the door, Spandau said, 'Get me that name and address,' then past him, 'Tina, let's get rolling on those calls.'

In a moment he could hear her. 'Good morning, I have David Spandau with Coren Security and Investigations returning Mr McKendrick's call, will you hold? McKendrick for you,' she said to Spandau.

Spandau picked up the phone.

'John, this is David Spandau. Look, there is nothing to worry about. We have everything under control . . .'

FORTY-THREE

Araz and Mitchell were in Mitchell's apartment watching TV when the door buzzer sounded. It was late, nearly 1 a.m. Araz and Mitchell looked at each other, then Mitchell went to the door and peered through the spyhole. He turned to Araz, made a 'I don't know who this is' gesture. Araz came to the door, looked out.

Savan.

'Who is it?' said Mitchell.

'Tell him it's Savan.'

'Tell who?'

'Quit fucking around,' said Savan, kicking the door. 'I saw him through the fucking window.'

Mitchell opened the door. Savan stood in the doorway for a moment, looking at Araz and then at Mitchell, smiling. He came in.

'What do you want?' said Araz.

'Did I interrupt anything?'

'Just tell me what you want,' said Araz, 'and then leave me the hell alone.'

'I just wanted to see,' said Savan.

He looked around, looked at the paintings, the artwork. Sauntered into the bedroom and stared at the Mapplethorpe photo of a man with his penis in a champagne flute. Came back into the living room.

'I just wanted to see,' he said, 'why a guy might want to suck another guy's cock. I still don't get it.'

'I don't know what you're talking about,' said Araz. 'He's just a friend.'

'You want to be friendly,' said Savan, 'don't stand so fucking close to the window. I was out there for a while.' Savan shook his head, opened the door, turned to Araz. 'I just wanted to see the look on your face,' he said, and walked out closing the door behind him.

'I'm so sorry,' said Mitchell. 'Maybe it's for the best.'

He started to put his arms around Araz, comfort him. Araz hit him in the chest, knocked him backwards over the sofa.

'You still don't get it,' Araz said. 'You still don't fucking get it.'

Araz went out, followed Savan onto the street where he was walking toward his car. Caught up with Savan, grabbed his arm. Savan shook it off.

'You tell him,' said Araz, 'you know what he's going to do.'

'You should have thought of that before you took up sucking dicks as a way of life.'

'I'm asking you,' said Araz. 'Please. For god's sake just keep this between us, okay? I'll quit working for Atom. I'll fucking leave. You get my place, you get everything, okay?'

Savan said nothing, walked around and climbed into his car. Araz pulled open the passenger door and leapt in.

'Please.'

'Get out of my car.'

'Please, you've got to help me out on this. He'll kill me. You know he will.'

'Get out of my fucking car!'

Araz reached out, meant to put his hand on Savan's shoulder, to make contact, to beg. Savan knocked away the outstretched hand and hit Araz with his fist, spun in the seat and kicked at him, trying to kick him back out the half-opened door.

On one of the kicks Araz caught Savan's ankle and held tight. Savan struggled and kicked with the other foot but Araz held fast and backed out the door dragging Savan with him. Savan grabbed the steering wheel, the gearshift, anything he could but Araz was bigger and his life was at stake. He pulled Savan out through the door. Savan fell on his back on the curb, his head still inside the car, his hands gripping the door post, struggling to pull himself back into the car.

Araz held on to Savan's ankle with his left hand and with his right hand he slammed the car door as hard as he could. Savan made an 'uff' sound but still held on and Araz slammed the door again, and again. Savan let go and slumped to the gutter with his head and neck resting across the foot of the door opening and Araz slammed the door again hard and heard a pop that sounded like Savan's neck.

He slammed the door two more times to be sure.

Savan didn't move. There wasn't much blood but Araz didn't have time to see if he was still alive. He looked dead.

It was a quiet street in the wee hours of the morning. Araz hoped nobody saw.

He opened the rear door and half dragged half stuffed Savan onto the floor in the back. The car itself hid them from the street. Trying to put him in the trunk was too exposed.

The keys were still in the ignition. Araz got in and drove, pulling his shirt cuffs down over his hands to act as gloves. He kept going over in his mind everything he'd touched. He drove to Topanga and had just pulled a little off the coast highway up into the canyon when in the now quiet he heard Savan making short 'ukk ukk ukk' gasping sounds from the back. Savan managed to crawl up the back seat and get his hand over to grab Araz by the hair.

Araz slammed on the brakes and Savan bounced forward on the seat and then snapped backwards and slumped back to the floor. Araz pulled over just off the road and went round and pulled Savan out onto the dirt. Savan lay on his back looking up at Araz making those 'ukk ukk ukk' sounds and Savan figured he might have broken his neck or crushed the windpipe. Savan waved his arms a little, like a beetle on its back. Araz opened up the trunk and found the tire iron. He looked down at Savan who was looking at Araz and knew what was coming. Araz said,

'Meat.'

He broke Savan's right leg at the shin. Savan let out a hissing sound. Araz broke Savan's left leg.

'Meat,' said Araz.

There was no other way to do it. It had to look like a mob hit, revenge, a show of force, a warning.

'Meat,' he said, and went to work on Savan's head.

'MEAT MEAT MEAT MEAT MEAT.'

He was splattered in blood but there was nothing to do about it. He dragged Savan round to the trunk and hoisted him inside and shut it. Savan looked dead. If he wasn't dead then he would be by the time anybody found him. Araz stood for a while collecting himself and then set about wiping down the car. He got out his cell phone and called Mitchell and told him where to meet him and to bring a fresh set of clothes. Mitchell was panicking and asking questions and Araz told him to shut the fuck up and just do it. Then he put the cell phone back in his pocket and started walking.

He was waiting in the shadows at the side of the road when Mitchell arrived. Araz jumped into the car. Mitchell stared at the bloodstained clothes.

'What have you done,' said Mitchell.

'Drive,' said Araz. 'Did you bring the clothes?'

'You killed him?'

'Drive the fucking car. You want to fall apart, do it later,' said Araz.

'Oh god,' said Mitchell. 'Oh god.'

Araz slapped him. Mitchell stared at him. Araz slapped him again.

'I'm telling you,' said Araz, 'that if you don't get the fucking car rolling you're going to be just as dead as he is.'

'I can't drive,' said Mitchell. 'I'm shaking too hard.'

Araz got out of the car, stood next to it quickly changing into the fresh shirt and pants. He wadded up the bloodied clothes, tucked them under the seat, then went round to Mitchell and dragged him out of the car by his hair. Araz climbed into the driver's seat and started the car. He looked at Mitchell, who just stood there.

'Get in,' said Araz.

'This is all wrong,' said Mitchell. 'We should go to the police. They'll understand. They have to.'

Araz thought for a moment, then got out of the car and put his arms around Mitchell. Mitchell sobbed onto his shoulder.

'You're right,' said Araz, 'you're right, it's all wrong, it's all fucking horribly wrong. But this is what it is. Anybody finds out about this, we both go to jail. They're going to think we did it together. So we have to get through this together, right? Right?'

Mitchell nodded.

'I love you,' said Araz. 'I've never said it before but I want you to know it now. We'll get through this together.'

Araz kissed him, looked gently into his eyes. Mitchell nodded again and went round and got into the car. They drove away. Araz reached out and took his hand and held it while Mitchell cried. Araz gave Mitchell's hand a loving squeeze and it was at that point Araz wondered if he would have to kill him.

Meat, thought Araz. Meat.

FORTY-FOUR

It was a postwar cottage on a quiet street in Studio City. Nothing fancy, maybe two bedrooms, but each house on the street had a yard and each yard had a tricycle or a swing or a scattering of toys that declared, a family lives here. It was Charlie's house, he'd lived there with his wife until she left him. Spandau wondered if living there ever bothered Dee. He thought it must, especially now. It would have bothered him.

Dee's Prius was in the drive. Spandau parked in front on the street and sat there for a bit, finishing a cigarette. He saw Dee push aside the curtain and look at him and flip on the porch light. He finished the cigarette then went up onto the porch and knocked at the door. It opened quickly. She'd been standing next to it, waiting.

'I'm glad you decided to come,' she said.

The instant he set foot across the threshold he knew it was a mistake, he should never have come. Spandau had managed never to meet Charlie, but he could now feel him everywhere. To be standing with Dee amid this swirling sense of another man, another lover, another husband, was squeezing the life out of him.

'Would you like a drink? A beer? I'm sorry, maybe you're . . .'

'Not on the wagon, no. It was never that bad. I wouldn't mind some coffee though, if it's no trouble. I haven't had much sleep.'

'I'll make a pot,' she said.

He followed her into the kitchen. Sat down at the table and thought: Charlie sits here, she makes him coffee like this. It was a small kitchen but neat and clean. Dee's handiwork everywhere. Some knickknacks on the wall Spandau remembered from their own kitchen. She set a pot of coffee brewing while he watched her. Her moves were slow and deliberate, as if she were demonstrating for the slow-witted how to use the machine. She knows how I'm watching her and she knows how I feel. He had never seen her commit a cruel act but to him this seemed cruel and pointless. If she doesn't love me then why am I here, why doesn't she let me go.

She poured a mug of coffee for him and for herself, brought them to the table, sat down across from him.

'You're not going to ask why I wanted you to come?'

'There are a couple of good reasons,' he said. 'Walter's dead. You'll want to know how that affects us looking for Charlie. And then, like you said in your messages, you're maybe a little worried about me.'

'I'm not worried about you stopping the search for Charlie,' she said. 'I know it has nothing to do with Walter. I know that it's just something you're doing for me.'

'I'm fine,' he said. 'Walter just finished what he started years ago. It's no real surprise.'

'When you leave here, what do you do?'

'I'll probably go back to the office. Walter has dumped me in the shit again. This whole thing is a nightmare. Nobody knows what happens now, and everybody is looking at me like I have the answers. I don't.'

'Why not go home,' she said.

'What is it you want, Dee? What great goddamn secret is it that you think you know?'

'I know you're afraid to go home,' she said. 'I know you don't live with her all the time, that you've still got the house in the valley, and that you won't want to go to either place tonight.'

'Are you suggesting I stay here?'

'If that's what you want,' she said. 'If that's what you need. But no, it's not what I'm suggesting.'

'You want me to cry on your shoulder? You going to give me a comforting little cuddle? Or maybe you're wondering by now if Charlie's ever coming back and you chose the wrong man.'

'Charlie will come back,' she said. 'You'll find him and you'll bring him back to me. This I know.'

'Why?'

'Because you said you would.' She got up, went over to a cabinet, and took out a bottle of bourbon. 'Fuck yoga,' she said, and poured some into her coffee. She looked at Spandau and he nodded and she poured a good dollop into his.

'You don't know a goddamned thing about love,' she said. 'You never did.'

'You don't think you were loved?'

'That's not what I'm saying. I know you love me. I know you loved Walter, and you love my mom and you loved Dad. There are all these things you do love, and I know that you love them with the whole of your heart. Maybe you love Anna, I don't know. I don't question that you love, but I do know you don't have a clue in hell as to what you're doing.'

'And Charlie does?'

'Charlie has many problems,' she said. 'That's increasingly obvious. But he's comfortable being loved. He doesn't have your passion, I'll admit that. But he also doesn't spend every waking moment waiting for me to stop loving him.'

'But you did stop, didn't you?' He nodded to the wall. 'You packed up your fucking little kitchen trivets and you left.'

'I never stopped loving you, David. You know this. You just want it to be simple and it's not. We never stopped loving each other, but we did wear each other out. You kept thinking I wanted you to live up to some ridiculous idea of maleness I had in my head. I didn't. I just wanted you to be you. But you resented the hell out of me for it anyway, and I resented you because I kept failing to make you feel loved. We just exhausted each other. It's not enough just to love. You've got to know how to do it.'

'This is from that year in therapy?'

'You're damned right it is. Maybe it'll boost your ego to learn that you were the major topic of conversation. You're the only thing I ever really failed at. Well, no. I never could draw and now there's Charlie too.'

She took a long drink.

'Remember the night your father died?' she said. 'I had to go find you. Mom and Dad, we were all out looking for you. You'd gone out for a walk and hours went by and I was worried sick, I called and called and you never answered. Finally you did, and you said you'd walked all the way to Topanga. I drove out there and got you to bring you home and you said no, you didn't want to go home. So we sat in the car and I held you and I asked you why you didn't want to come home and you said, "Because I'm never going to walk in the door and see him again." You said he was a bastard and a drunk and he beat you and your mother and your sister every day of your life but still you couldn't understand why you felt the way you did. As if you had a choice. That's the problem with you, David. You think you have a choice. Your heart just doesn't go in the direction you point it. It just feels what it feels and you have to live with it, especially when you can't follow.'

'Why am I here, Dee? I need to be working.'

'I didn't want you to be alone.'

'I'm not alone.'

'If you love her, David, then let her inside. You need to be with someone.'

'I don't have time for this.' He stood up. 'Do you know what you want?'

'Yes,' she said. 'I do. I want you to be with someone who can finally make you happy.'

'But it's not you?'

'No,' she said, 'it's not me.'

'I don't have time for this,' he repeated, and left.

FORTY-FIVE

Uncle Atom was on the warpath when Araz came into the office.

'Where the fuck have you been,' Atom demanded.

'You just called me, I'm here.'

'Where is your cousin?'

'Which one?' said Araz.

'Don't get funny with me, you pissant,' said Atom. 'Where is Savan?'

'How should I know? I have my own problems and Savan does whatever the hell he wants.'

'This isn't like him.'

'Maybe he's hungover,' said Araz, 'or with a woman.'

Atom picked up a heavy ashtray from the desk and threw it against the cinderblock wall, where it shattered loudly. The door flew open and Omar jumped in, ready to kill somebody.

'What the fuck do you want?' Atom said to him.

Omar shrugged his shoulders and gave Atom a confused look.

'Clean up this fucking mess,' Atom said to him.

Omar nodded and started picking up the pieces of glass.

'Not now, asshole,' Atom said. 'Give me a minute.'

Omar left holding a handful of shards. Atom turned to Araz and said,

'You.'

'Me what?'

'I put you in charge of things, you're the eldest, that's the way it's done. But you, I don't know about you. Things are fucking up.'

'How is Savan out fucking around somewhere my fault all of a sudden?'

'I don't know,' said Atom.

He handed Araz an address.

'This is an Indian casino up near San Jose,' said Atom. 'Your adopted deadbeat's been spotted up there. Take Tavit. Take the van. Don't fuck this up.'

'You sure you don't want to wait for Savan?'

'Listen to the way you talk to me,' said Atom. 'Listen to the way you talk to your uncle. This is the problem. You have no respect.'

'And Savan does?'

'Savan fears me,' said Atom, 'and that is the only kind of respect worth having. That way I'm in charge. Respect, it's about what the other guy feels. I don't give a shit what the other guy feels. I want what I want when I want it. That's the only way things get done. You should have learned that.'

Atom walked round the desk, stood close looking up into Araz's face.

'Do you fear me?' he asked Araz.

'Yes,' said Araz, but not quickly.

There was a very long and dangerous moment while Atom stood there studying Araz's face. Then Atom sighed deeply and turned away.

'Find this asshole,' Uncle Atom said over his shoulder. 'You can't find him you'd better think twice about coming back.'

Atom sat down at his desk. Omar went in as Araz went out.

'Now?' said Omar.

'Yes now,' said Uncle Atom irritably. 'I'm surrounded by fucking idiots,' shaking his head and going back to work.

FORTY-SIX

Walter Coren's attorney was named Bernie Silberman. He was a showbiz lawyer, in his seventies now but still sharp as ever. He had an office in Century City where the furniture looked as if it had been picked up at a garage sale and the walls were lined with signed photos of Bernie getting snuggled by every major actor of the last fifty years. Bernie was a legend and nobody gave a damn about the furniture when they knew you were the guy John Wayne came to when he needed to weasel out of a contract.

Bernie tilted his desk chair back a few inches and lit a cigar and told Spandau he could smoke if he wanted. Technically this was illegal in this building but then Bernie owned the whole thing. Spandau lit a cigarette and couldn't remember the last time anybody had let him smoke indoors. The smoke tasted sweeter.

'An awful thing,' said Bernie. 'You know he hated the Beverly Wilshire, right?'

'Something about wife number two getting naked in halls.'

'She was a pistol, that one, let me tell you. She cost him a pretty penny. Thank god she eventually married some Saudi, Walter was in love and couldn't wait for a pre-nup. Walter and his women. I used to tell him, Walter, if you need to piss away every cent you have, take up gambling or drugs, in your case it's cheaper than snatch. Walter was a smart guy everywhere but with his putz.'

'There was drink.'

'Walter started drinking when Number One left him. He was practically teetotal before that. You should have seen him. Handsome kid, like something out of Jay Gatsby. A real athlete. He rowed, did you know that? She put the spurs into him and that set the booze flowing. I watched it happen.' He blew a smoke ring and thoughtfully watched it float toward the ceiling. Then he said, 'Cancer. Walter was dying.'

'What?'

'Liver, prostate, bone, you name it. They didn't even have to open him up, no use. The X-rays looked like a satellite photo of Africa. He had three, four months left, max, and they weren't going to be pretty. I don't even want to think about the pain. The amount of dope they had him on alone should have killed him. A few more pills would have done the job. The Beverly Wilshire thing, that was Walter just being funny. He swore he'd get even. I remember when he said it.'

'I thought he was drinking.'

'Nah. His liver couldn't process it anymore, for, what, the last six months. And he couldn't take it anyway with all that dope. Walter died, my friend, as sober as a Mormon.'

Bernie had that rare talent, exclusive to the best attorneys, of

knowing when to shut up. He allowed Spandau to sit there. Finally
Spandau said:

'Why didn't he tell me, Bernie?'

'What would you have done? Walter needed someone to keep
the business going. He didn't want you worrying about that and
him too. He figured you had enough problems, am I right? Walter
also didn't want any goddamn fuss. And he would never have
gotten away with that Beverly Wilshire thing. Walter always knew
what he was doing.'

Bernie leaned forward, opened a thick file on the desk, leafed
through it.

'His estate is in good shape, he made sure of that. In fact he
had all this worked out long ago, so there's no question of him
being of sound mind or whatever. Everything is in good order and
there shouldn't be any glitches unless somebody comes out of the
woodwork to complain, which I don't see. No kids, no living
relatives, all the ex-wives taken care of or remarried. The official
reading of the will is next week, but barring unforeseen circumstances, you get just about everything. Walter wanted me to tell
you as soon as possible.'

Bernie paused to let this sink in.

'He's left a nice annuity to his cleaning lady, and there's some
bits to various friends – Pancho's gets a new kitchen, for instance
– but otherwise you've got the Palisades house and some other
real-estate holdings, and there are stocks and so forth. Walter was
well invested, so you're doing okay, my friend. You are sitting
pretty. And there's the business. It's yours, if you want it, with a
few minor stipulations. You can't change the name, for instance.
Walter was his father's name too. Walter was firm about that. The
company only passes to you if you keep to Walter's terms. If you
decide you don't want it, then I have instructions to close it down.
You're not going to pass out, are you?'

Spandau shook his head, got up, went to the window, stood
looking out. Bernie couldn't see his face.

'The bastard,' Spandau said quietly.

'The accountant is working on all this, so I'll have a better
breakdown for the official reading next week. So you've got some
time to digest all this, but I'll have to have your final decision by
then. Whatever you decide, Walter requests that you continue any

cases that are operational now. He specified the work you're doing for Frank Jurado and the Charles Marston case. He'd like you to see that they're completed. The finances are in place to keep things running as long as need be. Is this acceptable?'

'Sure.'

'He was a good man,' said Bernie. 'Better than he ever let on.'

'He was a master manipulator, is what he was.'

'Yeah,' said Bernie, 'it was one of the things I admired most about him. I could never figure out why he wouldn't go into politics.'

FORTY-SEVEN

Pookie, Leo, and Tina sat in the reception area while Spandau filled them in. When he finished, there was a moment of silence, then Leo said admiringly, 'Damn!' and Pookie said:

'Okay, if nobody else is going to ask this, what happens to the business? You're taking over, right?'

'I don't know.'

'Oh god, David . . .'

'It's more complicated than you know. There's Anna. There's a lot to be considered.'

'Walter stipulated that we finish whatever cases we have on our plates now. The money is there for as long as it takes. So we have time. If we do have to shut down, there's separation pay. Walter thought of everything. It won't be that bad. Everybody is taken care of.'

'What if I happen to like it here?' said Pookie. 'Like maybe I'm attached now.'

'We're all attached,' said Spandau. 'But you can become un-attached. As Walter would say, what you need right now is a healthy dose of Get Your Ass Back to Work. That goes for all of us.'

As they headed back to work, Leo said to Spandau:

'I've got that Oregon info you wanted.'

'You found me a location?'

'Location, name, address, the works.'

They went into Spandau's office. Leo logged on, up came the church website.

'The website's only been up for about a year, but Father Paul blogs nearly every day about something. Today what is it, let's see . . . Ah yeah, great, he's got about five hundred words here on watching the black squirrels playing outside. It's like reading *Bambi*, this guy and his little woodland creatures. This might, you know, actually be the most boring blog on the face of the earth.'

'The photo, Leo.'

'So it was a quick search through the archive for anything about Father Mike or Oregon. Father Mike goes fishing, Father Mike sends us a letter from Oregon, et cetera. It doesn't say where he goes except somewhere near Ashland, no names of who he stays with. But then here's a photo. Father Michael holding up a trout, caption says, "Leviathan captured in his own backyard!" Cute, huh?'

'Great, but how does this help us?'

'Hang on. Here's another photo, Father Mike chilling out in a BarcaLounger. "A well-deserved rest!" Jeez, I dunno if this guy is being sarcastic or he really is this lame. Some people shouldn't be allowed to blog if it's this stomach-turning. Look at the wood paneling behind him. I'm amazed people still do that. One more reason why Home Depot should be burned to the ground.'

'Leo.'

'Watch this.'

He clicked on the photo, then called up the technical information on the photo.

A few more key strokes and a map of Oregon appeared with two tiny red flags.

'You can see that the photos were taken not far apart.'

Leo began zooming in on one of the flags.

'This is so cool . . .'

Ashland, Oregon. Not far out of town was the river. As Leo went closer roads and street names appeared. He clicked again and the map turned into a satellite photo of a house and its surrounding area.

'Scary, isn't it?' said Leo. 'If we can do this, you have to imagine what the government is capable of. Rebecca Hamlin, 1444 Smithfield

Rd, Sparks Creek, Oregon. Age thirty-eight, one son, Michael, age fifteen. She works from home, has a mail-order internet business selling knitting yarns. There's a Facebook page but I only have public access to it. There are some photos, though. You want to see what she looks like?'

'No,' said Spandau. 'I've already seen her.'

FORTY-EIGHT

Anna said, 'You didn't come home last night. I notice these things.'

They were having lunch at Ago's on Melrose, out on the garden patio, where you could smoke. Half a dozen celebrities were sucking down nicotine and Pellegrino while having the usual moral dilemma over the menu. You're dying for the Nodino di Vitella al Balsamico but what you know you're really going to have is the fucking beet salad.

'It depends on what you mean by home,' Spandau said. 'I worked late at Woodland Hills. I had a load of stuff in the office there to go over. It's a mess.'

She looked at him for a moment, then looked at the menu.

'What are you going to have?' she asked. 'I'm having the beet salad.'

Spandau said, 'I'm having the Nodino di Vitella al Balsamico.'

'You're being spiteful, aren't you?'

'And the Castello dei Rampolla,' he announced, shutting the menu and laying it down.

'The whole bottle?'

'You're going to split it with me, beet salad be damned. You're going to need it.'

'Oh god,' she said. 'The news was that bad? I'm so sorry, David. But maybe it's all for the best. You know we've been talking about you going off on your own anyway and—'

'The official reading of the will isn't until next week. But unless somebody challenges it, which isn't likely, Walter left the whole enchilada to me.'

'He left you the agency?'

'The agency, the house in the Palisades, the real-estate holdings, the stocks and bonds. Just about everything.'

She was quiet. She stared at him. Her mouth opened, then it closed. Then she said quietly, 'Well, shit.'

'That pretty much sums up how I feel, as well.'

'The twisted, malicious son of a bitch.'

'I don't think he did it to piss you off.'

'Don't be too sure,' she said. She shook her head. 'He finally got you, didn't he, the bastard. He had to blow his brains out, but he won in the end.'

'What in god's name are you talking about. You're taking paranoia to a whole new realm here. The man was dying of cancer and he was in a lot of pain. I'm fairly sure he wasn't thinking of you when he did it. Walter did have other things on his mind, as hard as that is for you to believe.'

'You knew about the cancer?'

'No. I just thought he was drinking. I tore into him about it. I said some things. It was the drugs, the whole time. I thought he was drinking but it was the painkillers. Half the organs in his body were devoured. I can't imagine what it must have been like.'

'I'm sorry,' she said.

They ordered. Spandau asked for the wine to be brought quickly.

'I suppose it simplifies things.'

'What the hell is that supposed to mean?' he said. 'How do you figure that?'

'Your choices are made for you. He made them.'

'I haven't made any choices. Not yet anyway, not without talking to you. I'm not obliged to take over the business.'

'What happens if you don't?'

'Walter's stipulations are that it be dissolved. He didn't want anyone else running it. Whether I take over or not doesn't affect anything else. I still inherit and Pookie and Leo get a nice severance package. So no, he didn't pull a fast one and lock me into it. There's no pressure.'

The wine came. The waiter poured a thimbleful into Spandau's glass. Nobody was in the mood for the pretense of sniffing and he motioned the waiter to fill the glasses. The waiter seemed a little disappointed though in his experience only the assholes ever sent it back. The waiter eased away and Spandau attacked his vino with more than a little desperation.

'I don't see what there is to discuss, then,' she said. 'It's your decision.'

'I thought we might talk about it.'

'Like there's anything to talk about. Look, congratulations, you're a rich man now or whatever. Your options in life have greatly increased. I'm sure things are starting to look different.'

'Jesus, Anna, will you just say what the hell is on your mind?'

'How long have you known about this? I find it difficult to believe you had no idea, that he didn't at least drop you a few hints.'

'I found out about it today. And no, Walter didn't drop any hints.'

'You never thought what would happen if he died? I mean, the man was drinking himself to death anyway.'

'I never gave it much thought. I suppose I figured it would be like we've talked about, I'd start something up for myself. Something a little less stressful. I've been running things while he's been gone, and it's no picnic. Walter was good at the social-izing crap and I'm not, it's too high profile. And I don't like sitting behind a desk pushing papers around. That's not me.'

'So what's the problem? Don't do it.'

'It's not that easy,' he said.

'Why not?'

He didn't answer.

'You don't owe him anything,' she said. 'Especially not to spend the rest of your life running the Walter fucking Coren memorial detective agency. I'll bet he stipulated you can't change the name. He did, didn't he?'

Spandau smiled in spite of himself.

'I knew it. Even beyond the grave he's figured out how to take advantage of you. Are you sure he's dead? Maybe he's just set all this up and is shacked up somewhere laughing his ass off. I wouldn't put it past him.'

'He was my friend,' said Spandau. 'I know that doesn't mean a goddamned thing to you, but it does to me.'

Even as she said it, Anna realized she'd gone too far. Of course it was what she felt, but she hadn't meant to say it and now there was that look on his face, the look where his jaw muscles tightened and his brown eyes went a little liquid and she knew she'd hurt him to the quick and that he'd never quite forgive her. It was one of those moments where, in repair, you were now obliged to utter the real truth in spite of the dignity it cost.

'Are you going to leave me?' she asked him.

'Is that what you think?'

'In my experience,' she said, 'you should always get very nervous when someone answers a question with another question.'

'I'm not going to leave you,' he said.

'You're sure?'

'I'll have to check my calendar,' he said, 'but I don't think I've got it down anywhere.'

She tried not to cry, she really did. Tried hiding behind the upturned wineglass but there was just so long you could keep it there without actually drinking. When she lowered it she could feel the tiny landslides of carefully applied make-up.

'Shit,' she said.

'Anna.'

'You're all fucking weird lately, and heading off in the middle of the night. We don't talk anymore, we fight all the goddamn time and I have no idea why. You don't come home last night and now there's all this. You bastard, if you're leaving me then at least you could have the decency to be honest about it.'

'I'm not going anywhere. Anna, look at me. I'm not.'

She nodded.

'I have a choice,' she said, 'between sitting here and being really obvious about bawling my head off, or running through half of Hollywood trying to make it to the restroom. Which do you think is the better option?'

'I think I'd turn my chair slightly to the left,' he said, 'and just have it.'

Which is what she did. The waiter came with their salads and while her make-up looked like Emmett Kelly's she was past caring. Spandau held her hand across the table and she wouldn't let him take it away. The beet salad disappeared and Spandau drained the Chianti. She ate half of his lamb and slipped off a shoe to nuzzle his crotch under the table. Never pass up a chance to celebrate even the little victories.

FORTY-NINE

Oregon was damp and cold. Spandau found himself in yet another rented car, this one at least giving him a chance to stretch his legs. Rain splattered on the windshield as he followed the directions snapped at him by the GPS. 'Merge left. In half a mile, make a sharp right turn.' The female voice was cold, curt, and vaguely disapproving. Somehow you felt there was an implied 'fathead' silently tacked onto the end of every order.

He came over a rise and saw the creek and the house beyond. It was a relief to shut off the ill-tempered GPS. A small wooden bridge spanned the creek and rattled uneasily as he crossed. The house itself was a two-story clapboard structure a hundred yards slightly uphill from the water. A chain-link fence outlined most of the property. Spandau pulled off across the road from the front gate. Inside the fence a teenage boy with Down's syndrome played in the dirt with a set of metal toy trucks. Spandau got out of the car and the boy trotted to the fence to meet him.

'You're not the mailman,' said the boy.

'No,' said Spandau.

'I got a package coming,' said the boy. 'It's a fire truck. My mom got it on eBay.'

'Fire trucks are cool,' said Spandau.

'I'll let you see it when it comes,' said the boy. 'Fire trucks are cool.'

'You're Mikey?'

'How'd you know my name? I don't know you.'

'I'm a friend of Father Michael's.'

'He's a good friend,' said the boy. 'Known him all my life. Mom says he's grumpy to some people but never to me. He's going to live with us pretty soon.'

'He must like you an awful lot,' said Spandau. 'He's grumpy to me. Is he here?'

'He's in the house with Mom. You want me to get him?'

'Would you please?'

The boy turned to go into the house but already Father Michael was coming out the door. Rebecca Hamlin stood behind him.

'I figured you'd turn up sooner than later,' said Father Michael. 'You didn't strike me as the type who'd leave well enough alone.'

'Is he a bad man?' Mikey asked the priest.

'No, Mikey, he's just stupid and nosy. Why don't you go on into the house while I talk to this gentleman.'

Mikey went inside, but stood behind the glass weather door with his mother, watching.

'Am I going to have to physically throw your ass back into that car?' the priest said.

'We'd both look ridiculous in front of the boy,' said Spandau, 'and you know damned well I'd just come back. All I want to do is talk to her.'

'She doesn't want to talk to you.'

'Then let her tell me that.'

'The woman doesn't need any more trouble than she's got,' said the priest. 'I'm an old man but I'll give you more of a fight than you think, you walk past me.'

'I'm not going to fight you, Michael. But I'll talk to her now or I'll talk to her later. I have to know. It's my job.'

Spandau looked past Father Michael at Rebecca standing behind the glass. Father Michael turned too and Rebecca made a small beckoning gesture. The priest went to the door and they spoke. Rebecca and the boy disappeared into the house. Father Michael returned to Spandau.

'She says she'll talk to you,' said the priest. 'She just wants this whole thing over.'

Spandau opened the gate and stepped through. Father Michael laid his hand on Spandau's chest to halt him.

'Any grief comes to her or the boy as a result of this, and I will do whatever it takes to make you regret it.'

'I'm not looking to hurt her,' said Spandau.

FIFTY

He followed the old priest into the house. Rebecca sat on the couch in the living room, a place that was dark and worn in spite of the large glass patio door that looked out across the backyard to the creek. She was drinking coffee. A pot and what had been Michael's cup sat on the table.

'Why don't you take Mikey for a walk down by the creek,' she said to the priest. When she spoke, you could hear the soft, sliding vowels of Kentucky.

'Come on, big buddy,' said Michael, 'let's see if we can find that big old turtle again.'

'Would you like a cup of coffee, Mr Spandau?' she asked when they'd gone.

'Please, if it's not too much trouble.'

'Milk and sugar?'

'Black, please.'

She went into the kitchen for a mug, brought it back, and poured from the insulated pot already on the table. She handed him the mug and said, 'You might as well sit down.' He sat. 'You come to talk about Jerry, that it?'

'That's right.'

'How did you find me? I know it wasn't Jerry. Lewis maybe.'

Spandau didn't reply.

'I suppose I ought to ask you how much you know.'

'I know about you and Jerry. About that trip to San Diego. A little snooping around and it didn't take much to figure out the rest. I need to hear your side of it though. A lot still doesn't make sense.'

'I'm not sure I see why I ought to be talking to you at all. You want to bring up a lot of ugly things I'd just as soon forget.'

'But you can't, can you?' He looked around, a sweeping survey of their surroundings. 'Right now I could make a pretty good case that you've been blackmailing Jerry Margashack for the last fifteen years.'

'If that's true, then why would I need to put these things in the papers?'

Spandau shrugged. 'Maybe you want more and Jerry's having a hard time getting it to you.'

'You got it all figured out,' she said.

'If I had, I wouldn't be here now.'

She lit a cigarette from a packet on the table, never taking her eyes off his. She smoked for a bit, then finally said,

'I'll answer your questions, Mr Spandau. But you better be sure of what you ask, because I don't want to see you again. I mean that. You ask your questions and then there's an end to it, right here.'

'I can't promise you that.'

'You mistake my meaning. This is a promise I'm making to you, not the other way around. Now what is it you think you know?'

He recounted the story as Lewis had told it. 'How close is that to the truth?'

'The truth,' she said. 'Is that what you want? I'm not sure I know the truth. The Lord does, maybe, but not me. I'm still waiting.'

She smoked, sipped her coffee, crushed the cigarette into the ashtray with more force than was necessary.

'I'm asking you, is that how it happened?'

'Yes and no,' she said. 'Yes, that's the way I met Jerry. Yes, we started seeing each other on the sly. He was charming and he was fun and I was a cute little thing then, Mr Spandau, and I liked the attention. And I was cocky and I thought I had everything under control. I liked him but I didn't want to sleep with him.'

'You didn't find him attractive that way?'

'Oh I did,' she said. 'I would have slept with him eventually. I was no innocent, which of course was the problem. I'd had my share of men. I knew I was pretty, I knew what I had. But I also knew what he was like – or I thought I did – and that if I gave in too fast he'd lose interest. You could see that about him. He liked conquest, he liked a battle. If he couldn't find one he'd make one up.'

She stopped, stood up, went over to the patio door, and stood looking out at the creek and biting a cuticle.

'And San Diego? That's the way it happened?' he said, as if to remind her he was still there.

'It started out just fine.' She spoke without turning around, staring through the glass, worrying the fingernail, half talking only to herself. 'He was how Jerry can be before the Devil gets in him. You know him well, Mr Spandau?'

'A little.'

'Then you see what I'm talking about. He can be the most charming thing on earth. The Devil is like that, Mr Spandau. That's how he works his business.'

'You think Jerry Margashack is the Devil?'

'I think the Devil gets in him,' she said. 'I think the Devil's got a hold of Jerry Margashack and even now I still pray for his soul. It's hard, you know, trying not to hate, and I make myself pray. I make myself try to understand it all as part of God's plan.'

'San Diego,' Spandau gently prompted.

'I was going to sleep with him that night,' she said. 'I had it all worked out. I was like that in those days. It didn't make any difference he was older, more experienced. I was in command and I knew it. I wore this little dress, cut down low, tight. Oh, I was something in those days. I'd dangled the bait long enough, I was going to give him what he wanted. Just that one time, though,' she said. 'Just that one time though for a while. I'd give it to him and then I'd wait to make sure he wasn't sure. He was used to women always there, always sure to come back. I wanted to stay for a while, see. I wanted to be the one who stayed in his life for a while and I didn't want him to feel safe.' She laughed. 'Jerry, if he feels safe, he gets bored. I didn't want him bored, Mr Spandau. I wanted him to need me. I wanted to be like a drug to him. I wanted to be one of his addictions.'

'Were you in love with him?'

She turned, gave Spandau a surprised look.

'No,' she said. 'I've never loved anyone. Not like that. Not like you mean.'

She could see that he didn't understand. She walked over to him, stood next to his chair, looking down.

'I'm not a monster,' she said. 'I do love. But it came late, real love anyway, God's love, but there was never the kind you talk about me having for Jerry. All the men I had, I don't think I ever really felt anything. Not even lust. I knew what they wanted and sometimes I gave it to them because it came easy. But I never felt much. Not even the sex. Sometimes it was nice but I don't think I ever felt what they say you're supposed to feel. I don't know if that makes me strange. But I wonder how many women really feel this way. Maybe all that stuff we hear is just what they want us to think. They want you to think the earth is supposed to move and the skies to clear. It never did for me. It pleased me to do things to a man that made him mine, that gave me a sense of power. All men become children in bed, Mr Spandau. Did you know that? It's not the same for a woman. In bed a woman just becomes everybody's mother.'

'I think Freud said something like that.'

'I'm not an educated woman, Mr Spandau. I never read Freud. I'm just telling you what I know.'

Spandau waited. She lit another cigarette and began to pace. When she started to speak again, it was quicker, nervous, in bursts. She walked back and forth, from the glass door to the table, with a gaze that focused only on what she saw in her head.

'It was nice. He took me to this place in San Diego where he knew everybody. He spoke in Spanish, it was like he was one of the family. He didn't have to order, they just brought things, like he was some kind of royalty and he was used to it. He expected me to be impressed and I was. They made a fuss over me. I was the belle of the ball. I liked that. We ate, drank. I got a little drunk. More than a little drunk.'

'He was drinking a lot?'

'Jerry always drank a lot, and it was hard to tell how much he'd had or when he'd had too much. You never knew until too late. Sometimes you never knew at all. I'm not sure when it turned, or why. Maybe it was something I said. I've thought about it and I still don't know. I was flirting with him, being pretty obvious this time, giving him all the right signs that this was the night.

'It was fine, then suddenly it changed. Just like that. I think he was nervous. I think he was going to get what he wanted and he was nervous about it. He could be like that sometimes, shy. Or maybe he just got angry because he knew he was going to get what he wanted and the game was over for him. I don't know.

'Suddenly, snap, it turned, it was like the sky fell. He got quiet

and dark, then mean. Started snapping things at the restaurant
people in Spanish, I don't know what he said, but they backed off
and tiptoed around him like they'd seen it all before. He ignored
me, just drank, acted like I wasn't even there. I said maybe we
should go, it was a long drive back to LA. He gave me a look,
my Lord, if looks could kill. Then he turned away and went back
to his drink.

'I don't know what time it was we left. By this point I'd had
too much to drink myself and I just wanted to get home, get the
night over with, get home safe. I hated him, hated the thought of
him touching me. Made a promise I was never going to see him
again. If I hadn't been drunk myself I'd have never got into the
car with him.

'I don't know where we were, somewhere between Pendleton
and Laguna. He said there was a motel he knew nearby, a real
nice place, right on the water, let's go there. I said I just wanted
him to take me home. He said he was sorry, apologized over and
over. I said I just wanted to get home. He began to cry. Quietly.
But I could see these tears on his cheeks in the headlights of
oncoming cars. I felt, I don't know, I felt sorry for him. He said
he wanted to talk.

'He pulled off the road, down toward the beach. I didn't want
him to. He pulled off the road and I said I wanted to go on but
he just started talking. Crying and talking, talking not like a drunk
but like a man who's been possessed by a spirit, all these things
kept coming out. Told me he needed me, told me he desired me.
Told me he loved me. I knew then he wasn't drunk. It was something else. It was something that was inside him.

'I said, just take me home, we'll talk about all this tomorrow.
He said he loved me and touched me and I pushed his hand away
and then it happened, then I saw his face, the face of the Devil,
Mr Spandau, and he lunged at me. I got the door open and fell
out onto the sand and he come around the car after me and pulled
me down into the sand, had his hand around my throat . . .'

She stopped, wiped away the tears, went back to the door and
stood with her back to him.

'He cried after, tried to tell me how sorry he was. I got loose
from him, got up and ran down the beach. He come after me
calling but I ran and ran and when I stopped and turned around

he wasn't there. I don't know how far I ran. Maybe he just gave up, maybe he went back to the car to drive ahead and catch me, maybe he just left me. I never did know.

'I got back up onto the highway. I was drunk, half crazy, I didn't know where I was. Started walking on the side of the road. I think maybe I was going to walk to LA. I don't know. I tried to flag down some cars but nobody stopped. I was dirty, my hair was full of sand, my dress was torn, I kept pulling a piece of it over my breast. God had wanted it, the police would have stopped. But that's not what He wanted.

'This van pulled over. I looked in and there was this boy driving, practically not much more than a boy, he had this sweet blond face and I was so glad to see him, so glad. I got in and he drove me back to LA.'

'You lied about the second rape?'

'I needed the money. To be honest I wasn't sure anybody would care what Jerry did to me. I was afraid they'd think I had it coming.'

She paused, stopped pacing long enough to look at him, look deep into his eyes.

'People do the strangest things, don't they, Mr Spandau? Except it's not people, Mr Spandau, they don't have nothing to do with it except when we're weak. It's just God and the Devil, battling for souls, and the Devil just waits for you, just waits for the opportunity to ask you to dance.'

'You didn't hear from Jerry after that?'

'Oh of course I did. He called, tried to come round the very next day, hung around outside my apartment, called my friends. I wouldn't see him. Wouldn't see anybody, couldn't leave my apartment. I just lay there, didn't wash, didn't eat. People say it was shock. I don't think it was. It was just anger. Anger and helplessness. I lay there thinking of all the ways I could kill him, ruin him, make him pay.'

'You never saw him again?'

'He called me and I finally talked to him, told him if I ever saw or heard from him again I was going to the police, the newspapers, television, I'd sell my story to the whole world. I'd ruin him, I'd see him in hell. He knew I meant it and he stopped calling.'

'You got money from him before you left LA?'

'No, Jerry's lied about that, he needed to say something to Lewis, him and Lewis were friends. Lewis is a good man, he was my friend too, and that's why I went to him for the money. I knew he'd help me. There was nowhere else to go. And he did. I always thank him for that in my prayers. Not many people would have done that.'

'Where did you go when you left LA?'

'Back to Bowling Green, for about fifteen minutes. I was there for a few weeks. I had some thought I wanted to be with my family. It's the sort of thing you do, you hope while you've been gone they finally found something to give you, but they hadn't. Nothing had changed. A woman I knew invited me to Portland. I went there. She was gentle with me and I know what we did was against the scriptures but I was alone and I couldn't look at a man, couldn't think of a man without getting sick to my stomach. It was like that until the baby came.'

'Jerry's child.'

'That's right,' she said. 'There was no other man after Jerry. There hasn't been since.'

'What made you decide to keep it?'

'The voice of God, Mr Spandau.'

She saw the look on his face and laughed.

'You're not a Christian, Mr Spandau?'

'I'm not quite sure what I am these days,' he said.

'I thought about getting rid of it, I truly did. Thought about it all the time. Sally wanted me to, asked me how in the world I could even think of it, after the way it happened. Said it would ruin my life, would be nothing but a constant reminder of a terrible thing.

'I don't know if I can explain it,' she went on. 'It just felt wrong, and I knew it was wrong. I knew I wanted to have the baby. I didn't know what I would do after. I wasn't thinking about that. By that time I'd started reading the scriptures too, finding my way back to God. The closer I got to God the more I knew He wanted me to have it, that He knew what He was doing.

'Poor Sally was shocked, she thought it was horrible, she didn't want any part of it, didn't want to raise a rapist's baby. I don't blame her, I don't blame anyone. She had her own issues and God hadn't touched her yet. She was a good woman and good to me but there was no way to make her understand that I knew I was doing the right thing.

'There was no insurance, we were living off what Sally earned as a waitress. I did what piecework I could, made Lewis' money stretch as far as I could. I didn't do the usual tests, they probably would have shown me there was something wrong with the baby. I didn't know. I had no idea.

'Mikey was born, I knew there was something wrong, they took a long time bringing him to me in the hospital. Sally was there, when they told me. I didn't know quite what it meant, I was expecting something horrible, something like a monster, but they brought him in and put him in my arms and I knew I was holding an angel. I knew what it was all about then, I knew why I'd had this child.

'It was different for Sally. It was more than she could handle and I needed to find a home for myself and the baby now. There was no choice but to contact Jerry. There was nowhere else to go.'

'How did he react?'

'Quiet. Serious. I explained about Mikey. He asked me if I was okay, what I wanted to do. I told him I needed money. He wired some that day. A few days later I got a call from Michael. He said he was a friend of Jerry's, and that Jerry had asked him to help me out. He promised that everything would be fine. And it has been.'

'Did Jerry try to see you?'

'Yes.'

'You refused?'

'I haven't seen Jerry since that night in California, and I haven't spoken to him since that phone call to tell him about my child. He's never seen Mikey and he never will. The only contact either of us have with Jerry is through Michael.

'As far as blackmailing him, I don't have a need for it. We live simply and my business is good and the Lord provides us with everything we need. Jerry has always seen there's enough and if we ever needed more he's sent it. I never had to force him.

'As for trying to hurt him, well, that would take more time and energy than he's worth to me. I try not to hate him, Mr Spandau, and I work daily on trying to forgive him. I confess I haven't quite managed that yet, but I keep trying. And I also remind myself that he did give me a couple of important things. He gave me my child, and it was my child that has taught me love, real love, and he has

given me Michael. Through him God has given me the only real
family I have ever known, the only things I have ever really loved.

'Jerry Margashack has served the function God had for him in
my life, and I have no need or wish to think of him any more than
I need to, which is why your being here and asking these questions
is so pointless and upsetting. What God does with him now is
none of my business. Jerry carries around his own Hell, Mr Spandau.
You've seen this if you know him. He doesn't need me to find
him ways to suffer.

'Does this answer your questions? Because I'm going to have
to insist you leave now. You want to help Jerry, he's your problem
now and not mine. I won't waste any more of my life on it.'

Spandau stood up. 'I thank you for your time.'

'I want you to know I didn't do this for you, and I certainly
didn't do this for Jerry. I did it for Michael. He does love Jerry
and he's always seen something in him I could never find. But
I've done my favor and I won't do it again. You think I'm a hard,
cold woman, Mr Spandau?'

'I think you're trying to make sense of the world just like the
rest of us, Miss Hamlin.'

'My grandmother back in Kentucky used to say, "Honey, you
better have long arms if you're going to dance with the Devil."'
Rebecca held up her arms, shook them like a revival singer. 'These
arms ain't nearly long enough, Mr Spandau. Nobody's ever are. Not
mine, not Jerry Margashack's, not even yours. You remember that.'

Her arms fell to her sides. She looked at Spandau for a moment.
There was no trace of emotion, it was as if she'd emptied herself
and there was nothing left. She simply turned from him and walked
away, slowly climbed the stairs to her room.

FIFTY-ONE

In the yard the boy was playing again in the sand. Michael sat
a few feet away in a rusty metal lawn chair, smoking a pipe.

'You get what you wanted?' the priest said.

'More or less.'

'You believe now she's got nothing to do with all this?'

'I believe she's not the one trying to smear him,' Spandau said, 'but I wouldn't exactly say she's got nothing to do with it. I have a feeling that if you'd come clean I could wrap this whole thing up and get back to my own screwed-up life.'

'You give me too much credit,' the priest said around the stem of his pipe.

'You seem to be having this identity crisis about whether you're actually God or just some guy who works for him. I'm sure you think there's this elderly wisdom to what you're doing, but all it is really is just arrogance and monkeying around with people's lives. I don't mind so much you having me kidnapped, but I'm tired and I feel stupid and that does bother me.'

'Why don't you go back and talk to Jerry. Tell him you were here. Tell him what you know.'

'You haven't said anything?'

'I don't expect you to see it,' said the priest, 'but there is a process unfolding here and it's taken nearly sixteen years to happen. God takes His own time and uses whoever He feels. I admit I meddled a little in Cheney but it was a well-intentioned mistake. I didn't see the point in opening up this can of worms but you've got it rolling and now it has to be played out. I'm on the sidelines until I get a clear signal from the coach.'

'You don't know how strange it is,' said Spandau, 'watching you jump back and forth between playing Spencer Tracy in *Boy's Town* and Pat O'Brien as Knute Rockne. A real priest mimicking movie Catholics is just about as postmodern as I can stand.'

'They made real movies in those days.'

'Not like the sort of stuff Jerry makes?'

The priest made a face.

'Jerry's films never interested me. The world doesn't need one more movie about how bad things are. It's not true anyway, it's just an easy lie. The world is full of people who are trying to do the right thing. That's how we survive from day to day. Take a drive on any LA freeway and then tell me you have no faith in the prevalence of human goodness. You wouldn't be there if you didn't. Well, the whole of life is like that.'

'What about original sin and all that?'

'There you go again,' said the priest, 'talking about things you know nothing about. Leave the theology to the people who get paid for it. Believe me, you don't really need to know how many angels can dance on the head of a pin. Just worry about getting through your day doing as little harm as possible. That will keep you busy enough.'

'This the sort of pep talk you give to Jerry?'

'Jerry's like you are, always has been. Never listens to a damned thing. He's got to find everything out for himself. I can't tell you how exhausting it is to watch someone try to reinvent the wheel every day of their life. Meanwhile I take it that now you know the truth you're still not dropping the case?'

'I don't know,' Spandau said. 'Should you try to save someone who probably doesn't deserve to be saved?'

'This is where your own arrogance comes in. This talk of saving someone. That's not up to you. Just follow your own conscience and let God take care of the rest of it. If He needs your help, He'll ask for it.'

'I don't get it,' said Spandau. 'What is it that you see in him all these years? I can't think of a less likely candidate for salvation.'

'A good number of the saints,' said the priest, 'weren't exactly model citizens. It's never too late. I've seen a lot worse than Jerry ask for forgiveness.'

'Not from her,' said Spandau, nodding to the house. 'And I don't blame her.'

'That would just be one more thing,' said Michael, 'that you don't have a clue about. I could start making a list for you, if that would help.'

The boy came over with a toy steam shovel, handed it to Michael. A small pebble had jammed the bucket arm. The priest took out a pocketknife and patiently worked it loose.

'You going?' the boy asked Spandau.

'Yes sir, I am.'

'My mom don't like you.'

'This is a problem I've frequently encountered,' said Spandau.

'I don't think you're too bad though,' Mikey said and patted him on the arm.

'You'll see Jerry when you get back?' asked the priest.

'That's the plan.'

'Be sure to tell him I said to roll up his sleeves and get to work.'

'Is this supposed to make some kind of sense?'

'Never you mind. Just tell him. He'll know what I'm talking about.'

'You're very peculiar old man,' said Spandau, 'if you don't mind me saying so.'

Spandau opened the gate, went out. He turned and said, 'How many angels can dance on the head of a pin, anyway?'

'Three,' said the old man without missing a beat, 'but only if they diet.'

FIFTY-TWO

Spandau stood outside the door of Jerry's cottage. He could hear music inside. He knocked. Nothing, but the music went silent. He knocked again, louder. Nothing.

'Jerry, open the door. It's me, David.'

A hesitation before the door opened, while Spandau could feel Jerry standing on the other side of it, trying to make up his mind. Then Jerry appeared, beaming, a glass of scotch in his hand.

'Why, David Spandau, as I live and breathe,' he said in a mock-Dixie accent. 'Home from the wars are we? Is it true that mo'fucker Sherman burnt Atlanta? Or are the darkies finally in revolt?'

'Cut the shit, Jerry.' Jerry didn't invite him in, just stood there, smiling. Spandau pushed past him and into the room.

'Oh my my, who got his tail caught under a rocker?'

'I've been calling you all day. I've left messages on your cell phone, at the desk. The hotel says you've checked out. This doesn't appear to be true.'

'Working on a new screenplay. Needed a little artistic space. Nothing personal.'

'How's this for personal? I just got back from a long talk with Rebecca Hamlin. I met your son too, by the way.'

Jerry tried to keep that smile going but couldn't manage it. It wobbled for a moment and then fell apart altogether. He stood there blinking, looking up at Spandau, and his eyes changed and his shoulders fell as if the sand were running out of his body.

'Well,' said Jerry.

He gently closed the door, drained his George Dickel, went over and poured himself another. Sank that one. Poured another.

'How are they?'

'They appear to be well. You're not exactly a favored topic of conversation though. But I'm sure you know that.'

'The old man there?'

'Yeah.'

'He the one who sold me out?'

'No,' said Spandau. 'He even had your hometown constabulary rough me up a little to scare me off. He's convinced you've got a soul worth saving. My opinion is pretty much the same as Rebecca's. I think you're a miserable shitass who probably ought to be put down like a rabid dog. I wouldn't mind doing it myself. Nothing personal, of course.'

'You think she's the one sending out all this stuff?'

'She was the logical choice. But it's not her. She despises you, but she's shooting for less, not more. She doesn't think you're worth the energy it takes to keep hating you. Now that you and I are pals I can see her point. Anyway there's nothing in it for her, no real motive. She's got what she needs from you, she doesn't have to force it.'

'They get everything when I'm dead, you know. They get everything.'

'Everything meaning whatever is left over after drink, drugs, gambling, whores, and rape, and whatever other clever devices you can come up with to make the world a better place. I swear to god, Jerry, you are that mythical creature mankind has been waiting for, a one-man pestilence. Who the hell needs locusts or cholera when they've got you? One suggestion. Make some money first, then die. Cut them a break for once.'

'If that's what you came here to tell me, it's a waste of time. You're preaching to the choir. You're not saying anything I don't already know. The irony is, I'd have snuffed myself a long time ago if it hadn't been for them, knowing I had to keep going so they'd be okay. I've always managed to take care of them, get them what they need. They never lacked for anything, even if I had to scramble for it. They've kept me alive. Miserable, you're right. But alive.'

He rubbed his arms through the long-sleeved shirt. Turned to pour yet another drink. Said over his shoulder,

'Speaking of sucking down a bullet, I was real sorry to hear about your boss.'

Spandau grabbed him by the shirt collar and threw him backwards across the room. He hit the room-service cart and both went over with a great crash.

'You son of a bitch,' said Spandau. 'He's dead and you're alive.'

Jerry got to his feet, stood there waiting for Spandau to come at him. Spandau didn't.

'Come on,' said Jerry, smiling. 'Come on.'

'That's what you want, isn't it?' Spandau said to him. 'That going to make you feel better, me beating the crap out of you? That going to ease your guilt a little, get you through your night?'

'You and your fucking high horse,' said Jerry. 'You're a fucking joke. I don't know who the fuck you think you are, but the fact is you're still a lowlife cocksucker people like Jurado hire to peek through keyholes. They pay you to do their shit work. That's the fucking purpose of your existence, and you know it.'

'I'm not going to play, Jerry,' Spandau said. 'I quit. I'm out of here, case closed, gone. Rebecca is right. You're not worth the powder it would take to make the hole in your head.'

Spandau went toward the door. Jerry moved in front of him, put his hand against Spandau's chest and pushed him back.

'Come on, cowboy,' said Jerry, smiling. 'Do something. Stop talking. Show a little balls.'

He pushed Spandau again. Spandau took a few steps back, out of Jerry's reach.

'Not going to happen, Jerry,' Spandau said. 'You don't get off that easy.'

'You're not so hard to figure, cowboy,' said Jerry. 'You talk a good game. Fucking Gary Cooper, the honorable type in a morally ambiguous world. In itself a fucking cliché. Then you use it to try and cloud the fact that what you do is essentially pretty sleazy.' The fake southern accent again. 'Why, Mr Spandau, I do believe you're nothing but a dick-licking lowlife toady just like the rest of us.'

Jerry moved forward, Spandau moved back. Jerry stopped. Smiled, waited, rubbing his arms furiously.

Spandau watched him. He'd noticed it before, passed it off as a rash or nervous tic. It could have been anything. Spandau said, 'Michael said to tell you it's time to roll up your sleeves and get to work.'

The rubbing stopped as Jerry suddenly became aware of his hands. Jerry lowered his head, smiled, held his hands palms up in a gesture of surrender.

'The old bastard,' Jerry said, shaking his head.

'Let me see them, Jerry.'

Jerry stood there, smiling, looking at the floor. Spandau came forward, slapped him.

'Come on, Jerry. Let me see your arms.'

Nothing.

Spandau slapped him again. Jerry's head rolled to one side, he moved it back to look at the floor.

'Let me see them,' Spandau said.

Another slap.

'Come on. Let's see what it is you're hiding. Or do you like getting slapped around too much? This is what you like, isn't it? This is what makes you feel better.'

He looked up at Spandau. There was no smile, nothing but an empty face. Jerry unbuttoned his sleeves and rolled them up one by one. They were old scars, not new, and covered both arms like an irregular pattern of armor woven just beneath the skin, from wrists to where they disappeared into the turned-back cloth. Small tiny even craters that could only have been cigarette burns. Thin stripes of various lengths, razor or knife. It must have taken years.

Spandau looked. He went over and poured himself a drink while Jerry rebuttoned his shirt. Spandau sat down on the couch.

'You poor pathetic son of a bitch.'

'I was young,' said Jerry. 'Eventually I figured out that booze, drugs, and women could do a better job, if you were careful about your choices.'

'Jesus Christ,' said Spandau, shaking his head incredulously. 'I should have seen it. It was right there all the time. I should have seen it.'

Jerry refilled his drink. Flopped down in a chair across from Spandau.

'Why?' asked Spandau. 'You want to fuck up your life, your career, there are simpler ways. You've been trying most of them.'

'I don't expect you to understand. Anyway it doesn't make a goddamned bit of difference if you do. I didn't hire you.'

'Yeah, but you knew Jurado would. He had to protect his investment. I can't figure out who you wanted to damage most, yourself or Jurado.'

'Jurado is a shit, and it's a shit film, I don't care how many fucking awards they want to give it. It was a good script when he got it and it could have been something I could have been proud of. But it's not, and it's the first time in my life I ever sold out. Really just sold my fucking soul. But I'm getting old, and I'm tired, and there was Becky and the boy. There was all that. I was hoping the film would never get made, I'd just take my money and slink away. But shit sells. I'd forgotten that. The only time I ever made a film I wasn't proud of and it's my biggest hit. How's that for irony?'

'Why go to such lengths to fuck it up? Why not just take your money and walk away? Anyway, you get a hit and you're back in the game, the next film you can make the way you want.'

'Because it was wrong. It was all wrong, and from so many angles. It was wrong everywhere. I don't know if it was God. I don't even think I believe in God. But the whole thing did smell like divine retribution to me. God just sitting there laughing at me until I had to take matters into my own hands. It was beautiful. You believe in fate?'

'No.'

'Well, it's all about fate, the whole fucking thing. I don't know if I can explain this.'

'Try.'

'There was nothing else I could do. I couldn't say or do anything against the film. Jurado has me tied up seven ways to Sunday, I've signed shut-up clauses up the ass. I'd get sued, I'd never get my money, the whole thing. I have to do something, I have to stop this thing. This fucking abomination. This fucking travesty. I have to find some way to try and save my soul, because if this thing is a hit . . . I mean, I can't live in a world like that. You know what I mean?'

'I think so.'

'I figure the only way I can slam the picture is if I slam myself. Shit starts coming out about me, maybe public opinion changes about the film, maybe Jurado won't back it. If this film won an Oscar . . . I mean, I can't think of it, it's too horrible. What if it won an Oscar? What if I fucking won an Oscar? What if this fucking shit piece was the one thing people remembered me for?'

He stopped. Shook his head as if trying to clear it.

'I know this guy, name of Malo. Slick smart black dude. A fixer. You know the type. Knows everybody, connected everywhere. You want a kilo of Thai heroin or an unregistered howitzer or your deadbeat brother-in-law shoved off the top of the Roosevelt Hotel, he knows somebody who knows somebody. He hired this guy to break in here and lift some files off my computer. Part of my memoirs.'

'Memoirs?'

'Well, some stuff I planted anyway. I told him they were memoirs.'

'So the information's not true, then?'

Doesn't answer.

'Is the information true?' Spandau asked again.

'I couldn't give them lies,' Jerry said. 'The second anybody from the press got hold of this they were going to check it. They couldn't actually print anything from the files, but it gave them enough they could follow up, and there's no way they could trace it to me.'

'Let me see if I've got this straight,' Spandau said. 'You've concocted this whole Rube Goldberg affair in order to deliberately sabotage your own career?'

'I suppose if you want to look at it that way,' said Jerry, 'well yeah. You can understand why I wasn't real keen on giving you a lot of encouragement.'

'Michael was in on it?'

'Nah. He didn't have any idea what was going on until you started nosing around, then he thought he was protecting me.'

'There are simpler ways of fucking yourself up,' said Spandau.

'In this case name two,' Jerry said. 'I was looking to fuck up this movie and this was all I had.'

'Bullshit, Jerry. You don't have to be fucking Krafft-Ebing to see this.'

'So it cost me a little,' Jerry said. 'You don't think I deserve it? You see that kid? You know how it happened.'

'That's not the point.'

'Then what is the point?'

Spandau's mind raced. He didn't actually know.

'I've met some truly whacked-out individuals in my life,' said Spandau, 'but you are the king of all head cases. I've got to hand it to you.'

'Think about it. This is Hollywood. You do anything on the up and up and nobody believes you. It makes sense.'

'No it doesn't,' said Spandau helplessly. 'I'm not exactly sure why, but it doesn't.'

'The question is, now that you know, what are you going to do with it? You going to take it to Jurado?'

'You're goddamned right I am. Somebody's got to put an end to this madness. This is epically insane, Jerry. There's something almost biblical about it, which is what's making me so uncomfortable. It's hard to tell just how nuts you really are, but you're up there with the great ones. You can't go around winding people up like they were your personal clockwork toys.'

'Sure you can,' said Jerry, 'me and practically everybody I know has made a career out of it. Look, you tell Jurado and he's going to cut me up into ribbons. He's going to ruin me.'

'Listen to yourself. Listen to what you just said. Dear mother of god, have you no idea how bonkers that is? You want to be punished but you want to be the only one who does it. What's so amazing is that you've managed to get half this town to take part in a masochistic fantasy the size of a Cecil B. DeMille movie.'

'Don't do it,' said Jerry. 'I'll stop the leaks. That's all Jurado is concerned about. You'll have done what you were hired to do.'

'Kiss my ass, you crazy bastard. You're not calling the shots anymore. How does it feel now?'

'You're going to force me to do something drastic. I'll do what your boss did. I'll fucking kill myself, I swear to God I will.'

'No you won't,' said Spandau. 'This is all just a fucking movie to you. You kill yourself before it's done and you don't get final cut.'

'That,' said Jerry, 'is a shitty thing to say.'

FIFTY-THREE

'**W**hat?' said Jurado. 'I want you to explain this all again, very slowly.'

Spandau did. It made no sense the second time either. It would make no sense no matter how many times he told it.

'That sick twisted bastard,' Jurado said when Spandau finished again. He was smiling and there was more than a little appreciation in his voice, of one professional for another. For some reason Spandau had expected something darker.

'Next thing is for Jerry to contact this guy and plug the leak.'

'No,' said Jurado. 'I don't want him to do that.'

Spandau was quiet. After a while he said very patiently,

'That isn't what you want.'

'Of course it isn't,' said Jurado. 'I never said it was. I just said I wanted to know who was doing it. I never said anything about stopping it.'

'I'm going to sit down,' said Spandau. 'It's been a long day.'

'I admit I thought about it at first,' Jurado said, 'but then I found out how much publicity this was generating. It's all over the place. People hate his guts. It's fucking brilliant.'

'And this is wonderful how?' asked Jurado's assistant, who was too fascinated to keep her mouth shut.

'Because,' said Spandau, 'by the time the movie is in actual release they'll have forgotten they hate him and all anybody will remember is Jerry's name and the name of the movie.'

'Exactly,' said Jurado. 'Nobody remembers why anybody is famous. They just remember that they are. No no no. I don't want to stop the leaks, I just want to be able to control them.'

'And you've got Jerry by the balls.'

'Well, I had him by the balls anyway,' said Jurado. 'This just gives me a much better grip.' Spandau had never seen him this happy. He was glowing.

He had not told Jurado everything. He had not, for instance, told him about Rebecca and the child, or the scars on Jerry's arms, or Father Michael's concern over the state of Jerry's soul.

Spandau rubbed his eyes.

'I'm sure this won't be the last time I say this,' he said, 'but you fucking people deserve each other. You really do.'

He sighed, stood up.

'You'll have a report and an accounts statement by the end of the day tomorrow. If you will forgive me I'm about to be sick on behalf of the entire civilized world.'

'If you wouldn't mind,' Jurado said to Spandau. To his assistant he said, 'Mandy, will you give Mr Spandau and me a moment? And as you're leaving would you ask Fred and Arturo to come in?'

She left, giving a nod to two large and familiar bruisers to step inside and close the door.

'Not again,' said Spandau. 'Hello, boys.' They nodded to him. To Jurado he said, 'They look thinner. Are you not feeding them? The price of horse chow gone up?'

'In regard to your bill,' said Jurado, 'certainly I'll cover any justifiable expenses and your time. That's fair. But whatever additional payments or bonuses you may have worked out with your former employer, those have nothing to do with me. I'm being generous here since I'm not entirely happy with the way this turned out. There seems to have been a lot of unnecessary travel involved.'

'What if I just sue you.'

'Ah well,' said Jurado merrily. 'Your dear and presently *dead* employer might have been able to do that. But as you are nothing but hired help and the proprietor of your company is, as I say, *dead*, there is ergo no longer a company or a leg for you to stand on. It appears you are out of a job as well. Imagine that.'

Spandau smiled, looked at the carpet, shook his head ruefully.

'Well, I've got to hand it to you,' said Spandau. 'Between you and Jerry, you've made me look like a complete asshole.'

'I think you're underestimating yourself,' said Jurado. 'You don't just look like an asshole, I believe you're showing some real dedication to the role.'

'I know when I'm whipped. As they say, discretion is the better part of valor.'

'Spoken like a true loser,' said Jurado. 'You fucking hit me, you pathetic fucking nothing. I can't imagine you ever thought I'd let you get away with that. Good luck finding a job, by the way. I'm going to smear you like shit on a sidewalk. You'll spend the rest of your days chasing skate rats at a mall somewhere in Utah.'

Spandau reached into his jacket pocket for his cell phone.

'Will you excuse me for a moment? I have to make this call.'

He dialed Anna's number.

'David, where have you been? I've been worried sick.'

'We'll talk about all this later, sweetheart. I just wanted to call and tell you I've decided to go for it, that thing we talked about.'

'You're going to do it. You're sure?'

'I confess I wasn't until just a few moments ago,' he said, 'but I've just had this sort of revelation. I just wanted you to be the first.'

'I love you,' she said.

'I love you too.'

'Kiss?'

'Kiss,' he said, and hung up.

'Well, that was delightfully stomach curdling,' said Jurado. 'Will she love you castrated and weeping in your cowboy boots? Give her my regards by the way. Tell her I know where she can find a real man.'

'I'm sure you do,' said Spandau. 'Probably the same bovine paradise where you found these two specimens.'

Spandau starts to leave.

'That's it?' said Jurado. 'No John Ford histrionics? No punches flying, giving me the opportunity to have my associates here beat the crap out of you again?'

'Sorry, not this time.'

'That's too bad,' said Jurado. 'But it is wonderfully satisfying to piss down on the vanquished from a great height. *Ciao*, baby,' he said as he slammed the door. Spandau could hear self-satisfied chuckling from the other side.

In the parking lot Spandau took out his cell phone again.

'Bernie, hi, this is David. As my first official act as the new head of Coren Security and Investigations, I'd like for you to phone Frank Jurado first thing in the morning and tell him we're suing the shit out of him for breach of contract. On the other hand, why don't I drop by in the morning and we'll make the call together on your speakerphone. I want to hear the sound of water being suddenly cut off from somewhere above me. I'll explain everything when I see you.'

FIFTY-FOUR

A raz pushed the van up Highway 5 toward San Jose. Tavit was making him crazy. They had to stop for Tavit to pee every five minutes. Tavit himself wondered aloud why he had to pee so often, but every time they stopped he came back to the van with a fucking bladder-buster of a soda and a candy bar or something. There was no point talking to someone like this and Araz had his mind on other things. It was about lunchtime when they hit Salinas and Tavit had an imperative need for Mexican food. They stopped at a taco franchise on Highway 101 and he watched Tavit eat like a sumo wrestler with a tapeworm. He ate like a pig, he did everything but rub it on his body.

'You're not eating?' he said to Araz, who sat there sipping at a Diet Coke.

'You're going to get sick,' Araz said to him.

'I'm nervous,' said Tavit. 'I always eat like this when I'm nervous. Aren't you nervous?'

'No,' lied Araz.

'Anyway,' said Tavit, 'I got a stomach like cast iron. I can eat anything,' and downed an entire jalapeño to make his point.

FIFTY-FIVE

I t was an Indian casino near Milpitas. They pulled into the parking lot and Tavit said,

'What is the plan?'

'The plan?' said Araz. 'The plan is we go in there and find the bastard and get our money. That is the plan.'

'Should I bring the gun?'

'No,' said Araz, 'please do not bring the fucking gun. Where is it?'

'In the glove compartment.'

Araz thought for a moment, then put the gun in his jacket.

'What if he runs? Don't you think he might run?'

'Of course he'll fucking run. Wouldn't you run if you owed eighty-five grand plus interest and someone was about to fuck you up for the rest of your life?'

'So if he runs?'

'You fucking chase him,' said Araz.

Tavit appeared to agree with the logic of this.

They went inside.

'You remember what he looks like?' Araz said.

'Yeah,' said Tavit. 'Should we fan out?'

'Fan out,' repeated Araz. 'There are two of us, Tavit, how much of a fucking fan out is that going to be? Just stay with me. I don't want to be looking for two assholes at once,' though Araz didn't actually say this last part aloud. At least he didn't think he did.

It wasn't a big place and it didn't take long to spot him. When they did, Charlie was standing at a blackjack table talking to a young man and a girl. Anyway they were talking to him and he was picking up his chips and shaking his head no, over and over again. The girl was pleading with him about something and Charlie happened to look up and see Araz and Tavit walking toward him. It took a second for it to register. Charlie scooped up what he could of the chips, dropping about half of them, and ran for the exit. He was nervously struggling to unlock his car when they reached him. He started to run again but they caught him between the cars and started pounding on him.

'Leave him alone!' It was the guy Charlie had been talking to. The girl was with him.

'This is none of your business,' said Araz, while Tavit continued to hammer the shit out of Charlie.

'We mean it,' said the girl. 'Back away.'

They were fucking do-gooders, nothing to worry about.

'Get rid of them, will you,' Araz said to Tavit.

Tavit stopped beating Charlie, Araz picked up where Tavit left off. Charlie looked pretty bad and he leaned against a car to keep from falling. This set off the car's alarm, which was unfortunate. Araz was going to drag Charlie back to the van when he heard Tavit let out something like a pained squeak. Araz turned to see Tavit maybe ten feet away from the guy and girl doing some kind of dance. Then Tavit fell down and Araz saw the thin wires running from Tavit's chest to a small box in the girl's hand. Tavit lay on his back with his eyes wide open, shaking. They all stood there looking down at Tavit for a bit, and this reverie was broken only by Tavit emitting a loud and seemingly endless fart.

'What the fuck,' said Araz, realizing that whatever order there might have been in the universe just gave way. He pulled out the gun and pointed it at the girl. 'Drop that thing or I am going to shoot you dead.'

The girl dropped the Taser. Araz went over and kicked it skidding across the asphalt and the wires came loose from Tavit. This however did not stop him from shaking.

'I'm sorry,' said Pookie. 'It's really not supposed to do that. Maybe I had it turned up too high. Is he an epileptic or anything?'

Araz went over and kicked Tavit.

'Get the fuck up.'

Tavit tried to speak, couldn't, just kept shaking.

Araz looked up at the heavens. He more or less believed in a God but was decidedly pissed off at him for all this.

'Pick him up,' he said to the girl and the guy. They stepped forward to pick Tavit up.

Araz turned to Charlie and Charlie was gone.

Life is but a sport and a pastime, says the Koran.

FIFTY-SIX

Pookie and Leo were in the back of the van. Araz had the presence of mind to take their cell phones away and threatened again to kill them dead. Tavit was in the passenger seat unsteadily holding the gun at them but nevertheless holding it. The tip of the pistol bobbed and weaved like a conductor's baton.

'You sure he ought to have that gun?' said Leo.

'No,' said Araz, 'but if he shoots you it's her fucking fault, not mine.'

Araz threw the cell phones off into the brush as he drove.

'That phone,' said Pookie, 'was hand-dyed pink Moroccan goatskin encrusted with diamonds. It took weeks to have it ordered through Neiman Marcus.'

'Shut the fuck up,' said Araz. To Tavit he said, 'How are you doing?'

'Harghh,' said Tavit. He farted again and the atmosphere was directly redolent of not quite internally processed burrito.

'Jesus,' said Leo and Pookie, gagging simultaneously.

There were indications of other gastric problems as well but Tavit himself seemed unaware of them. The entire van smelled like the Guadalajara sewer system.

'Where are we going?' asked Pookie.

'Somewhere we can talk,' said Araz. 'You let him get away and now you get to help me get him back.'

'We have no idea where he is,' she said.

'We are going to find out pretty soon,' said Araz.

He looked at Tavit, who wasn't shaking as hard now.

'You doing better?'

'Yah-hargh,' nodded Tavit.

Bip.

'How about a rest stop,' said Leo, 'for god's sake.'

Araz laughed. This was meant to display disdain when actually he felt only like crying.

FIFTY-SEVEN

Araz drove up into the Santa Cruz mountains. He pulled off the road and while Tavit wobbled the gun at them Araz taped their hands behind them.

'Which one of you,' said Araz, 'is going to tell me where he is?'

'I've been telling you,' said Pookie, 'that we don't know.'

'Your IDs say you're from LA. You were looking for him and you found him. Why?'

Nothing.

Araz sighed.

He studied them both and then he hit Leo.

'Leave him alone,' said the girl.

He hit Leo again.

'Stop it,' said the girl.

He hit Leo again but this time the girl said nothing, just bit her lip and glared at Araz with hatred.

'Who is the boss here?' asked Araz. To Pookie he said, 'I think you are the one in charge.'

He put a piece of tape over Pookie's mouth and watched the boy's eyes grow wide with fear.

'Ah,' said Araz. 'I see.'

Araz stood behind Pookie, grabbing her by the hair, turning her to face Leo. He reached round and cupped his hand on Pookie's breast and gave it a squeeze.

'Not much here,' he said, 'but she's not bad looking. Have you fucked her yet? I don't think so. I think she's the sort who'll only fuck you when she's ready.'

'Leave her alone,' said Leo, 'please.'

'I'll bet she hasn't even let you see them,' said Araz. 'Well, now is your chance. You can thank me later.'

He began to unbutton Pookie's blouse.

'No,' said Leo. 'No.'

Araz took out a knife and flicked it open. He started to cut the front of Pookie's bra. Leo lunged forward but Araz moved the knife to Pookie's throat and Leo stopped.

'I will kill her,' said Araz. 'You tell me what I need to know and you both walk away. Why were you looking for him?'

'His wife hired us to find him. She's worried. She knows you guys are after him.'

Araz nodded.

'How did you know where he was?'

'We got a tip. Somebody spotted him in the casino.'

Somebody is playing a fucking game, thought Araz.

'Where is he going?'

'I don't know.'

Araz put the fine edge of the knife underneath the bra between Pookie's breasts.

'I will throw her down and fuck her while you watch,' said Araz, 'and then I will have to kill you both.'

Leo looked desperately at Pookie. She shook her head. Leo said to her,

'It's not fucking worth it, Pook. Not with you.'

To Araz he said,

'He's got a girlfriend up here, in Mountain View. He's probably with her.'

'Ah,' said Araz.

And while Araz did not actually see God smile, Araz thought he did see the corners of God's mouth rise just a little.

FIFTY-EIGHT

'I think I have shit on myself,' said Tavit.

'What do you expect,' said Araz. 'You eat like a fucking pig, you shit like one.'

'It's her fault,' said Tavit. 'What do I do?'

'Put something under your ass,' said Araz, 'and shut up.'

Crystal Ellerbee lived in the suburbs. It was a nice small house that looked just like everybody else's. Charlie had parked down the street, as if nobody would notice.

'He's not,' Araz said to Leo and Pookie, 'exactly a fucking genius, your boy.'

'What are you going to do to him?' Pookie asked.

'I am going to take all his money,' said Araz, 'and then I'm going to rearrange most of his internal organs. Whether he dies or not is going to be up to him. All I really care about is the money. To me,' added Araz, 'he's just meat.'

'He was losing again when we found him,' said Leo. 'I don't think he has much.'

'Just what I needed to hear,' said Araz. 'You can do this?' he said to Tavit.

'Yeah, I'm okay.'

'Stop shitting.'

'Okay.'

'They move,' Araz said to Tavit but looking at Leo, 'you kill the girl first.'

Araz walked up to the house and onto the porch. The door was unlocked. Araz walked in. Charlie and Crystal were sitting at the dining-room table having coffee.

Charlie, as expected, saw him and took off into the back of the house.

The fucking woman jumped up and got in Araz's way. She was tall and the years had put on a few pounds. Araz wrestled with her. True fucking love. He hit her and threw her across an ottoman and kicked open the bedroom door to find Charlie going out the window. Araz grabbed Charlie's leg and was trying to pull him back in. That's when he felt the sharp pain between his shoulder blades and turned round to see Crystal staring in horror at her own handiwork. She wasn't so much looking at Araz as at the three-inch steak knife standing up in his back. Araz glanced in the bedroom mirror. He tried to reach the knife but couldn't and he didn't honestly expect any help from her. The knife hadn't gone in very far but shuddered when he moved and sent lightning bolts of agony through his body.

Araz walked quickly out of the house with the knife wobbling every step. Charlie was hotfooting it down the street to his car, coming up past the van. Araz yelled at Tavit to stop him. Tavit got out of the van, still wobbly on his pins, and stepped in front of Charlie. Charlie, the high-school football star, lowered his shoulder and in passing knocked Tavit on his ass in the middle of the street. Araz did a sort of Quasimodo jog to Charlie's car and was beating rather half-heartedly on Charlie's window as Charlie tried to start the thing again. Araz was blind with pain and could feel the blood seeping down his back into his waistband. Much of whatever enthusiasm he might have had was now gone. Charlie got the car going and ran over Araz's right foot.

He watched the car drive away, just stood there bleeding and watching it go. Then he turned and did his humpbacked limp back to the van, where Tavit and Leo and Pookie all stood watching him.

'Would you mind?' he said to Pookie, turning his back to her. She pulled out the knife with a brief jerk. 'Thank you,' he said.

It vaguely dawned on him that the girl had managed to free herself but hadn't run off. She took the steak knife and cut the tape on her partner's hands.

The van's passenger door was open and Araz sat down in it wearily.

'Things are going very ugly for me,' Araz said to her.

'I can see that,' said Pookie.

'What do we do now?' asked Tavit. 'Should I kill them?'

'No,' said Araz. 'Let them go. It doesn't matter now.'

'He was never going to kill us,' Pookie explained to Tavit.

'Really?' Tavit said, looking at Araz.

Araz nodded.

'Too many witnesses,' Pookie said to Tavit. 'Would you mind please standing just a little downwind?'

Tavit moved.

'He almost raped you,' said Leo.

'But he didn't, did he? Look, anything happens to us and the whole world knows exactly who did it. It was all a bluff.'

'You can't be sure.'

'Of course I'm sure,' said Pookie, though she wasn't.

'We're fucked, aren't we?' Tavit said to Araz.

'Yes, we are,' said Araz. To Pookie he said, 'Why don't you go. You've caused enough trouble. I'm fucked. Everything is fucked.'

'Atom is going to kill you,' said Tavit. 'He thinks you're a fucking Jonah, is what he says. He's going to turn everything over to Savan.'

'Yes, that's right, Atom is going to kill me but I'm fucking well going to make sure I take your shit-stained ass along with me.' Araz took the gun away from him. 'In fact I think I might kill you myself. I've got nothing to lose. Why are you still here?' he said to Pookie.

'I can help you,' said Pookie.

'What the hell are you talking about?' Leo said to her.

'Remember what David told us, about the uncle? David wanted to make contact with him anyway. That's one reason he wanted us out of it. David has some kind of plan. I can't help you,' she said to Araz, 'but I think our boss can. I need to make a phone call. Unfortunately my phone has been misplaced.'

Araz made the effort to stand up. He dug into his trousers pocket and pulled out his cell phone, handed it to her. What the hell, it couldn't get worse.

Pookie took the phone, said thank you, then kicked Araz in the balls. Araz doubled and sat back down.

'That,' said Pookie, 'is for my one of a kind pink Moroccan leather and diamond-encrusted phone,' and made the call.

FIFTY-NINE

S alvatore Locatelli was having a bite in his Thousand Oaks restaurant when Spandau showed up. Two of Locatelli's bodyguards stopped Spandau at the door.

'Let me see him,' Spandau said.

'Let him come,' Locatelli called from his booth in the back of the room.

The two men frisked Spandau and then let him through.

'Exactly what sort of fucking game are you playing at?' Spandau asked him. 'You tipped off both me and Atom about Charlie being up north. I just got a call from my people and it's goddamned lucky for everybody nothing happened to them. Especially goddamned lucky for you.'

Locatelli wiped his mouth with the crisp cloth napkin. He took his time. Then he leaned back and looked Spandau in the eyes.

'First of all, you don't want to raise your voice to me, it makes all these people around me very nervous and somebody is liable to shoot you just because you make them jumpy. The other thing is that you never threaten me especially when it's a bullshit threat you and I both know you can't back up. It makes us both look stupid and it puts me in the position of having to make you eat your words. This, as it happens, I would prefer not to do. Not yet anyway. You want to sit down?'

'No.'

Locatelli shrugged.

'I'm sorry about your friends. I admit I made a bad call on that one, I thought you were the one who'd be going after him. I didn't figure on your labor-management skills. I thought it was a good chance for you and Araz to meet. Who ended up with him?'

'Charlie skipped again—'

'He's like a fucking ferret, that one, isn't he?'

'But Araz and my people are on their way back down here together.'

'Ah,' said Locatelli. 'That's interesting. So it worked out well after all. Very good.'

'As well as a near-bloodbath can ever be. And Charlie is still loose.'

'Charlie has never been my problem,' said Locatelli, 'and he really isn't yours either. There are far bigger fish we need to be frying. Sit down, Texas, have a glass of wine.'

'No,' said Spandau again.

'Perhaps you are misreading my body language,' Locatelli said. 'I'm not asking you.'

Spandau sat. Locatelli motioned and one of the men brought over a glass and a bottle of Chianti. He filled the glass for Spandau and backed away.

'Somehow you always wind up in the extremely fortunate position of doing me a favor,' said Locatelli. 'I don't know how you manage this. Lots of people tell me I should have killed you a long time ago but I am inclined to think we share a guardian angel. Before you head swells let me assure you that if the guardian angel has to make a choice it's going to be my ass over yours. This is where theology and common sense part company.'

Locatelli took a sip of wine. He stared at Spandau until Spandau picked up his glass and took a drink as well.

'Early this morning while you were having your cornflakes somebody found the body of Araz's cousin in the trunk of his car down in Topanga. His head was bashed in and his arms and legs broken. Somebody is trying to make it look like we did it, which we did not, but you, me, and everybody on the planet knows this is how Uncle Atom is going to see it. Like I told you before, Atom has become a great source of irritation to me and this thing has happened at the worst possible time.'

'How is Atom reacting?'

'I don't think he knows about it yet. My police contact told me and they're holding the information back from the press. The point is that when Atom does find out all hell is going to break loose. Atom is crazy and he's going to come after me and mine to make a point. Once he does that there is no talking anymore and the shit, as they say, will fly. I am going to have to kill half the Armenians in Los Angeles. It will look like that fucking Turkish thing all over again. I would like to avoid this.'

'You know who did kill the cousin?'

'Oh sure,' said Locatelli. 'I can't prove it but it's got to be Araz. Savan, the dead one, was nosing around asking questions about Araz, about who he saw, about his sex life. He was ambitious, more like Atom than Araz ever will be. Thank god the fucker is dead, because he was jockeying to push Araz out and set himself up to take over after Atom kacks. Atom is not one of your more liberal thinkers and if he found out his next in line was light in the loafers he wouldn't hesitate to bury him somewhere. In a surprising bit of ruthlessness I think Araz whacked him. It's all kind of biblical really. I have to say I'm a little proud of him. This means he's somebody I can deal with.'

'What do you want me to do?'

'You are going to set up a meeting.'

'No,' said Spandau.

'Give this some thought, Texas. Araz is the key to all our problems and right now he's got his tit caught in the wringer and needs help. I need to neutralize Uncle Atom or LA is going to look like fucking Rwanda for a while. Atom will surely find out about Savan and about Araz's sexual preferences and either one of these is enough for Atom to snuff him. Araz gets dead and both your pals, Charlie, and that loon Margashack are still up shit creek. There is no other way. I've been telling you this from the beginning.'

Spandau thought. He downed the glass of wine. Locatelli motioned for the bottle. Spandau drank another one. Said,

'How is this supposed to work.'

Locatelli told him.

SIXTY

They were in a motel in Camarillo. When Spandau got there Leo and Tavit were playing gin rummy and Pookie was changing the dressing on Araz's knife wound. Leo kept watching Pookie. Savan was a big, good-looking guy. Watching Pookie touch Savan's naked back did not make him happy.

Spandau introduced himself, they shook hands. Spandau said to Pookie and Leo,

'Why don't the three of you get something to eat. There's a restaurant down the road.'

'I'm not hungry,' said Tavit.

'Come on,' said Pookie. 'There might be something cool in the Happy Meal.'

'Go on,' Savan said to Tavit. 'It's okay.'

They left.

'You want a drink?'

Araz nodded. Spandau went over to the minibar, opened it, looked.

'Scotch, bourbon, what?' said Spandau.

'Any vodka?' asked Araz.

'Vodka it is.'

Spandau poured vodka and scotch into paper cups. Handed the vodka to Araz, pulled up a chair, sat across from him.

'You are in trouble,' Spandau said to him.

'No kidding,' said Araz, taking a drink. 'The good thing is that it can't get much worse.'

'This is where you're wrong,' said Spandau. 'They found Savan's body this morning and it doesn't take Perry Mason to figure out that you did it.'

'Prove it,' said Araz.

'I don't have to prove anything. The fact is that sooner or later Atom will find out about your boyfriend and that Savan was trying to out you. This is the conclusion that Atom is going to make and Atom is going to come after you.'

'Okay, fuck it,' said Araz. 'I've been thinking about this. The only chance I've got is to turn myself in and go state's evidence. Nobody gives a shit about Savan and if I can help shut down Atom maybe I can even walk, go witness protection or something. Nobody can prove I had anything to do with Savan and they aren't going to want to if I give them what they need.'

'It doesn't have to go that far. First of all, what's going to happen with Charlie?'

'Once Atom finds out he got away again, his patience is going to be at an end. This asshole is just making everybody look bad, and the awful part is that he's not that smart. He's just stupid lucky, is all. But Atom is going to take him out before he creates any more embarrassment. With Locatelli breathing down his neck he can't afford to look weak. That's really what all this is about.'

'What if we can fix this.'

'How?'

'By getting rid of Atom. By putting you in his place, where you belong.'

Araz thought. Drank his vodka. Held up his empty cup. Spandau went back over to the fridge and brought back a vodka shooter, opened it, poured it. All the time Araz watched him carefully.

'You work for Locatelli,' said Araz.

'Does it make any difference?'

'Not really,' said Araz. 'What is all this going to cost me?'

'A spirit of détente,' said Spandau. 'A new and better world for all of us, an atmosphere of trust and cooperation. Something your Uncle Atom is shitty at. The hope is that you have more sense.'

'He's a crazy bastard okay,' said Araz.

'And you call the dogs off Jerry Margashack and Charlie Marston. They're off the hook, the accounts are reset to zero.'

Araz shrugged. 'Sure. I'm just anxious to see what sort of moves you think you've got. Atom isn't stupid, and he's like a fucking wild animal with his nose in the wind. Anything you try he's going to smell a mile off.'

'I want you to meet with him.'

'Oh sure,' said Araz. 'That's going to fly.'

'The police haven't released the information on Savan yet. We've got maybe twenty-four hours hopefully before Atom hears about it. Then he's going to start putting things together. If we do this fast it might work.'

'What am I supposed to do?'

'Call him. Tell him you fucked up, you want to come home but you're scared. You want to talk to him, somewhere neutral. You want to be reassured.'

'Why would he go for this? What the fuck does he care if I come back at all?'

'Savan is missing, Tavit is with you. Atom's lost his three top guys and he's worried about throwing down with Locatelli. Right now he's got nobody in charge on the streets and every operation he's got is a sitting duck. He may not trust you but he needs you. For the time being, anyway.'

'You don't think he's going to worry about a setup?'

'Sure, but he's only worried about you setting it up. I hate to say this but your uncle doesn't have a shitload of respect for your talents. Whatever you might have up your sleeve he isn't going to worry much about it.'

'Ha,' said Araz, smiling. 'You've done your homework.'

'He underestimates you. That's what we're counting on, that's his weakness. And he'll be curious. He needs to have you where he can see you.'

'You've got it all planned out,' said Araz, 'and I don't really have anything to lose, do I?'

'What about Tavit? Where does he stand in all this?'

'I can control him. He doesn't want to face Atom any more than I do. He'll do what I tell him to do.'

'Suggest a place to meet. He'll want you to come to the butchery but he'll expect you to say no. You suggest someplace else and then he'll say no. Haggle a little but let him select the place. If it doesn't work for us we'll change it. He'll expect that.'

'We set this up and it works, what happens to Atom?'

'Is this something you expect to lose sleep over?'

He considered Spandau for a while.

'You don't like this, do you?' Araz asked him. 'I mean, it's like a moral thing for you, isn't it?'

'I do what has to be done. Most of the time I don't much like it.'

'Atom says we don't have souls. I don't know one way or another. I don't like violence unless there's no other way. It's not a moral thing, that's all shit. But most of the time it's unnecessary, just stupid and bad business. Atom doesn't see this. He's seriously fucked up. That part of him is missing.'

'That's why you need to be there instead of him.'

'So that's it,' said Araz. 'That's your key, that's where you come into all this. It's a crusade. You're trying to address the fucking moral balance of the universe.'

Araz laughed. Spandau let him laugh. Then said,

'Make the call.'

SIXTY-ONE

I t worked just the way Spandau said it would work.

Araz didn't have to pretend to be frightened when he spoke to Atom. The quivering voice was legitimate. Araz was apologetic but scared. Wanted to come home but was afraid to after everything Atom had said. Atom suggested he come to the office, they could talk there. No, said Araz, he couldn't do that. It had to be someplace public. They finally agreed on that. And someplace not far away.

Now it was evening and Araz sat in a Starbucks on Santa Monica. Sat there framed in the window, for all the world to see, as public as it gets, looking like an Edward Hopper painting to the hundred cars that passed every minute.

Waiting.

SIXTY-TWO

'H e looks like an Edward Hopper painting, don't you think?' said Locatelli.

They were in a French restaurant a few doors down and across the street, but from their table they could still see Araz sitting in the cafe.

'You're giving art-history lessons now?' said Spandau. 'While you're in such an informative mood, you might try telling me why I'm here. This wasn't part of the deal.'

'Think of this as my moment of triumph,' said Locatelli. 'I wanted you to share this with me. You can help me gloat. This man has been a pain in my ass for years.' Locatelli surveyed the menu. 'Try the Daube Provençal. They put the orange peel in it. It's the only fucking place in town that gets it right.'

'You eat here a lot, do you?'

'I own it,' said Locatelli. 'You want something made right, you just buy the factory. Otherwise it's market-driven economics and the law of entropy. You leave things alone and they naturally turn to shit. The Medici knew this.'

'It doesn't bother you, what's about to happen?'

'You mean am I like Uncle Atom? A fucking monster? You know better than that. I've got a wife I love, sons, a daughter. I believe in God but I also believe you're supposed to take care of your own. I let this man live and how many people do you think are going to die? The world will sleep better and you know it. And not that I don't trust you, but it would be truly amiss of me to let you out of my sight at this point.'

Spandau stared out the window at the cafe.

'You might want to be a little less obvious,' Locatelli said. 'You look like you're waiting for a bus. Relax. There won't be any great drama. Atom can't do anything to him there and Araz isn't going to leave with him. The whole thing is just to get the crazy bastard into the open. My guys will grab Atom on the way back to his car, and as far as you're concerned he decided to retire to Bali. End of story. I'm telling you, try the daube.'

Locatelli looked out the window.

'Ah,' he said. 'The trout has arrived. You see that guy over in the doorway, the big ugly one, out of sight? That's Omar and somewhere on his person there is a large knife. You see what I told you? Atom was supposed to show up alone. Does this tell you anything? The bastard is cheating already. Not that anybody thought he wouldn't. Atom smells a rat. Araz is dumb enough to actually leave with him and Omar would slice him like a loaf of mortadella.'

SIXTY-THREE

Uncle Atom stepped into the cafe. Or rather he stopped in the doorway, paused, like he was stepping into a dentist's office. He looked around distastefully. Then he put his foot over the threshold and walked slowly toward Araz.

'I hate these places,' said Atom, sitting down. 'It's everything that's wrong with this country. Artificial light, artificial coffee, artificial people. Just look at them. Let's get this done quickly. What do you want?'

'I want to come home?'

'So who's stopping you?'

'I admit I fucked up.'

'You did.'

'The bastard got away again and then there's all that money I owe to you and you said a lot of stuff that made me very nervous before I went up north.'

'There's got to be discipline,' said Atom. 'You are my blood, but you've got to learn, there's got to be discipline. You are my right hand, I need you, but you can't be weak. It's my place to teach you. That's the way it is. You think I'm too hard but the world is hard.'

'You said some things.'

'You got a thick head,' said Atom. 'Sometimes you just got to knock things into a thick head. That's all I was trying to do. This is stupid. Come home. We'll go sit in the office, drink real coffee, talk.'

A homeless guy came into the cafe. Tall black man, dreadlocks, a torn army jacket that looked like it had been rolled in seven kinds of grease. Atom looked at him with something that could only be described as hatred.

'I need some sort of guarantee,' said Araz.

'You want a guarantee,' said Atom, 'then take a look at that living piece of shit. You don't come home, you end up like that. Where you going to go, hah? What will you do? You walk out on your family, you abandon them, this is what happens. This is what the world does to you.'

There was some altercation about the bathroom. The homeless guy wanted to use it and the young prick behind the counter didn't want to let him, said it was for paying customers only. The homeless guy dug around in several dozen pockets, produced some change, slapped it on the counter.

'What do you want to buy?' said the kid. 'This isn't enough for anything.'

'For god's sake,' said one of the customers, a young woman. 'Be human. Let the guy use the bathroom.'

The kid shrugged.

'Flush, will you,' said the kid.

The homeless guy trundled toward the rear of the cafe.

'Come home,' said Uncle Atom. 'You don't want to be like this. You don't want to let the world do this to you.'

They could smell the homeless man as he passed them. Years of piss and sweat. Atom made a sour face.

'I need to think,' said Araz. 'I need some time.'

Just before the bathroom door the homeless man stopped and turned around. Araz looked up and saw the gun. He watched the man shoot Uncle Atom in the head first and as the gun turned to him Araz's last thought was not really a thought at all but a vast weariness that the world should actually be like this.

SIXTY-FOUR

There were four shots in all, two pairs, like a simple poker hand. Pop pop, pop pop. They heard them but it was, as Locatelli had said, nothing dramatic. It was really the screams that got their attention. Spandau looked out the window like everybody else. You couldn't see either Araz or Atom now, they were hidden behind large connecting spiders of cracked glass and crimson stains that inched their way toward the floor. Spandau stood up, like there was something he could do.

'Sit down,' said Locatelli firmly, 'unless you want to spend the next fifteen years in jail.'

Omar had moved from his spot in the doorway, ran to the entrance of the cafe, but saw what had happened and melted back out into the crowd that was gathering. You could see him on his cell phone, calling god knows who.

'You son of a bitch,' Spandau said.

'There was no other way,' said Locatelli.

'It doesn't make any sense. I mean, everything we planned, what was supposed to happen . . .'

'There was no other way,' Locatelli repeated. 'You wanted everything to be done offstage and I'm sorry about that, I truly am, but this is as much you as it is me and frankly I resented the idea of you walking away all smug and able to lie to yourself. You want to know if I'm a monster and no, this is how it feels, Texas, we get to share this one. And like I say, it's not that I don't trust you but I needed an insurance policy. Otherwise I have to be afraid of you and I just can't have that, Texas, I just can't. It was this or the other thing. Your guts may hurt for a while but once again you get to stay alive.'

'It doesn't make any sense.'

'Stop saying that,' said Locatelli. 'Somewhere in that reptile core of your brain you knew damned well what had to happen. Why the hell would I want to remove one dangerous man and then replace him with another? Araz takes over and in six months you think he's not going to be as big a pain in the ass for me as Atom ever was? He was too smart for his own good. Unfortunately his luck was shit. That gay friend of his was already talking. How do you think I found out?'

'You think you've killed the whole operation? I thought the point was to have someone in there you could deal with? Now it's just wide open, somebody else steps in and you've got no control. What the hell is the sense in that?'

'Use your imagination, Texas. It's like the royal fucking family. There's a chain of succession.'

'What are you talking about? There's nobody left. There's just . . .'

It was a moment before he got it. It was too funny.

'Tavit's not the brightest crayon in the box, but with a little help he'll do. In fact he's exactly what we need. If Araz could waltz him around like a pony, imagine what I can do. It's brilliant.'

Spandau stood up, threw his napkin onto the table.

'Sit down, Texas. Have something to eat. Some wine. We'll get a little drunk.'

'No matter what you tell yourself,' Spandau said, 'you're no better than he was. Maybe you're worse. He was crazy. You're just fucking pure evil.'

'You just crossed the line and you're scared,' said Locatelli. 'You just helped murder two men and nobody's giving you the option to pretend you didn't know. Welcome to my world. Maybe it will take you a while to deal with it but you will and no matter what happens things are going to look different from now on. Everything is shades of gray, Texas. How long was Walter trying to tell you that?'

'One of these days,' said Spandau, 'I'm going to kill you.'

'Maybe,' said Locatelli, 'but I doubt it. If it truly worried me you'd be dead before you stepped out that door. You've finally lost your innocence, Texas, and there is a brave new world out there for you and we are going to be of much use to each other. You can count on it.'

Spandau left the table and stepped out into the street. It was like a circus now. The sirens, the gathered patrol cars, the pressing crowd, the craned necks. Everybody loves a circus. An officer with a bullhorn warned people to stand away from the yellow cordon that was being unwound. Spandau turned and through the restaurant window watched Locatelli giving his order to the waiter. Every now and then in his life, holding Dee or Anna, Spandau felt he had touched something holy, something radiantly good that gave his life some kind of meaning, that made it possible to go on. Maybe he couldn't tell you what God looked like, it's true. But for the first time in his life he could now describe, in intimate detail, the face of the Devil.

Spandau's phone vibrated. He looked at it. A text message. From Anna.

Come home, it said. Come home.

SIXTY-FIVE

They sat around Dee's kitchen table, drinking coffee. Dee said,

'So he's not coming home.'

'We didn't get much of a chance to talk to him,' Pookie said. 'Like I say, the other two showed up and he took off. You can't blame him.'

'You don't know where he went? You don't know where I could contact him?'

'That's the last we saw of him. He's very clever, Dee, he got away from all of us.'

'But he's safe now, you say? You're sure of it?'

'The guy he owes the money to is dead. There's nobody looking for him now,' said Spandau.

'What about the money?'

'The slate is clean. The guy he owes it to can't try and collect on it anymore.'

'I'm sorry we didn't get him back,' said Pookie. 'We did what we could.'

'It's worked out well enough,' Dee said. 'I mean, when he hears, he'll come back. Or at least he'll call and I can tell him.'

'That's right,' said Pookie. 'He'll hear about it and when he calls you tell him it's okay about the money now, he can come home.'

'He's still out there somewhere,' said Dee, 'gambling away what little we have left.'

'I'm sorry, Dee, there's nothing to be done about it,' said Spandau. 'He can come home now. You can at least start all over. Maybe get him into therapy again.'

'Strange,' said Dee. 'All I could think about was the money he owed, and now that's resolved it doesn't feel as if we're any farther along. There was something about the whole situation that never seemed quite real in the first place. What do I do now?'

'Be patient,' said Spandau. 'Wait. He'll call soon. Then he'll be home. You'll have him back.'

'Thank you,' said Dee.

'We didn't do much of anything,' said Spandau. 'Uncle Atom had the good fortune to get himself killed. It worked itself out.'

'I know you're lying,' said Dee. 'And I know you well enough not to ask too hard. I suppose it was always like that, wasn't it? You trying to protect me and me making sure I didn't ask too hard in case you actually told me the truth. You protected me then and you're protecting me now. I don't think I ever saw that so clearly before.'

'Would it have made a difference?' Spandau asked her.

'Yes,' she said. 'I think maybe it would have.'

'I have to go,' he said.

'I'll come with you,' said Pookie.

'When he comes back, maybe you'd like to meet him. All this and it just dawned on me you've never actually crossed paths.'

'No,' said Spandau. 'It's probably best left just the way it is.'

She put her arms around Spandau, leaned into him, kissed him gently on the cheek. Whispered to him, so soft and close that only he could hear, 'Maybe another life.'

He nodded.

Let go of her.

Went out.

SIXTY-SIX

'Well,' said Pookie once they were outside, 'that was some fancy lying.'

'What is there to tell her,' he said. 'You want to explain about what he was doing in Crystal Ellerbee's house? Or how the sonofabitch probably helped kill three people? There's just no way to explain all that and she's right, she doesn't really want to know. And I don't want her to. Maybe he loves her. I don't know. Maybe everything will work out all right for them. That's not my problem. I'm just not going to hurt her anymore.

She's wrong. You only get the one life and it's too goddamned short as it is.'

He walked with Pookie to her car.

'When are you coming back to work?' she asked him.

'I don't know that I am.'

'You've got to make up your mind, David. You can't sit on the fence forever. You've got to either grab it or let it go. Like it or not, it's yours now. You have to decide.'

'I'll be in on Monday,' he said. 'I'll take the weekend to think about it and, anyway, there's something I need to do.'

Pookie nodded. She hugged him. He hugged her back.

'God,' she said, 'you are so dumb.'

'I know,' he said. 'I know.'

SIXTY-SEVEN

Pam Mayhew, Anna's younger sister, was in the kitchen making a pot of coffee when Spandau came in. Pam and Anna were Texans by birth, and came from a ranch family that, like Spandau's, considered coffee as a sacramental liquid and the basic fuel of everyday life. Sand in your grub might be forgivable, but screwing up the java could get you injured.

Pam didn't say hello, just glanced at him when he came in and went back to the coffee. She was a smaller, younger version of her sister. Blonde, well built, and spirited, she was a knockout in her own right. But Anna had something else, that inexplicable other thing, that her sister lacked. Pam was pretty and sexy as hell, but Anna possessed a quality that drew people to her, made her unforgettable to complete strangers for reasons even they couldn't describe. It had always been this way, and if Pam envied her she never let it show. She was a smart woman and Spandau felt she simply understood the burden of it, having watched all the pain the mixed blessing had caused her sister.

'She's out by the pool,' she said coolly.

'Are you mad at me too?'

'None of my business,' she said. 'But damned right I am.'

'Is there a specific reason or just on general principles?'

'I'm just giving you fair warning if you're fixing to hurt her, which it seems to me you are about to do.' Like Anna, when she was angry the otherwise subdued Texas twang kicked up a few notches. 'I will hunt you down and kill you where you sleep. You want coffee?'

Anna was stretched out on a lounge reading a script when he came out carrying the mug of coffee.

'When I said come home, I sort of thought it might be the same evening.'

'I'm sorry.'

'I waited. You really shouldn't make a girl beg. She won't thank you for it.'

'Is it too late?' he asked her.

'To come home? No, not if you mean it. Not if you're going to stay. I can't take the up and down, David. I have a life and I'm offering to share it with you. But even if you don't want it it's still my life and it's the only one I've got.'

He sat on the pool deck next to her chair, resting his head in her lap. Her fingers toyed with the hair on the back of his neck.

'I talked to Pookie,' she said. 'Now she tells me you're still undecided about whether or not to go on with the agency. I thought you'd worked all that out.'

'I thought I had too,' he said. 'But there are new developments.'

'What sort of developments?'

'The kind that makes me think Dee was right. That it's ultimately a destructive and dehumanizing way to make a living, and that I probably ought to be ashamed I'm any good at it. It occurs to me that maybe the only reason I'm any good at it is because there's something flawed about me in the first place.'

'What would you do?'

'I don't know. I've got Walter's money now. I suppose I could do anything I want. Buy a ranch, raise horses. Sell rare cowboy books. Or I could just sit around and drink beer.'

'You could have done those things anyway.'

'Then why didn't I do them.'

'Walter.'

'Loyalty to Walter had nothing to do with it. I stayed because I wanted to stay. I stayed because I needed to. Walter understood that. But I hate what I've become. I can't stand who I am anymore.'

'Then stop. You just said yourself you can do it now, it's easy, there's no reason to stay.'

'It's just not that simple.'

She threw her arms up in frustration.

'I do not understand you. I just do not fucking understand you at all. Why keep doing something that makes you hate yourself?'

'It's hard to explain,' he said. 'I'm not sure I can. It's just that maybe I'm not the man I always thought I was. Maybe this is what Dee and Walter both saw in me, except Dee had to run from it and Walter knew he could put it to use.'

'You're a good man, David. The best I know. You're exhausted, you're still reeling from Walter's death. Give yourself a little time. Or is it something else? What's happened, David? What's wrong?'

'I don't know who I am anymore and I can't run away from it. That's the thing. If I leave now, if I run away from it, I'll never know, it'll always follow me. The only way I can find out is just to stay with it, to plough through and see if I can come out the other side.'

She took his face in her hands.

'Something's happened to you, David. Tell me what it is.'

'It's nothing,' he said. 'A kind of midlife crisis, I think. That's all.'

'Whatever you want to do, I'm here for you. You know that. But you need to be sure. If it's ever going to work between us, you need to know you made the decision for your own reasons, not mine.'

There was a long silence. She held his face and studied it. Then she pulled her hands away and stepped back and said,

'This is you leaving me, isn't it?'

'I'm just going back to the Woodland Hills place. For a while.'

'You're not dumping me?'

'No. I'm just grabbing a little space.'

'If that's what you want.'

'I have to go away for a couple of days. I'll be back on Sunday. We'll talk. There's some other business I have to finish.'

'It's not another woman, is it?'

'I wish it were that simple,' said Spandau.

'I love you,' she said.

'I could never figure that one out,' he said.

'I thought maybe I could help you with it,' she said, 'but it doesn't look like I'm doing so hot. Look, I'm not Dee. I'm a tough old broad. You don't have to be afraid for me, if that's it.'

'I think I probably do,' he said. 'That's just the point.'

SIXTY-EIGHT

There were boxes in the attic of the Woodland Hills house. Dee had taken a few with her when she left, but the rest were his, and the dates and notes on the cardboard cartons were probably as close to an autobiography as he would ever get. He was not so much a collector as an accumulator. Collection implied some sort of order or purpose. Spandau's life had neither. It was as random as the contents of these boxes around him.

He shifted them around, opened a few. It was like archaeology, like diving backwards through time. College, high school, the army. Photos of his parents, his sister, friends and relatives he'd not thought about in years. Finally he located the box he was actually looking for, and carried it downstairs.

He opened a beer and went out into the backyard. The tattered carcass of another dead fish lay just outside the pond. He waited for the usual anger to rise but it didn't. All that came was a great, sad weariness that threatened to wash his legs from under him, and he fell into a chair and sat staring at the pond. One more notable failure but this was the first time he blamed himself and not the raccoons. Why hadn't he seen the answer before? It wasn't the goddamn raccoons, it was him. It was him all the time. The raccoons just did what raccoons do, however ghastly and inconvenient it appeared to us humans. This was their nature, this was the way it worked, and you could rant and rage and fire guns into the air but nothing was going to change this. It was Spandau who was the guilty party. How many fish had died? A dozen maybe in the last couple of years? All placed there by Spandau, all swimming around happily, just waiting to become a carnivore's midnight snack, because Spandau was too stupid and too arrogant to give up a fight even common sense told him he'd never win.

Somehow, he thought, I've got to make peace with this thing, and he wasn't sure if he meant the fish or Dee or Anna or Pookie or Leo or the two men whose deaths he helped advertise across a cafe window. A whole chain of lives he'd failed to protect. Before another nightfall he'd go out, get a tank, bring the fish inside. Or better yet, he'd give them away, find them a home with somebody who had more sense than to get them hurt. That's what you did if you cared about things. You put them first, you got them the hell out of harm's way. And if you were the thing that was hurting them, well, you just moved your own sorry ass, however much it hurt.

SIXTY-NINE

He stood at the gate, looking at the house. They were in there. They saw him. Curtains moved.

He stood there for a long time. It began to rain. A curtain was pushed aside and he saw, for a moment, her face.

It was raining hard now. The front door opened and Michael came out.

'You're a determined bastard, I'll give you that,' said Michael. 'But there's no point to this. She won't see you. Nor should she. There's nothing else to be said. Exactly what the hell is it you want anyway?'

'I'm not sure, exactly,' Spandau laughed. 'But I think it might have something to do with forgiveness.'

'You come up here asking her to forgive him, it's a waste of time. You can't really expect it of her.'

'I'm not talking about Jerry,' Spandau said. 'I'm talking about me.'

'You? Aside from being a general nuisance and sticking your nose in everywhere it doesn't belong, there's not a whole lot for her to forgive.'

'Just tell her. Please.'

Michael shook his head, turned, and went back into the house. It was a while before she came out, wearing a thin raincoat and holding a newspaper over her head.

'What is it you want from me, Mr Spandau? Michael says you're asking my forgiveness but I don't know what you're talking about. You've done nothing to me that I need to forgive.'

'I wanted to ask you because I'm not sure anybody else would know what I'm talking about.'

'It's raining, Mr Spandau, and you still haven't told me what you want.'

'Do you think – one day – you'll be able to forgive him? Do you think that's possible? I'm not asking for him. I'm asking for me.'

'God forgives us all,' she said.

'It's not about God,' he said. 'It's about you. As a human being. Do you truly think you're capable of that kind of forgiveness?'

She thought. The rain beat an irregular tattoo on the newspaper above her head. She said,

'Yes, I believe I will. I believe one day I will. I believe that kind of forgiveness is possible. I couldn't live if I didn't. I don't think any of us could. We make so many mistakes, we take so many wrong paths, we are so weak and the temptations are so strong. You read your Bible, Mr Spandau, and one of the things you realize is that we don't get thrown into Hell. We just bury ourselves there, we fall through being weighed down by all the things we can't manage to forgive, all the things we can't let go of.'

Spandau nodded.

'Is this what you wanted to hear?'

'It will do,' he said.

'Go home, Mr Spandau,' she said. 'Go back where you belong and take care of the things you love. The forgiveness will come. Sometimes it just takes a while. I've been waiting fifteen years. I expect I'll have to wait a while longer, but I'm not so far away as I once was. I can tell you that.'

She reached out, put her hand on his chest.

'I will pray for you, Mr Spandau. But you go on now. You get on with your life and you let me get on with mine.'

She turned, went back into the house. Spandau looked up and saw the boy and the priest watching him together from an upstairs window. The boy waved. Spandau waved back. Spandau went to his car and opened the trunk and removed the cardboard box. He went back to the gate and leaning over placed it just inside. Then he went back to his car and drove away. He imagined the boy and the priest and the woman looking out the window at the box sitting there in the rain. Maybe they'd come out now, maybe they'd wait until the rain had stopped. He thought they'd probably wait. He knew there was something wonderful about the box sitting there, full of possibilities, teasing them against their will.

How long, Spandau asked himself, do you wait for forgiveness? She'd been working on it for fifteen years, more likely all her life. How long before you forgive yourself, how long before you allow others to forgive you? And what the hell are you supposed to do in the meantime?

There was not, he realized, much in his life he had not fucked up. Dee was right, his life did seem to be little more than a series of betrayals. It was what he did best. You start out with the best of intentions but end up waylaid by your own nature. You think you've got a shot at being some kind of good man in a bad world but maybe this is just goddamned arrogance. What happens when it dawns on you that maybe you're the shit everybody ought to be avoiding? I fucked up my marriage, I'm fucking up with Anna, I can feel that already slipping sideways. I left my best friend to die alone and in pain and then blamed him for it when I was just too self-absorbed to see. Now there are two men murdered that I'm responsible for and I don't feel a thing, not a goddamned thing. This is what scares me. A good man would feel something but I don't. Spandau envied the people in the house. Envied them their hope, envied their conviction, right or wrong, that it was still possible to live and love and somehow pass on through the horrible things we do to each other.

What they'd find when they did come out and tear open the soggy box was a fire engine, old, a little rusty, the red paint more than a little faded, but built in an America when people still believed things ought to last. Spandau remembered the boy had been waiting for his own fire engine. Maybe he'd got it by now. It didn't matter. Rusted and faded though it was, the small metal vehicle connected the boy to a past where things like truth and honor and family still seemed to mean something. It connected the boy to Spandau's world, or at least the world he'd grown up in – the world he still carried with him even if he'd betrayed it. Maybe the boy would never know it, but Spandau would. Maybe Father Michael would too. He was a clever old bastard. He'd know damned well the gesture had to mean something. Maybe he'd know that Spandau had just passed on to the boy the best part of himself. And that it was, however pathetic, a gesture of hope.

SEVENTY

He drove all Sunday and reached Anna's that night. There was nothing to say, and she was wise enough not to ask again. They hardly talked, though he found himself compelled to tell her over and over that he loved her. They made love and afterwards she could feel something desperate in the way he clung to her, the way some part of his body needed to touch her as if fearing she'd float away, when the truth is that it was him who was going.

I've lost you, she thought. At least part of you anyway.

He'd filled a small box with his belongings. Better to do it tonight, it would be harder in the morning.

No, he wasn't leaving her, he was just moving back into his own place.

Yes, they were still a couple, they'd still see each other, they weren't breaking up.

Then why is it, she thought, that some part of you has gone and the rest is waiting to follow?

'Will I see you tomorrow?'

'There's a lot I have to do,' he said. 'I'll call you.'

Oh god, she thought. Oh god.

She let him go. Kissed him, walked him to the car. Waited until he was out of sight before she fell apart.

Sank to the sidewalk and sat there crying.

Pam came out of the house, went over to her sister, sat down next to her, and draped her arm round Anna's shoulders.

'He's not worth it,' said Pam.

Anna reached up and gave her sister's hand a gentle squeeze. 'How long have we been doing this?'

'What part?'

'The part where they leave me and you tell me they're not worth it.'

Pam thought.

'Your ninth birthday party. Larry Burrows kissed that little slut Sophie whatsername and you ran out and hid in the barn loft and threatened to burn it down. I brought you out a glass of Ovaltine and we ended up hanging out and dropping lit matches on the chickens. I was five.'

'You're lying this time, though.'

'Yeah, pretty much,' said Pam. 'You didn't tell him, did you.'

'I don't want it to be the reason he comes back. If he comes back.'

'What happens if he doesn't?'

'I'll have it anyway. I've had two abortions, both because the fathers were assholes and I didn't feel I could love their offspring. David is maybe the most emotionally confused man I have ever met but he's good and true and for the first time I want to keep at least a part of him no matter what.'

Pam stood up. She held out her hand. Anna took it and struggled to her feet, grunting.

'I feel like the Hindenburg already. I'd axe you to death right now for a glass of wine and a smoke.'

'Come on, my little fertilized flower. I'll make you a glass of Ovaltine. If we can find some poultry to victimize, so much the better.'

They headed arm in arm to the house.

'Best Actress Oscar, my ass,' said Anna as they went inside. 'If the bastards could only have seen me tonight.'

SEVENTY-ONE

On Monday morning Pookie, Leo, and Tina were in the office when Spandau got there. He wasn't sure what he expected, but when he walked in it was like another business day, same old, same old. Casual greetings, they looked up from their work, said hello, put their heads back down. Better this way, he thought. Smooth transition, no muss no fuss, we're all pros here. Pookie was even wearing a business suit.

'You've got me,' Spandau said. 'Who are you today?'

'Oh,' she said, 'it's just a suit.'

He opened the door of his office and saw the candles, the rose petals scattered everywhere. They'd elevated his office chair on cinder blocks and draped it in gold-trimmed velvet, a makeshift version of an emperor's throne. A circle of laurel hung from the ceiling just above where his head would be. His desk was covered with food. The centerpiece was a small roast pig replete with apple in mouth. Tucked between the knuckles of one baked trotter was a card. 'Welcome home, you redneck bastard. Julien.'

'Ascend to your rightful throne, O Great Caesar!' Pookie said from the door. A sheet was wrapped around her like a toga. Spandau climbed up into the chair. Leo and Tina came in, draped in togas as well, chanting, 'Hail, Caesar!' and bowing. They filed around the desk, stood beaming across at him.

'We exist to serve your wishes, my liege,' said Leo.

'Shall I feed you sweetmeats from my own gentle hand?' Tina asked seductively.

'Peel me a grape,' said Spandau.

Tina popped a grape into his mouth. He clapped his hands.

'Bring on the dwarves, freaks, and the dancing women,' he commanded.

'Oh,' said Tina, 'you mean business as usual then?'

'Exactly.'

Leo and Tina peeled their robes, lined out, and shut the door behind them. Pookie remained.

'You're going to do this then? No kidding?'

'Yep,' he said.

'Not that I'm not utterly ecstatic about it, but would you mind if I asked what settled it for you? Because when you walked in here today I was pretty sure it was General MacArthur bidding farewell to the troops.'

'Because it's there,' said Spandau, leaning back in his chair and putting his feet on the desk. 'Because a man's gotta do what a man's gotta do. Because I want to be able to enter my house justified.'

Pookie glowed. She loved these games.

'Okay, the first is George Mallory talking about Everest, why he wanted to climb it. The second is from *High Noon* but I think it might be a common misquotation, I have to look it up. That last one is Joel McCrea in *Ride the High Country*. I've always loved that line.'

'Clever girl.'

Spandau tossed her a grape. She popped it into her mouth, chewed thoughtfully. Then,

'You don't have a clue, do you?' she said brightening. 'It's a completely emotional decision, isn't it? You had no idea what you were going to do until just now.'

'There are wheels within wheels, girly girl. Still waters run deep. All prophets lack honor in their own homes.'

'Who said that?'

'I did, just now. See what I mean about depth.'

'Codswallop,' said Pookie. 'You don't wear your emotions on your sleeve, you carry them around on a sandwich sign. Oh, don't look at me like that. It's one of the reasons we all love you.'

Pookie smiled, put her arms behind her back, marched round the desk like the private-school girl she was to kiss Spandau softly but ever so chastely on the lips.

'You will conveniently forget,' she said over her shoulder as she walked to the door, 'that ever happened.'

She paused in the doorway. Did a half turn, gave him a fierce look. Said,

'And if you ever, ever, call me girly girl again, you die.'

She shuddered and closed the door behind her.

Spandau sat for a while in the quiet room. Pookie was right, as

usual. He had no idea. When he walked in this morning he still
didn't know, didn't have a clue. He'd been yo-yoing up and down
all night but had convinced himself to leave by the time he opened
the office door. Then suddenly all that changed. What changed it?

Spandau looked down at the pig on his desk staring mournfully
up at him. It was probably the pig that did it, which made as much
sense as anything. The pig looked so ridiculous sitting there that
Spandau was overcome by a sense of kinship. Neither of us belong
here, bub, but it is here somehow we have both ended up. Pigs
had waddled foremost into his mind. Meg had called him a gentle
swine in the restaurant, which had now led to him recalling a pig
hunt long ago in the hills outside of Flagstaff. His uncle Jim had
taken him, Spandau was ten maybe, and had strayed off to get
lost and wander panicked on his own until Jim found him sitting
on a rock and crying. Jim hugged him in relief then gave him a
quick clip on the ear and told him that whenever you find yourself
bewildered, you damn fool, don't wander around like an idiot but
sit down and wait until somebody finds you, most times they'll
be looking.

Spandau had to admit this was not much on which to base a
life-altering decision. Unfortunately, however, it was just about all
he had. Having admitted to himself that a more bewildered man
probably never trod earth, it struck him that he ought to wait, to
just sit down somewhere and wait for some thing, some body, to
find him. Looking around the room – at the pig, at Julien's card,
thinking of Tina and Leo in their togas, Pookie's kiss, Dee, Anna,
a dead friend who knew Spandau better than he knew himself and
had forced on Spandau a decision he was too cowardly to ever
make – he began to suspect something already had.

In a few moments he heard phones ringing, the mail being
delivered, people coming and going. There was a knock at the
door, it opened, Tina stuck her head in, said, 'Huntley in the
conference room,' and closed the door again. Spandau took a
moment to survey his new kingdom. There were worse ways to
be, alone was one of them. He took a deep breath. He'd climb
down from his throne, pick up his lance and shield, and sally forth
into the real world at last. But first, first before anything, he'd pick
up the phone to tell Anna he was finally coming home.

EPILOGUE

. . . it absolutely must be fired by the end of Act Three.

It was an easy job, they said, down in Compton. The warehouse of some fucking camel jock, import export, full of fucking rugs and shit. It was a desktop PC, they were after the account books. Poor fucker's wife was divorcing him, resourceful bitch, she wanted the accounts in case he was lying. Of course he was.

The lock was nothing, she'd furnished the code for the alarm. Inside, down the aisle, up the metal stairs at the far end to the office on the landing. A fucking cakewalk, he loved these. There had to be a coffee mug somewhere in the office. He was going to whack off into it.

Captain Midnight was almost to the bottom of the stairs when the lights went on.

Well shit.

'Surprise, surprise.'

He looked up to see Malo on the landing outside the closed office door.

'What the fuck are you playing at, you stupid coon,' said Captain Midnight.

Malo shook his head, clicked his tongue. He pushed open the office door to let out the two mastiffs, who loped down the stairs.

'Feets don't fail me now,' said Malo.

Malo watched the look of terror as Deets saw the dogs coming. Deets did like this Wile E. Coyote move, where his shoes literally spun for purchase on the slick concrete floor. Deets was halfway down the aisle to the outside door and thought he might make it when the dogs caught up with him, just about the way Malo had imagined it all these weeks.

Once they'd knocked Deets down there was no getting up. Big fucking dogs. Deets flopped around as they tore at him. He didn't, for once, have the opportunity to shoot his mouth off.

This was a happy extra as far as Malo was concerned.

Malo sauntered down the stairs and over to where the dogs had him pinned in the middle of the floor. One had Deets' entire knee in his mouth and the other was in the process of consuming his throat. Malo stood there for a while and watched. Then he said,

'Woof woof, motherfucker,' and went home.

"WET EYE" DIRECTOR DIES IN CAR CRASH

Augugst 29 – Crescent City, California (AP) – Cinema legend Jerry Margashack, who both wrote and directed *Wet Eye*, an Oscar contender and one of last year's most successful films, died early yesterday morning in an automobile crash just outside Crescent City.

The fatality occurred at 5.35 A.M. Tuesday on the Pacific Coast Highway ten miles north of the town. Authorities are not yet clear if the cause was accidental or suicide, and are awaiting further investigation into Margashack's state of mind just prior to the crash.

According to Whitman Lowes, a logging truck driver who witnessed the accident, Margashack's Jaguar XK8 was heading south in the opposite lane when it failed to take a sharp curve 150 feet above the shore.

Lowes stated that, as he passed the Jaguar, he saw Margashack slumped forward onto the steering wheel as if he were unconscious. But he also claims that Margashack's hands were still in place on the wheel, indicating that Margashack may have been conscious and in control of the car.

Lowes commented that the Jaguar seemed to speed up as it approached the 45 mph curve and was going perhaps 75–80 mph when it struck the retaining barrier and plunged over the edge.

After a preliminary autopsy of Margashack's body, county coroner Ken Alvarado said there appeared to be no evidence of alcohol or drugs, or that Margashack had succumbed to death by natural causes leading to the crash.

Alvarado said the body would be removed to Los Angeles, where a more detailed investigation would take place, though at present death by suicide has not been ruled out.

Alvarado noted that the director's chest and arms were covered by scars from burns and lacerations that clearly existed on the body prior to the crash. Some of these were recent enough to remain unhealed, suggesting that Margashack may have had a long history of self-harm.

Margashack's agent, Ann Michaels, declined to comment on her client's recent state of mind, but said that, when the fatality occurred, he was on his way back to Los Angeles from Medford, Oregon, where he had gone to visit friends.